A TALE OF
RED RIDING
RISE OF THE ALPHA HUNTRESS

TO: Elizabeth!

A TALE OF
RED RIDING
RISE OF THE ALPHA HUNTRESS

The Alpha Huntress Series

Year 1

Neo Edmund

PART ONE

CHAPTER 1

Red wondered if the moon was on fire when she caught a glimpse of it in the midnight horizon. It loomed like a blazing crimson titan, high above the towering treetops of the majestic forest. As impossible as it sounded, she believed that lunar spirits were calling out to her. She could hear their distant voices beckoning her further down the dark dirt path she'd been riding on since earlier that afternoon.

"Show me the way!" Red shouted at the moon.

With each mile she traveled further from the city, and the deeper into the woods she ventured, the hope in her heart grew ever stronger. It felt as if she was waking from a mundane dream she'd been dreaming her entire life. There was no clear reason to think the direction she was traveling would lead to her grandmother's house.

In her heart, she knew it would.

The giant trees and overgrown brush caused the path to become dangerously narrow. The ground was paved with jagged rocks, unexpected dips, and slippery puddles. Red had to fight tooth and nail to keep the wheels of her little motorcycle upright. She knew that slowing down would be the smart thing to do. One false move could be disastrous, and there was little chance of rescue so far away from the safety of civilization. Ignoring these sensible notions, she squeezed harder on the throttle.

"Playing it safe won't get me to where I'm going tonight," she said aloud.

The roar of the motor penetrated deep into her chest, making her feel like a fearless predator on the hunt. Hope for a new life filled with love and adventure was her prey. A great warrior was awakening from deep within her and taking control. The darkness was no longer obstructing the path from her sight. It wasn't that she could see the giant trees surrounding her like a canyon—she could feel them.

Her thoughts drifted away as the aroma of wild roses aroused her senses. The wonderful scent spawned a surge of emotions that warmed her heart and soul. Distant memories of a time long forgotten came rushing back in a flash. In her mind's eye she saw a collage of amazing places that felt somehow familiar.

There was a mysterious cottage hidden deep within the woods ...

A temple that housed supernatural forces of unimaginable power ...

An ivory palace that sat atop a hill ...

And a metropolis with wonders far beyond her wildest dreams ...

For the first time in her fifteen years, Red was free of the cares and concerns of growing up as an orphan in the big city. Then, in the blink of an eye, the moment of bliss escaped her. A furious roar thundered out from behind. It sounded like the engine of another motorcycle, one far more powerful than Red's. The deep rumbling gave her such a fright that she nearly lost control and crashed into the trunk of a towering oak. Taking a quick glance back, she saw the blinding glare of a single headlight approaching.

Seconds later, a *mysterious rider* sped up beside her. He cranked his throttle hard, making his engine roar out like an untamed beast. The rumbling vibrations made Red shudder with both fear and excitement. From what she could make out under the dim moonlight, he wore a black leather jacket, gloves cut off at the fingers, ripped jeans, and knee-high riding boots. Something about him felt oddly familiar to Red, as if she had once met him in a distant dream.

"Do I know you?" Red asked.

She tried to get a look at the rider's face, but the tinted visor of his black helmet masked it. The only feature she could make out was his long, brown hair rippling over his shoulders. Her curiosity turned to angst when she noticed him glancing down at her hip. Her short green skirt flapped around in the wind. She didn't need to see his face to know that he was checking her out.

"Peep show's over!" Red shouted.

Squeezing down on her throttle, Red accelerated ahead of the mysterious rider. For the next few minutes, she tried with relentless intent to ditch him.

She cut under low hanging branches …

Shot across slippery puddles …

Sped flat out down a steep hill …

And even made a daring jump over a pile of fallen logs …

But it made no difference how hard she tried, the rider stayed right behind her.

If things weren't complicated enough, Red could smell a hint of danger in the air. She had no doubt that the startling scent was coming from the mysterious rider. It made her blood boil in a way that she'd never known. *I just have to know who he is*, she thought.

Red decided that if she couldn't ditch the rider, then she would do whatever it took to unmask him, even if it meant having to play dirty. She slowed down enough so he could cut alongside her. Once again she could tell that he was checking her out from behind his dark visor.

"Would you show me your grungy mug already?" Red said. She reached into a wicker basket tied to the back of her motorcycle. When her hand emerged, it held a few wild berries that she had picked earlier that day.

The rider glanced down at her hand, then back up to her face. Unsure of her intent, he gave a shrug.

Red flung the berries at the rider, causing them to splatter all over the front of his helmet. He *grunted* and flipped his visor up so he could again see. Red glanced his way, excited to get a look at his face. Before she got the chance, he accelerated ahead. Adding to the insult, he cut into a puddle and squeezed his throttle, spraying a shower of mud right into Red's face.

"Watch it, you stinking jerk!" Red shouted.

The rider waved an arm high to let her know he had done it on purpose. Red clenched her teeth and squeezed her throttle to the max, pushing herself beyond all rational limits to keep pace with him. Deep down inside she knew that doing so came with a big risk, but her pride simply refused to let him win the night.

I'm going to catch him, and nothing can stop me, she thought as she pushed the accelerator as far as it would go and the bike's vibrations spread throughout her body.

No sooner had she thought it than Red caught sight of a massive tree a few hundred yards ahead in the road. The trunk was twenty feet around and surrounded by jagged black boulders and thorny brown bushes. The giant branches swayed in a methodical rhythm, like arms dancing in the night breeze.

The fiery explosion Red expected to see when the rider reached the tree never came. Instead, there was a glaring flash of white light. It took every bit of will Red had to keep her eyes open. When the light finally faded away, the mysterious rider had vanished from sight.

The instant Red's hand reached for the brake, a distant voice spoke out in her mind. It was the spirits that inhabited the tree, telling her that they stood as guardians to a world hidden on the other side. If she stopped now, there would never be another chance to find her family, nor would she discover the truth of who she was. It was a fate, Red thought, worse than the ultimate risk of facing the tree head-on.

With only seconds before it would be too late to stop in time, a fear greater than any she had ever known before overcame Red's heart. She knew speeding head-on into a tree was pure madness, but stopping sounded worse than the dreadful disappointment of waking from a dream at the best part.

I can't go back now, Red thought.

Red's life had been exactly the same for as long as she could remember. She was an orphan without a last name or any family to speak of. All she knew of her past was that her father had abandoned her on the steps of a church when she was five years old.

For ten years, she had lived in every orphanage in the city. Most stays were short-lived and rarely pleasant. The endless moving from place to place left her feeling quite unwanted. She quickly learned to avoid getting close to people, as it always led to disappointment and heartbreak.

This all changed when a letter arrived by messenger late on a mid-summer's night. It was from a woman called Grenda Stalk, who claimed to be Red's grandmother. She insisted it was time for Red to return to her hometown of Wayward on a matter of great urgency. The directions given stated that Red would find the way if she had the courage to trust her heart.

After days of agonizing over the letter, Red came to believe it was merely a cruel prank. She couldn't find any public record of a woman called Stalk, nor did Wayward appear on the maps in the city library. Red did her best to forget about the whole thing, but this proved to be impossible as her mind became clouded from dreadful dreams.

It wasn't long before Red couldn't sleep a wink. Whenever she closed her eyes, she saw a burning red moon in the sky and vicious wolves chasing her into the forest. It always ended with a faceless young man who stood engulfed in flames, demanding that she set him free or he would haunt her till the end of her days.

The headmistress of the orphanage would never allow Red to return if she went off in search of her family. Well aware of the risk of ending up homeless, Red snuck out the back window during the night. With no direction in mind, she hopped on her trusty little motorcycle and sped off into the darkness, taking along only a small basket of food and a bag of coins she had been saving to buy a new dress.

For a full day, Red sped around the countryside beyond the borders of the city. She traveled for miles through the scenic hills overlooking the suburbs. By late afternoon, she even risked venturing along the isolated back roads used by merchant drivers and shady travelers who opted to avoid the main highways.

As the warm day faded into a chilling night, Red feared the chances of finding Wayward had escaped her. Just when she was ready to give up the search and return to her life of loneliness, she came upon a desolate wooded path. On it was a sign that appeared to point toward Wayward Woods, though it was far too faded to say for sure one way or the other.

Red was certain that if she dared venture down the road very far, there would not be enough fuel in her tank for a return trip. It took little debate for her to decide that the potential reward outweighed the risk. With renewed hope in her heart, she buried her fears and headed off into the unknown realm of the forest.

No more than an hour later, she was speeding toward the great tree that blocked the path.

The instant before she would have crashed to her demise, the spirits of the forest spoke in her mind.

Only one brave enough to risk everything will gain anything on the journey ahead.

A startling chill overtook her body as the spirits peered deep into her heart and soul. They exposed her every last hope and dream … deepest desire … closely guarded secrets … and even a few dark deeds. They were judging Red. If they didn't deem her worthy to pass, this would be the last thing she would ever do.

I'm not afraid, she answered them.

Blaring white light blasted into Red's eyes as a mystical portal opened in the great tree's massive trunk. She had survived the perilous trial of the forest. The spirits would now reward her bravery. As her motorcycle sped into the light, Red looked down and saw the tree's roots, stemming deeper into the ground than anybody could ever dig. All around her were glowing gold rings that revealed the tree was as old as the Earth itself.

"Welcome home, Red Riding!"

In a flash, her passage through the portal was over. The moon now loomed directly overhead like a great lunar spirit watching over the forest. It sat on a backdrop of a million twinkling stars. A glowing blue comet soared across the horizon, so close that Red felt as if she could reach out and snatch it from the sky.

The sight was so majestic that she needed to stop to get a better look. Her wheels skidded on the wet, moss-covered ground until she came to a halt in the middle of a small meadow. It was hard to make out all the details of her surroundings under the pale moonlight, but clearly nothing about this world was like the concrete city she had left behind. It was enchanted with the sort of magic she knew so well from her favorite storybooks.

The crisp air smelled of wild flowers, savory berries, and countless other wonders Red looked forward to discovering. For a moment, she sat with her eyes closed, taking in all the sounds of the night. Countless creatures could be heard stirring all around her, chirping, croaking, grunting, and growling. There was no doubt Red was far, far away from the grasps of the hands that would try to pull her back to the world she had so eagerly fled. She just knew that her grandmother's house had to be nearby.

As long as I trust my heart, somehow I'll find the way.

Just then, in the near distance, a deep howling erupted. In any other place it would have been safe to assume it was the ravings of a wild animal. Red would have even believed that now if not for a distinctive scent lingering in the night breeze. She had smelled it while racing through the woods alongside the mysterious rider. It didn't make a bit of sense to her why he would be howling like a wolf, but on that night in the enchanted woods, Red knew anything was possible.

CHAPTER 2

Once again, the howling of the mysterious rider echoed through the trees. This time it was much closer than before. Red's heart fluttered in nervous anticipation as she listened to his melodic song. On the surface it sounded sad and lonely, but she could also sense undertones of anger that could not be ignored. If she stayed around any longer he would find her, an idea she found both startling and exciting.

Red rubbed an affectionate hand down the side of her little motorcycle. The vibrations of the still rumbling warm engine gave her a feeling of comfort. "If there's danger to be faced tonight, I'm glad I have you to carry me away to safety."

The forest went deathly silent. The creatures that had been merrily enjoying the night fled the meadow. Red knew that she ought to do the same. If not for having already decided that it was a night for risks, she certainly would have.

The deep roar of an approaching motorcycle erupted, the thundering of its powerful engine making even the trees shudder. Before Red could ponder fleeing again, the mysterious rider was upon her. Her heart skipped a beat as he rolled to a stop at the far end of the meadow. He sat for a tense moment, staring at her through his dark visor. Red took a nervous gulp as she tried to find the courage to speak.

"Hey there." Red said with a crack in her voice.

The rider cranked his throttle. It was more than loud enough to drown out her voice. Red was sure he had done it with the intent of silencing her. This might have intimidated her under normal circumstances, but on that night, it consumed her with an unexpected rush of irritation.

"No need to get all rude about it," Red said.

The rider again cranked the throttle, making his engine roar out.

"Fine, if you don't want to talk to me, then get lost."

The rider slowly shook his head as if he found her words amusing.

Red gritted her teeth. He'd only been there for a few minutes and was already getting on her nerves. "Are you just going to sit there giving me the creepy stare-down, or say something?"

He yet again let his engine roar. Red gave him a hard glare and squeezed her throttle, making her motorcycle's little engine roar as well. He didn't hesitate to meet her challenge by letting his engine roar right back.

That was all Red could take. The rider had ignited a fire in her heart that she had never before known. "If that's how you want it, why don't you show me what you got, Wolf Boy?" she shouted.

Without hesitation, the rider hit the throttle hard and began speeding straight at Red. She wasn't about to let him intimidate her now, so she squeezed her throttle and sped right toward him. As the distance rapidly closed between them, Red realized she'd made a huge mistake. The rider wasn't going to be the first to flinch.

As much as she hated to admit it, there was a big difference between courage and stupidity. A mere second before impact, Red made a hard turn. She let out a *yelp* as her tires lost traction on the wet grass. Her motorcycle fell on its side and slid a dozen yards before coming to a stop.

"That stupid crazy jerk is so going to get it," she said.

In a whirlwind of anger, Red stumbled to her feet. The sight of her favorite dress caked in mud was enough to make her *growl*. She'd saved up for six months to buy the outfit, and now it was ruined. She wanted to give the rider what she considered a well-deserved kick in the butt, but figured a guy unhinged enough to pull such a crazy stunt wasn't somebody to scuffle with.

Red watched with a mix of nervousness and irritation as the rider rolled to a stop nearby. He turned off his engine and shoved down the kickstand with his boot. She tried to get a look at his face as he pulled off his helmet and used his black shirt to wipe the mess of berries away from his visor, but he had an innate ability to keep his identity concealed in the shadows.

"Would you just drop the mysterious man routine already?" Red shouted.

The rider slammed down his helmet on the seat of his motorcycle. He stood looking at the ground for a tense moment, likely trying to calm himself. As he strutted over toward Red, he cracked his neck from one side to the other. Red stood up straight and did her best to look fearless. When his face finally came into the light, she was surprised to find he was just about the same age as her.

"Oh my!"

Red felt a bit lightheaded as she fought the urge to swoon. The rider's long brown hair waved in the wind over his handsome face. A scar ran from below his left eye, all the way down the length of his cheek, giving him a rough and tough edge. His eyes appeared to be copper-colored, though it was hard to tell for sure in the pale moonlight.

"You okay there, Little Red?" The rider had a deep, scratchy voice.

Red gave him a suspicious glare. "How do you know my name?"

The rider cracked a grin and pointed to her long red hair. "I didn't, until you just told me."

Red grabbed a lock of her hair. "Oh, you called me 'red' because …" She stopped herself short, both annoyed and embarrassed.

He took a step closer. "So tell me, Little Red, where are you headed so late in the night?"

"Not your business, Wolf Boy."

The rider gave Red an odd look. "Why do you keep calling me *that*?"

"I don't know." The way the rider glared at Red made her feel oddly uneasy. "Maybe because of the way you were howling earlier, Wolf Boy."

"Did it frighten you, Little Red?"

"Bored now."

"Are you?"

"Totally. So why don't you get back on your big, bad bike and get lost already."

Red turned her back on the rider and walked over to her fallen motorcycle. As she strained to pull it up onto its wheels, she could feel him watching her every move. It took all her willpower to resist the urge to look at him. There was no denying that she was smitten by him and she didn't like it one bit.

"So you got anything yummy in your goody basket, Little Red?" the rider asked.

Red grumbled in irritation. "What are you going on about, Wolf Boy?"

The rider reached down and tried to open the basket tied to the back of Red's motorcycle, but she smacked his hand away.

"Never without my permission, Wolf Boy."

"Whatever you say, Little Red." The rider gave Red a smug grin as he backed away.

"Look, buddy, if you're going to hang around acting all creepy stalker-like, the least you could do is help me get my poor little man out of the dirt," Red said.

"You don't need my help. You *should* be plenty strong enough to pick up that tiny trike."

"Don't push me, Wolf Boy." Red pulled and pulled on her motorcycle with all her might, but she just couldn't lift it more than a foot or two off the ground.

"Pathetic. I know you can do better than that, Little Red."

"Stop saying my name like that." Red stomped over and stood inches from the rider's face. "You hear me, Wolf Boy?"

"You're cute when you're angry, Little Red. But you need to calm down."

"Caln Down!" Red's fist flew wild, pummeling him in the arm.

The rider groaned. "Ouch. That hurt a lot."

"Well you had it coming, Wolf Boy."

The rider's face tightened and twitched. He was clearly fighting the urge to lash out. This was enough to make Red shudder in fear. She figured that if he had any dangerous intentions in mind, this would be enough to set him off.

"Listen, I'm sorry," Red said. "I've never in all my life done a thing like that."

The rider rubbed his sore arm. "For a first hit, it sure had a lot of *wham* behind it."

"I don't know how that could be. I'm totally weak."

"I'm thinking you're a lot stronger than you realize, Little Red. That hit is going to leave a serious mark."

"If I'm so strong, why can't I even pick up my own bike out of the mud?"

"Because you're trying instead of doing, Little Red."

"Now where have I heard *that one* before, Wolf Boy?"

"Stop calling me that." The rider stomped over and grabbed the handlebars of Red's motorcycle. With one hand and an effortless heave, he pulled it up onto its wheels.

"*Wolf Boy!* What big muscles you have." Red was so embarrassed by the girly tone of her reaction that she smacked herself in the head.

The rider flexed his muscles. "Think nothing of it."

"Already forgotten." Red hopped onto her motorcycle. "Now, if you're done with this creepy little game, it's time for me to go anywhere away from here."

"Leaving so soon? Don't you want to stay around and pick flowers or something, Little Red?"

"Whatever that means." Red stomped her boot down on her motorcycle's kickstarter, but the engine didn't start.

"You're wasting your time. That bike ain't going anywhere unless you plan on pushing."

Red clenched her teeth. "Look, I get it. You think you're all that and know everything there is to know. This time you're totally wrong. My boy will start for me." She again kicked the starter, with the same frustrating result.

"Your bike is a boy?"

"A little one, but definitely a male. Not like your little missus over there." Red again kicked the starter. Still nothing.

The rider looked at his motorcycle with a curious eye. "You're saying that great big machine is a girl?"

"Does the idea of that threaten your manliness, Wolf Boy?"

"No. It just explains why she gets all temperamental once a month."

"Oh, that is so *not* funny." Red kicked the starter, this time unleashing all of her angst. The motor just would not start.

"You can kick that thing all night. It's just not going to happen."

"What makes you so sure, Wolf Boy?"

"Your fuel line is busted." With a smug grin, the rider strutted away toward his motorcycle.

Red glanced down to the underside of the gas tank. The fuel line was indeed snapped in half. "This is all your fault, you know?"

"Whatever you say, Little Red." The rider mounted his motorcycle and kicked the starter. The engine fired up with a thundering roar. "There's a repair shop in town, but it won't be open till morning, and it's a long walk."

Red looked around at the dark forest, debating if it would be worse to deal with being stuck alone in the middle of nowhere all night, or to ask for help from the stranger she believed was responsible for her predicament.

"So do you want a ride or not, Little Red?"

Red had to fight the urge to tell him where she thought he should go. "You're not going to try to make a move on me, are you?"

"I make no promises."

Red had never felt so conflicted. Going with the rider could be dangerous, but staying in the forest alone felt just as risky. "Fine. I just need to do something real quick."

"Make it quick." The rider revved his motor. "I ain't got all night."

"Just chill out for a second." As much as Red wanted to argue with him some more, she felt it best not to push the fates any further. She knelt down by her motorcycle and rubbed an affectionate hand over the seat. "I'll be back for you just as soon as I can, my little man."

The rider revved his motor. This time it had a clear tone of impatience behind it.

"Okay, okay, I'm coming." Red took a deep breath to dismiss her fears as she walked over to join the rider.

"Put this on so I don't have to look at you." The rider shoved his helmet onto her head.

"What about you, Wolf Boy?"

"What about me, Little Red?"

As Red climbed onto the back of the rider's motorcycle, she did her best to hide her attraction to him. The seat was small, forcing her to press her chest up against his back. She was startled to find his body temperature was far hotter than hers—or anyone she had ever touched.

"So where we going, Little Red?"

"I was on my way to a place called Wayward. Ever heard of it?"

The rider grinned. "Heard of it. You're right in the middle of it."

Red's face lit up with a smile. "Finally, some good news for a change. I'm looking for somebody called Grenda Stalk. I have no idea where she lives."

"Then it's a good thing I do," said the Rider.

Red took a nervous gulp. "If it's not too far, would you please take me there?"

"I can do that. First you gotta answer me one thing." The rider looked back to Red with narrowed eyes. "Who is she to you?"

"From what I understand, she's my grandmother."

"Is that so? And for what reason are you going to see the old girl?"

"How about we file that one under none of your business, Wolf Boy."

"How about I just leave you out here and whatever happens will also be none of my business."

Red bit down on her lip to hold back another snarky remark. "If you must know, I got a letter from her asking me to come live with her."

The rider let out a belting laugh. "I should have known."

"Is there something odd about that?" Red couldn't tell if he found this humorous or upsetting.

"Nothing odd about it at all." The rider revved the engine hard. "But you better hang on tight, Little Red. It's going to get bumpy from here."

CHAPTER 3

As the mysterious rider raced at top speed through the dark woods, Red tried to keep track of the direction they were traveling. They passed a field of wild berries ... a hillside covered from top to bottom in sunflowers ... and a small river with a rickety old bridge. Even with these landmarks committed to memory, she knew the chances of finding the way back to her motorcycle on her own were not good.

"I have a feeling my little man is totally doomed," Red mumbled.

"What are you complaining about?" the rider asked.

Red hadn't noticed how tight her arms were wrapped around the rider until she felt the muscles in his chest tense up. "Is there something wrong with you, Wolf Boy?"

"Want me to make a list, Little Red?"

The rider shut off his headlight and cut the motor. They coasted for about fifty yards before he hit the brakes and skidded to a stop. Red could again hear the creatures of the night stirring all around. The dark woods were alive with a symphony of peculiar sounds that felt like music.

"End of the line." The rider spoke not much louder than a whisper. "Your granny's house is about a mile ahead."

Red could see his eyes surveying the area. It was certain that he was nervous about being there. She considered asking him why, but wasn't sure she wanted to know.

"I guess I should thank you." Feeling a bit nervous, Red stepped off the motorcycle. She returned the helmet to the rider.

"Don't make a thing of it. And don't make a habit of it either," the rider said.

"Will I ever see you again? Or should I just kiss my little man goodbye?" Red tried to keep her tone civil, but it came out more like an accusation.

"Little man?"

Red rolled her eyes in irritation. "You know, my motorcycle."

The rider gave Red a sarcastic grin. "I guess you'll just have to wait and wonder."

"I'll be sure not to hold my breath," Red muttered.

They locked eyes for a tense moment. Red would never admit to it, but she wanted him to say something snarky or annoying that would get her blood boiling again.

The rider finally looked away. "As long as you stay on the path you'll be safe. Don't think about straying even a little bit."

"You don't have to tell me twice." Red gazed down the dark path. The way the shadowed trees swayed in the wind made it look dreadfully creepy.

"Hope you mean that, because you wouldn't be around for me to tell you again."

Red wrapped her arms around herself as a nervous chill ran down her spine. "I didn't get your name."

"You already know it, Red Riding." The rider fired up his motor and revved the engine hard. He squeezed the throttle and sped away.

"See you around, Wolf Boy." Red bit down on her lip as she watched him fade away into the darkness. Part of her was glad to see him go, and part of her wanted him to stay. It wasn't until he was gone from sight that she realized what he had called her.

"Wait. Why did you just call me Red Riding?"

The name *Riding* echoed out in Red's mind. Whoever had abandoned her at the church as a child didn't mention her last name. They had pinned a note to her dress that only said *Please take good care of my Little Red*. Making it even more confusing, the rider said that she already knew his name. It sent her mind spinning into a wild frenzy of hopeless speculation.

Doing her best to dismiss these confusing thoughts, Red turned her attention to the dark path she hoped would lead to her grandmother's house. It took all the courage she had to stand up straight and begin walking.

The strange cackling and gurgling of creatures scurrying about in the near distance were enough to keep her on the straight and narrow. She even opted to wade through an ankle deep mud puddle rather than stepping around it, because the edges extended beyond the safety of the path.

After a couple of minutes of walking, Red spotted a light glowing through the window of a small cottage. She took a careless step off the path to see around a tree that blocked her view. An ear-piercing shriek screeched out in the nearby bushes.

To contain a startled yelp, she pressed a hand over her mouth, standing as still as possible. Another piercing shriek wailed out, followed by a vicious roar, and then the sound of flesh being chomped and shredded. It was so terrible that it made Red shudder with fear.

In a whirlwind of panic, Red dashed as fast as her feet would carry her. The path was so dark that she could only hope not to slip or step into a hole and end up with a twisted ankle—or something far worse.

After a lingering moment of terror she feared would never end, she reached a forest clearing outside the little cottage. A quick glance back at the path behind her revealed there wasn't a sign of anything sinister chasing after her.

As Red caught her breath, she took in the sight of the stone cottage residing in the clearing. It was hard to make out all the details in the night, but something about it seemed almost unreal, as if it could only exist in a fantastic dream. Judging by the cracked and crumbling walls, it had been there for hundreds of years. Still, something about it was also safe and inviting, as if she had finally arrived home from a long journey.

It took a bit of coaxing to get her feet moving again. With each step closer to the porch, Red was astonished to find that the air felt warmer and warmer. The cold breeze that had been blowing on her faded away.

Standing at a safe distance from the door, Red peered through the front window, hoping to catch a glimpse of somebody inside. From what she could tell, the furnishings were about what one would expect to find in the home of an old lady.

It took one more deep breath for Red to find the courage to step up onto the porch. For a tense moment she stood with a fist raised, trying to convince herself to knock on the door. It suddenly occurred to her that it could be quite dangerous to call on a stranger in middle of the night. In a place that was so far from any sign of civilization, something bad could happen to her and nobody would ever know about it.

"Sure hope I don't end up in some creepy old witch's oven," she muttered.

Red knew that her fears, however sensible, were trying to hold her back. The idea of turning away now was just ridiculous, so without further hesitation she knocked two times on the wooden door. She waited no more than a brief instant without response before knocking again. A moment after that, she knocked again, and still again. The lack of a response was just maddening, although in truth only a brief instant had passed.

As the seconds dragged on, Red paced around, considering her options. She pondered trying the doorknob to see if it was unlocked. That was just a little more risk than she was willing to take, at least at this point.

Glancing down, she noticed a rather large doormat with the word *WELCOME* embroidered on it. Something about the gothic style lettering was familiar. She wasn't sure if she had seen it in a dream or a distant memory, but the thought felt all too real to deny.

Could it possibly be?

It only took a single calming breath to find the courage to raise a fist and knock three times. After a second of pause, she knocked twice, and finally three times more. There was the sound of a lock clicking, and then the door creaked open by way of unseen forces.

Topping the oddity of the situation, Red was bewildered to see the doormat now read *ENTER*. It was nearly more than her nerves could endure. Part of her wanted to dash away in haste, but she had come too far. There was just no way she wouldn't see this through.

"Hello?"

Red took a cautious step over the threshold into the dimly lit house. She stood breathless, waiting to hear a response, or at least a sound that would imply somebody was home. The room was so abnormally silent that even the warm fire burning in the stone fireplace didn't make a crackle or snap.

"I got a letter from Grenda Stalk."

The sound of her voice didn't pass any further than her lips. If it weren't for the sights of the room feeling so comfortably familiar, the strange phenomena might have been enough to make her dash right back out the door. It took every bit of courage she had to take another step or two into the room, and she was careful not to venture too far inside.

Her reluctance vanished in an instant upon catching a glimpse of an old photo on the fireplace mantel. She dashed over and snapped it up, gazing for a lingering moment at what could have been her mirror image.

Red noticed several other photographs of the same girl on the mantel. They showed her life, spanning from the age of a small child and all the way up to a young adult.

The final photo at the end of the mantel was the most startling of all. The woman was in her early twenties, holding a red haired infant in her arms.

Red's face lit up with a smile warmer than any that had ever graced her face. She was fairly certain that she was the little girl and the woman was probably her mother.

The front door slammed shut with a bang.

Deathly startled, Red dropped the photo as she spun around. The normal sounds one would expect to hear came rushing in. The fire that had burned in silence was now crackling away. Even more startling, she could hear tiny footsteps scampering around in the shadows.

"Is someone there?" Red asked.

Hands trembling beyond her control, Red picked up the photo from the floor and placed it back on the mantel. The footsteps again scampered around, though there still wasn't a sign of anything or anybody that could be making them.

"I was invited here by Grenda Stalk."

Red began a cautious search of the room, first peering behind the sofa, then under the coffee table, and finally behind an old bookcase. Though she did not find anybody hiding in these places, the mysterious scampering sound continued. This led Red to the troubling thought that whatever was in the room with her had to be either too small to see, or was invisible.

"My name is Red."

A *bong* erupted, that sounded like somebody slamming a fist down onto the keys of a piano. Red spun around and looked to an old upright piano sitting in front of the picture window. She dashed over to get a look behind it, certain she would catch somebody hiding there. All she found was a tiny, white mouse nibbling at an old crumb of bread.

"Are you the one making all that noise?" Red asked.

The mouse looked up at Red in such a way that she wondered if it might actually speak. Its peculiar expression was enough to give Red a chill. After a tense moment, the mouse turned away and fled through a small crack in the wall.

"That was quite strange," Red said.

"You don't know the half of it." A woman's voice spoke from behind her.

Red spun around and was startled to find a strange creature standing there. It was three feet in height, covered from head to toe in puffy white and grey fur.

"Booo." The furry creature said.

Red screeched at the top of her lungs. She somersaulted backward, high into the air, and landed in a crouch on top of the piano. Through clenched teeth she let out a dangerous *growl.*

"That was quite a feat you just pulled off there," the furry creature said.

"What are you?" Red asked.

"Oh, dear. I hope my winter coat didn't startle you." The furry creature proceeded to take off a bulky fur coat and nightcap, revealing the body and face of a kindly looking old woman with thick glasses and her grey hair tied up into a bun.

"I see." Red grimaced, feeling a little embarrassed.

"Why don't you come down off the piano so we can have a nice hot cup of cocoa? You still like extra marshmallows, right?"

Red snapped back to her senses, startled to find she was crouched on top of the piano. "How did I get up here?"

"The *how* isn't as important as the fact that you *could*." The little old woman scampered into the next room.

Red tried to recall how she had gotten on top of the piano. She was quite certain it couldn't have been the result of a leaping somersault. Even as the image of executing the move replayed in her mind, over and over again, she just couldn't believe it was possible.

Carefully sitting down on the top of the piano, Red then slid down to the floor. Her mind was abuzz with a thousand questions as she approached what she somehow knew to be the kitchen entryway. A wonderful aroma was coming from inside that awoke her senses.

She smiled and stepped through the doorway into the tiny kitchen. Every little thing about the room felt so familiar that a tear escaped her eye. She slid a hand over the surface of the dining table and somehow knew that it had been fashioned from the trunk of a large oak tree.

"My father made this," Red said.

She then approached a tiny cabinet near the stove. Inside, the shelves were crammed with glass jars and other oddly shaped containers.

"My granny used these to create all sorts of strange concoctions," Red said.

A porcelain teapot began to whistle on an old black iron stove. The pantry door swung open and the little old woman scampered out. Red watched as she dashed over and took the teapot off the fire. The little woman filled two teacups with steaming hot milk, then scooped in a generous portion of melted chocolate. She topped it off with plenty of puffy marshmallows. The smell was so wonderful that it made Red's stomach rumble with anticipation.

"Don't just stand there with your jaw to the floor," the little old woman said. "If you've got something to say, you might as well just say it."

Red clenched her trembling hands as she sat at the table. "Well, it's just that I'm not entirely sure you are who I think you are."

"Not to worry, my dear. I'm going to help you remember everything." The little old woman put a cup of cocoa in front of

Red. "Not that it's all going to come back in one night. Honestly, you were so young, you might not ever remember all of it."

"I see." Red strained to ask the question she was agonizing over. "Are you my grandmother?"

The little old woman sipped her cocoa. "You used to call me granny, but it's been so long I'll take what I can get."

"So that would be a 'yes?'"

"That is a great big yes. I am your granny, Grenda Stalk. So with that, your next question has to be …" She gestured to Red.

"Why did you wait so long to call me here? And why now?"

"Jumping right to the big one first. I was hoping we could work our way up to that one."

"I don't mean to be pushy, but I've come a long way. You were the one that called me here."

Grenda downed her entire cup of cocoa in a single gulp. "I just figured you would want to know what happened to your parents. Or how you ended up living in all those orphanages. Or what the story is with that giant tree you had to pass through. I can't wait to hear the tale of how you pulled that one off."

Red gave Grenda an odd look. "You know about that?"

"Of course. The tree's purpose is to make sure not just anybody can cross the borders of Wayward," Grenda said.

Red considered this and nodded. "I suppose that makes sense."

"I know you're confused, Red. I guarantee this is all going to be a lot more confusing before it starts to make any sense at all."

Red was about to ask what that meant, but she felt like it might be best left for a later conversation. "What did happen to my parents?"

"Why not take a sip of your cocoa before we get to that one."

"Oh, I had nearly forgotten." With a fond smile, Red picked up the cup and inhaled its wonderful aroma. Growing up in orphanages, it was rare to be able to enjoy even the simplest of luxuries. "I know this smell."

"You should. I used to make it for you nearly every night."

"I wish I could remember that." With her eyes closed, Red took a sip of the cocoa. The instant the magnificent flavor touched her lips, a flood of memories filled her mind.

She saw herself as a child of age two, sitting in the same spot she sat now, sipping cocoa from the cup she now held. Her mother was cooking breakfast at the stove with her back turned away. Across the table sat her granny, ten years younger, mashing up herbs with a stone mortar and pestle.

Red then heard the sound of the front living room door swinging open, followed by heavy footsteps clunking across the wood floor. The voice of a burly Irishman called out:

"Little Red, come see what I brought home for you."

Red leaped up in a thrill of excitement. She was sure that the voice could only belong to one person.

"Papa."

CHAPTER 4

"Papa? Where are you?"

Red dashed into the living room expecting to see her father, though without a single memory of him she couldn't even guess what he might look like. Her heart sank when she discovered nobody around. Not ready to give up, she shot over to the front door and pulled it open.

"Papa, are you out there?"

"Your father is not here," Grenda said as she entered from the kitchen.

"That can't be. I heard his voice call out my name so clearly." Red slumped in disappointment as she closed the door. "How can that be?"

Grenda placed a comforting hand on Red's shoulder. "You've had quite an adventure just getting here. Why not get some sleep and we can talk more in the morning?"

Red was more exhausted than she had ever been. The idea of going to sleep was tempting, but there were so many questions that she needed answered. "I just can't wait, Granny. Please tell me what happened to my parents."

"My dear, you're home now. I'm not going anywhere."

Red nearly broke into tears. Her granny calling this place her home was the most comforting thing she had ever heard. For the first time in her life, all of her cares and concerns faded away. She cracked a little smile and nodded in agreement.

"That's a good girl." Grenda gestured toward the stairs. "Your room is all ready for you."

"My room." The words were music to Red's ears. She could never recall having a room of her own. In the orphanages, she had to share a room with five or six other children. "Which one is it?"

"Just head on up. You'll remember easy enough."

Grenda extended her arms for a hug. Red hesitated before she finally embraced her granny. The feeling was more comforting than she could have imagined. It was the first time she could recall hugging anybody. It's just not a thing that happened in orphanages.

"Thank you, Granny."

"Welcome home, Red."

Grenda turned away and headed back into the kitchen.

A surge of anticipation filled Red as she approached the staircase. With each step up, she got just a little more nervous about what might be awaiting her at the top. She tried to imagine what her bedroom might be like. It was safe to assume that it was probably quite childish considering she hadn't stepped foot in the door for nearly ten years; not that it mattered a bit, for the simple reason that it was hers.

In the upstairs hallway, faint hints of moonlight peering in through a small window at the far end provided the only light. Red did a quick search of the walls for a light switch, but instead found an old glass lamp mounted on a wall. A closer inspection revealed it didn't have a cord or switch. She realized she hadn't seen a sign of anything in the house powered by electricity. It made her wonder if she would have to get accustomed to living without such modern conveniences.

From a rickety old bookshelf, she picked up a candle and a box of wooden matches. It took a few moments of fumbling around in the dark before she was able to light the candle. The faint flickering of the flame provided just enough light to see what was around her. Standing in the center of the hallway, she could make out the outlines of four identical doors. She looked to each of them, but none felt familiar enough to brave opening it.

Closing her eyes, she tried to imagine herself as a young child walking the hall on the way to her room. The distant memory she was searching for finally came. With a hint of doubt, she approached the door nearest to the stairs. A strange tingling sensation filled her body as she reached out for the doorknob. It felt as if the house was looking right into her heart to assure she belonged there.

Her mouth curved into a smile as she pushed the door open. The candle provided just enough light to make out the features of the room. It was indeed childish, just as she had suspected, but was also wonderfully ornate. The smell of cedar wood hit Red's senses as she took in the sight of the handcrafted furnishings with finely carved details. The wallpaper had images of red birds flying through puffy white clouds.

All through the room were handmade dolls, along with a collage of colorful stuffed animals, from bears to frogs, and a few other creatures that were not so easy to identify.

Red approached a wooden rocking chair and picked up a beaten-up rag doll. "I named you *Neoprene*. You were quite the mischief maker."

A small desk stacked high with fairytale books caught Red's attention. With a gleaming smile, she dashed over and grabbed a book from the center of the pile. It was titled *The Dragon Princess*. The cover had a faded picture of a young girl standing next to a gigantic green dragon. "This was my favorite story."

The spine cracked a little as Red opened the book. It was worn and brittle from being well read and much loved. Browsing through the pages, she recalled insisting Grenda read it to her every night before bedtime. The specifics of the tale were a little foggy in her memory.

From what Red could recall, it told of a young girl who set out on an adventure to put an end to a dangerous dragon. It had been making a lot of trouble for the people of her village. When she finally met the beast, it turned out that it was merely trying to make friends with the villagers, but his massive size and fiery breath created all sorts of trouble. The girl befriended the dragon, and together they saved the land from a terrible tyrant king. She was crowned the princess of the dragons and kept the land safe for all of her days.

As Red sat the book down, she noticed a few crayon drawings tacked to the wall. The first was a scribbly image of a small child with red hair, standing between a man holding an axe and a woman wearing a red cloak. "I bet that was me with my mom and dad."

She was fairly certain the next drawing was of herself as a small child, along with a boy and girl of similar age. They all had big smiles and were waving. "I think we were the best of friends. I wish I could remember your names."

The final drawing was the most peculiar of all. It depicted a little girl in a red cloak holding the hand of a boy with the face of a wolf. Something about it was so chilling that it made her feel lightheaded. After a lingering moment of staring at the image, she shook it off and turned away.

Red came face-to-face with her reflection in the cracked glass of a full-length mirror. It was a dreadful sight to behold. Dry mud caked her face and dress. Some kind of weird, sticky goo was in her hair. She picked up a fluffy towel from the dresser and tried to wipe herself clean, but it was a hopeless effort that just smeared the mess around more than it got it off.

As much as Red wanted to continue exploring her room, she'd become so tired it was hard to keep her eyes open. She was relieved to discover that her bed wasn't child-sized, as she feared it might be. It was large enough that a full-grown adult could sleep in it with room to spare.

She slipped off her sandals and let her tattered dress fall to the floor. The fluffy feather mattress was the softest thing she had ever lain upon. It was so warm and comfortable that she was overcome with a feeling of safety the likes of which she had never imagined possible.

The moment was/seemed so perfect that she feared it was nothing more than a wonderful dream. The thought of waking up in the orphanage brought a sinking feeling to her stomach. Dismissing this dreadful thought, she blew out the candle on the nightstand. It wasn't more than a moment later that she drifted off into blissful slumber.

Or, so Red thought …

A thundering crash echoed all around, causing Red's eyes to snap open with a fright. She looked up to discover the ceiling of her bedroom was no longer above her. Instead she saw the blazing red moon on a backdrop of a million twinkling stars in the midnight sky.

Her head was aching with so much pain that it was hard to think straight. Even through blurred vision it was clear that she was again in the forest meadow, in the same place she had the head-to-head encounter with the mysterious rider.

A few feet away, her little motorcycle was on its side with the front wheel still spinning. Not far from it, a motorcycle tire trail was leading away into the forest, but there was not a sign of the mysterious rider.

Red's body ached as she pushed up to her feet. She was so dizzy that each step forward made her feel more nauseous than the last. Of the many thoughts jumbled around inside her throbbing head, one stuck out above all. She feared that the journey to her granny's house had all been a dream.

The sky above ignited with fiery red light. Red looked skyward and gasped in fear as a massive explosion erupted on the moon's surface. It sent countless shards of blazing rocks scattering in every direction. At first, they looked like thousands of falling stars zipping across the night sky, ready to grant the wishes of those who gazed upon them. Red smiled and made a silent wish that she would find the happiness she had desired for so long.

The moment of bliss turned to terror when the twinkling moonstones began popping and exploding in the atmosphere, and plummeted toward the earth like blazing comets. Red could not stay in the meadow any longer, so with no direction in mind, she ran as fast as her feet would carry her. It wasn't long before she was once again racing down a dark path deep in the woods.

The ground rumbled as the moonstones slammed into the earth and exploded on impact. The air rapidly filled with so much smoke that it was hard for Red to see a thing beyond her nose. With the forest ablaze all around her, she feared there would be little chance to escape.

A burning shard of moonstone hit the ground not more than a few yards away, blowing a tree into a million flaming splinters. Red covered her face and ran as fast as she could in the opposite direction. It wasn't long before she was gasping and choking from the smoke filling her lungs.

Just when things couldn't get any worse, she reached the edge of a steep embankment. A blazing rock pelted the ground nearby, causing a shockwave that knocked her over the edge. Tumbling down the grassy hill, head over feet, her efforts to stop the fall proved useless.

When she finally stopped, it came with a hard flop that left her breathless and flat on her back. It took a painful moment of gasping and wheezing before she was able to come to her senses. With the aid of a splintered tree branch, she strained to get to her feet. Her leg was throbbing from a sharp pain shooting up her thigh. She wasn't sure if the muscle was twisted or the bone was broken, but there was no chance she would be able to run with such an injury.

Using the branch as a crutch, she stumbled onward, each step requiring relentless determination as the pain grew worse and worse. After stumbling for another mile or so, a blaring red light suddenly erupted up ahead. It wasn't like the amber flames that had burned so brightly earlier in the night. The pulsating glow emanated from deep within the trees. What was causing it, Red did not know, but it was beckoning her toward it.

The need to find the source overwhelmed Red so much she forgot the pain in her injured leg. Whatever was calling to her was growing louder with each passing moment. The final steps required her to push through thorny bushes, ripping her clothes to shreds and leaving her covered with cuts and scrapes.

When she emerged into a forest clearing, she saw a glowing red stone that sat atop an ancient pedestal. Somehow its identity was as plain to her as anything she had ever laid eyes on.

"The Omega Gem."

The scorched red stone wasn't much larger than a gumball. At face value it appeared to be nothing more than a worthless chunk of rock, yet the power it emanated was anything but ordinary. Red could feel its energy crackling in the air around her. She knew without doubt that it was a force unparalleled by anything on Earth.

"Why are you calling to me?"

As Red reached out to pick up the gem, a furious roar erupted from behind. She spun around to see a powerful white wolf perched a fee yards away, showing its razor-sharp fangs, ready to pounce. The deep rumbling growls of more wolves erupted from all sides.

Red looked around as four more wolves emerged from the trees. Each must have weighed at least two hundred pounds and had its own uniquely colored coat—black, grey, brown, and yellow.

"What's happening to me?"

Red's senses spiked as her body began to twitch with strength she had never before known. She was astonished to see three-inch, razor-sharp claws protruding from her fingertips. A pair of canine fangs was forming inside her mouth. Hair began growing all over her body, from the tips of her pointy ears all the way down to her elongated wolf feet.

Letting out a furious roar, the white wolf lunged forward to attack. Red raised a claw to smack the beast in the face. An instant before it connected, she snapped awake in her bed at her granny's house. She swung her arm wide, so fast it made a whooshing sound like a knife cutting through the air.

Red leaped to her feet and dashed to the mirror. She let out a huge sigh of relief upon seeing she wasn't covered in fur and had no fangs. With her heart still pounding in her chest, she stumbled backward and flopped down on the bed. Reaching up to scratch an itch on the back of her neck, the tip of her fingernail poked into her skin like a sharp needle. The fear of what this might mean was more than enough to set her heart racing even faster.

Slowly holding out her trembling hands, she discovered razor-sharp claws protruding from her fingers. They were shrinking down and gone within seconds, but the fact that they were ever there was enough to send her mind spinning into a frenzy of confusion. For the next several hours she sat awake, pondering how much of what she had experienced was merely a dream, and how much of it might have been real.

CHAPTER 5

Red awoke at the break of dawn with a sense of calm she had never known. In the land of Wayward, her future was a mysterious path of unknown possibilities. Whatever she would become there didn't frighten her. It had to be better than being tossed around like a rag doll from one orphanage to another. In the city, she would have eventually fallen into a mundane life of hard labor or waiting on tables. For the first time, she actually felt hopeful about the future.

Looking down at her dress lying tattered on the floor, Red whimpered a little. She couldn't imagine having to put the thing back on in such a sorry state. It was certain she would need something new to wear, or at least something not ripped apart at the seams.

With a blanket wrapped around herself, Red opened the bedroom door and peered into the hallway. The scent of fresh baked pastries woke her hunger like a starving beast. Her empty stomach grumbled with anticipation over what awaited her in her granny's kitchen.

"Red, are you awake?" Grenda called from downstairs.

"I am, Granny," Red called out. "At least I think so."

"I made up a hot bath for you, if you're interested."

"Oh, yes. That would be the best thing ever."

Red had never felt so dirty in her life. There wasn't an inch of her body that wasn't covered in filth. Her hair felt like vermin had crawled into it and built a nest. The constant itching had been another problem she was doing her best to ignore.

"It's the door at the end of the hall," Grenda said. "I put a change of clothes in the bathroom closet for you."

Red dashed down the hallway and pushed open the bathroom door. The sight of an old cast iron tub filled to the brim with steaming water was more than she could have hoped for.

Just before getting into the tub, she stopped cold and locked the door. In the orphanages, forgetting to do this was an invitation for trouble. It felt a little foolish to feel the need to do this in the safety of her new home, but she wasn't ready to let her guard down just yet.

As Red stepped into the hot water, she was certain that the day would be the finest of her life. She committed to the creed of always being grateful for things even as simple as a hot bubble bath. This was a luxury as rare to her as receiving gifts on Christmas morning.

Dipping her head under the water brought a moment of silent tranquility. Her thoughts drifted away to a time long ago. She recalled sitting in the tub as a child, her mother by her side, singing a lovely folk song. It was the most vivid memory Red had ever experienced from her childhood. She could only hope that in the coming days, the house would grant her many more memories of her life.

By the time the water grew cold, Red had washed her hair twice and scrubbed every nook of her body. She wished she could stay there all day, but the time had come to step out and face her new world.

The towel she dried off with was the softest thing that had ever touched her skin. It was quite the opposite of a place she had once lived where the towels were made of scratchy burlap.

The next order of business was hanging inside the tiny bathroom closet. The change of clothes Grenda had put there for her to wear was a troubling mystery. It wasn't a big secret that grannies don't always share the same fashion sense as their granddaughters.

With no other choice, Red resolved to gratefully wear whatever was waiting for her inside. Slowly opening the closet door, her eyes lit up with delight. The most wonderful green dress she had ever seen hung inside, made of crushed velvet with crisscrossing ribbons that laced up the front.

The aroma of fresh roses rushed Red's senses as she rubbed the soft fabric against her face. Letting out a shrill of joy, she slipped the dress on and was astonished to find that it perfectly fit her every curve.

Red gasped in bliss when she caught a glimpse of herself in the mirror. The dress was the same worn by her mother in one of the photos on the mantel downstairs. She pulled the towel off her head to let her red hair dangle down. The sight of her reflection brought a blissful smile to her face. She looked nearly identical to her mother.

If ever there was such a thing as a perfect day, Red felt she was living that day in all its glory. She began to hum the tune that she recalled her mother singing to her as a child. While the words were unknown to her, the melody felt hauntingly familiar. She would have stood in front of the mirror for endless hours, if not for realizing that she could now see her mother anytime she wanted to.

Red stepped out of the bathroom and headed downstairs. In the living room, she took a moment to look at her mother's photos on the mantel. She tried not to assume the worse about her mother's fate, but suspected it was grim, considering the way Grenda had dodged the question. This led Red to wonder what became of her father after he ditched her on the steps of the church.

In her granny's kitchen, Red gasped at the spread of breakfast delicacies waiting for her on the table. She dashed over and began to pile a plate high. If it hadn't been days since having had a proper meal, she might have felt a bit greedy for taking so much. But instead, she called out, "Granny, this all looks so wonderful. I hope you'll join me in this fine feast."

Red bit into a blueberry biscuit and waited eagerly for a response. "This is the best thing I've ever tasted."

Next, Red stuffed a luscious strawberry in her mouth and savored its sweet juices.

"Where are you, Granny?"

Red stood from the table and walked over to the pantry. Upon opening the door, she expected to find Grenda inside. Instead, there was nothing more than small shelves well stocked with cans and jarred preserves. There wasn't nearly enough space for a person even as small as Grenda to fit, but she distinctly remembered seeing her granny step out of it the night before.

When Red turned back to the table, there was a note sitting next to the plate she had just been eating from. She shook her head in outright denial, refusing to believe that she'd been so busy enjoying the delicacies that it had gone unnoticed.

In a dash, she grabbed the single sheet of parchment and unfolded it. The handwriting was the fanciest she had ever seen and just as difficult to decipher. From what Red could gather, Grenda had needed to head into town for some reason or other and wouldn't return until just before nightfall.

Dwelling in her disappointment, Red wandered the house, snooping around in the closets and cupboards. Grenda had a fascinating collage of strange objects stored away, many of which had no clear purpose.

In a large oak chest, Red found a stack of dusty photo albums, most filled to the brim with pictures of her mother, spanning from birth to adulthood. There were also plenty of Grenda in her younger days, and she was exceptionally attractive.

At the bottom of the stack was an album containing photos of Red as a child. One showed her sitting in front of a cake with five candles, with a boy and girl of the same age standing at her side. *Red, Dote, Ash, Age 5* was written on it in faded ink. Red could only wonder if these children were relations or friends, but judging from their joyful smiles, she suspected they were the best of friends.

By the time she'd finished looking through the albums, a glowing smile had overcome her face. The photos sparked memories that held many wonderful feelings. The one troubling thought she could not shake was that there wasn't a single photo of a man who could be her father. Red was sure there had to be a good reason, but that question could not be answered until Grenda returned, and that was still hours away.

In the early afternoon, Red decided to venture outside. The woods surrounding the house were far less menacing by day. The weather was so perfect that she wanted nothing more than to hop on her little motorcycle and go for a long ride. It was quite upsetting to think that her little man was sitting alone in the woods, unwatched and well out of her reach. She could only hope that the mysterious rider would soon return to help her retrieve it.

The path Red had walked down the night before looked safe and inviting in the daylight. It took her only a brief moment before deciding there could be no harm in taking a short stroll.

Each step she took came with a new and wonderful fragrance to enjoy. The sounds of the forest were a delight to her ears. Birds sang cheerful melodies, unlike the mindless squawking of those that lived in the city. It wasn't long before she felt that her perfect first day in Wayward was getting back on track.

"Red Riding." The muffled voice of a man called out from the near distance.

Deathly startled, Red stopped cold in her tracks. Holding her breath, she looked all around. The area was so thick with trees and shadows, whoever it was could have been two feet from her and she wouldn't have known it.

"Is somebody there?" Red said, no louder than a whisper.

"Over here," the man said. "Come quick."

"Is that you, Wolf Boy?" Red thought it might be the mysterious rider, although the voice didn't sound as she remembered. "I'd like you to take me to my motorcycle."

"I don't know anybody by that name," the man said.

"Then who are you and how do you know me?" Red asked.

"If you want to see me, you have to come and find me."

"Why don't you just come out and show yourself?" Red stood for an impatient moment, waiting for a response. Nothing came. "Well if that's the way you're going to be, I'm heading back home."

"Fine. Run right back to your granny's house like a frightened little girl."

Red grunted in angst. She knew venturing off the path came with a lot of risk, considering she didn't know her way around the woods. It wouldn't take much for her to get lost and not be able to find the way back.

"Don't tell me *you're* afraid, Little Red."

"Who said I'm afraid?"

The man sang out, taunting her, "Little Red Riding is a fraidy cat. A foolish girl. A little brat."

"Hey, I'm not a fraidy cat."

"Fraidy cat, fraidy cat. Little Red is a fraidy cat."

There wasn't a chance Red would walk away now. She just had to know who was calling to her, even if doing so meant taking a big risk.

"I haven't got all day, Little Red fraidy cat."

"Fine. But this better be good."

As Red ventured off the path and into the woods, she did her best to note landmarks in hopes they would help her find the way back. She passed a hollowed log ... a pile of black stones ... and a tree with a large nest holding a family of chirping baby bluebirds.

"You're almost here. Hurry, quickly." The man's voice sounded close now, and much deeper than before.

"I'm going as fast as I can. Would you tell me your name?"

Again there was no response. Red knew it would be best to stop this foolishness and return to the path. She had walked in a straight line, so doing an immediate about-face should lead her back to safety.

"You're not thinking of running away like a little fraidy cat, *are you?*" the man asked.

Red's need to prove her courage overpowered her sensibility. Venturing onward, she noted a tree bent over into a curved arch, with the top touching the ground. She thought such a large landmark would be easy to spot on her return trip to the path.

"If you won't say your name, at least tell me how you know who I am," Red said.

"Don't be silly. Everybody in Wayward knows who *you* are, Red Riding."

Red stopped cold. This had gone far enough. "If you refuse to tell me who you are, I'm going straight back to the path."

"Is that so?"

"Yes, it is. Now what's it going to be?"

"Fine, go back to the path. *If* you can find your way."

The temperature dropped so quickly that it made Red shiver and shake. In only seconds, she could see her own breath as she exhaled. There was no doubt she had made a dangerous mistake.

Red did a quick about-face and started walking as fast as she could in a straight line. Her eyes searched for the arched tree she had passed only moments ago. She desperately wanted to see the nest of bluebirds—or the pile of black rocks—and the hollowed out tree, but none of these things were anywhere to be found.

"Keep going. The path can't be far now," the man said with a snicker.

"Would you just leave me alone already?"

Red walked even faster, but she was gasping for breath and shivering from the unnatural chill in the air. Whoever her unknown stalker was, it was sure he had done something sinister to prevent her from finding the path.

"Don't tire yourself too much, Little Red. I like my meals to have a little fight in them."

His words pierced Red's ears like a knife. She had traveled so far to find her granny and still had much to learn of herself. The idea of her journey ending in such a foolish way was unacceptable. She knew it was time to stop running and face her stalker head on.

"Don't give up too easily or I'll be disappointed," the man said.

"Who said I'm giving up?"

Red piled a few small stones near her feet. She then snapped a branch off a tree, creating a jagged stake about a foot in length. With her makeshift weapon concealed behind her back, she struck an innocent pose. "I'm waiting, unless you're too much of a fraidy cat to show your face."

"Don't fear, little dear. I'll be there to meet you just as soon as I can."

"Don't make me wait too long."

After a silent moment passed, a nearby patch of bushes began shuddering. When her stalker emerged, he was nothing more than a decrepit old man. He stood hunched and walking with the aid of a twisted wooden cane. Red felt disgusted by the sight of his withered skin and long and crooked nose.

"Well, hello there, Little Red Riding. The master didn't tell me you were going to be so darn pretty," the old man said with a raspy voice. "This is going to be so much fun."

Red eyed the old man oddly. "Master? Who are you talking about?"

He pointed to the moon hovering high above. "It doesn't matter because you're not going to be around long enough to ever meet *him*."

Red cringed at the man's foul stench. It reminded her of rotten eggs. She then spoke in a childish tone. "Gee, mister, I thought you were going to be something big and scary, like a hairy troll or a smelly old orc."

"You mean *I* don't frighten you, Little Red?" The old man approached her, standing only inches from her face.

"Not even a bit. You look much too nice to be dangerous." Red's body temperature began to spike as a primal force deep down inside took control.

"Would it give you a fright if I said I had eaten men twice your size and many times your strength?"

"I can't believe a sweet old man like you would harm even a butterfly."

The old man snickered. "Then you are a fool, and you will die as one."

Red giggled like a child. "You're funny. I like you." She wanted to drive the stake into his heart, but her instincts warned her to wait for the perfect moment. "I think we should be friends." She fluttered her eyelashes. "Would you like to play a game with me?"

"We're already playing a game, Little Red. My game. I always win."

His mouth stretched open twice as wide as a normal man. The sight brought Red's blood to a near boil, but she somehow managed to maintain her endearing smile.

"Have you ever kissed a girl, mister?" Red giggled. "I like kissing boys more than anything in the whole world."

The old man twitched in impatience. "Little girl, do you have any idea what I am?"

"Granny said if she catches me kissing one more boy, I'm going to get a spanking," Red said with a mischievous grin.

The old man's massive jaw dropped open. He twitched in disbelief, unable to resist the lure of Red's childish charm.

"Mister, would you like to kiss me?" Red gave her lips a pucker.

The old man trembled with excitement. "This better not be some kind of trick, or I'll make you regret it in ways you could not possibly dream."

"Whatever do you mean?" Red asked with a nervous crack in her voice. "I just thought a handsome man like you would be willing to grant me just one little kiss. Especially if you're going to eat me."

"Fine, if that's what you want." The old man looked around to make sure nobody was watching. "Don't think I'm going to let you go over a little peck on the lips."

"I'm waiting." Red leaned forward. "Please don't disappoint me."

The old man began panting like a dog as he moved in to kiss Red. His face was so hideous that she lost the fight to keep her eyes open. As soon as his clammy lips made contact with hers, Red's heart was overcome with furious intent. With a powerful yank, she grabbed the old man by the coat and pulled him close.

Their eyes snapped open at the same instant.

"Now who's the foolish one," Red said with a *growl*.

She stabbed the sharpened end of the branch into the old man's chest. His mouth opened wide enough to swallow a person whole. He made a desperate grab for the stick, but Red kicked him to his knees. She watched through stone-cold eyes as he transformed into some sort of goblin with scaly, wart-laden, green flesh.

"Looks like I win this game," Red said.

The goblin grabbed Red by the hair. He pulled her head towards his mouth with all his might. Red struggled for a terrifying moment as she got closer and closer to his razor-sharp teeth. Red raised a foot and kicked the stake deeper into his chest. The beast groaned and fell backward.

"You may have won this day, Little Red." The goblin looked up to the moon. "He's coming back to Wayward, and one way or another, you're going to help him."

"Who is coming back?"

"You'll see soon enough."

"Maybe so, but you're not going to be around when it happens."

Red picked up one of the stones she had placed near her feet earlier and hurled it with all her might. It hit the goblin in the forehead so hard his eyes rolled back into his head. The vile creature that would have ended her life dropped to the ground with a thud.

Red stood trembling as its decrepit body withered up and turned to dust. The triumph of the battle overwhelmed her with a feeling so primal that it was impossible to resist a calling deep from within. "What's happening to me?"

She looked down at her hands. Razor-sharp nails protruded from her fingertips. Empowered with immense strength, she swung an arm wide, slashing her claws through the trunk of an oak tree. With her arms raised high, she looked at the moon. The voices of the lunar spirits called to Red, and this time she knew how to respond. The howl that came from her was so deep and loud that it echoed out through the entire forest. When it was finally over, she dashed away at lightning speed, leaving behind only a gust of wind in her wake.

CHAPTER 6

"Wake up, Red Riding."

Red's eyes opened to see a million stars twinkling in the night sky. It was a majestic sight she could never enjoy under the blaring lights of the concrete city. The air was shivering cold, and yet she was burning with sweat, as if she'd been running for hours. "Where am I?"

A masculine voice with an Irish accent spoke. "The *where* isn't as important as the *why*."

"So *why* am I here?"

"*That* is the big question. I suspect you're not going to much like the answer," the Irishman said.

"Try me."

The Irishman took a deep breath. "If I had to give it my best guess, I would say a dark force did something sinister to get you here."

"How did I know you were going to say something like that?" A rather harsh odor hit Red's senses and made her already queasy stomach churn a bit. "Look, whoever you are, I'm thinking you're in serious need of a bath."

"I hate to break it to you, Red, but that odor is coming from you."

"Yeah right." The idea of this was so absurd that Red shrugged it off. Just to be certain, she held her arm close to her nose. "Oh, rank. I smell like a wet dog."

"Don't worry. The stench will be gone before you know it."

"Fabulous."

This didn't give Red a bit of reassurance as she pushed up to a sitting position. Her vision was somewhat blurred, making the details of her surroundings unclear. From what she could tell, she was outside a temple, constructed of grey stone and towering well above the tree line. There were stained glass windows that depicted celestial images of the moon in its eight phases. "What's the story with this place?"

"When you regain your senses, I'll do my best to explain," the Irishman said.

"I can hardly wait." Red could just make out the outline of a burly man standing over her, though her vision was still too blurry to see if he was human. After all that had happened since her arrival, she thought it best not to assume anything. "Listen, whoever you are, if you're going to try to eat me, you should know that I just slayed a goblin."

The Irishman belted out a laugh. "Well, one day you will have to recount the tale for me. Not that such a triumph is unusual for a woman of the Riding Clan."

"How do you know my name?"

"Everybody in Wayward knows who you are." The Irishman extended a hand.

Red cracked a smile, feeling quite safe in the company of this stranger. She took his hand, which was three times the size of her own and rough with calluses. His raw strength felt quite astonishing as he pulled her up to her feet.

"Easy there, muscle man. You trying to pull my arm off?"

"I'm so sorry. I was under the impression that you were a rough and tough girl that could slay a goblin."

"Okay, okay, leave the sarcastic wisecracks to me." Red took a few quick stretches to loosen her sore muscles. "I know people around here don't always like to give their names. If you could tell me yours, I'd appreciate it."

"You can call me Ethan. I hope in time you will come to also call me friend."

"Ethan is a good name. I could use a friend right about now."

"Then you have one in me, Red of the Riding Clan."

"What is this *Riding Clan* business you're talking about?"

"Your family has a long heritage of great heroism and honor in Wayward. You should take great pride in knowing that their blood flows through your heart."

"Maybe if I knew more about my family, I would understand what that means. Would you tell me about them?"

Ethan stood up straight like a soldier saluting a general. "It would be my greatest honor to aid the Alpha Huntress."

"Alpha what?"

Red's vision had cleared up enough to be able to make out Ethan's features. He was well over seven feet in height and more than twice her age. His face was rugged and handsome, accented with a thick red beard. Leather armor covered his massive muscular chest and a huge axe hung over his back.

"Now I know I must be dreaming again," Red muttered.

"I can assure you that this is no dream. Though I suspect you've had some rather confusing ones since your recent arrival."

Red took a half-step back. "How do you know that *exactly*?"

"I knew your mother. Since you are her spitting image in both looks and wit, I would guess I know you just as well as I knew her."

"Knew her? Does that mean she's … you know … not alive anymore?"

Ethan took a long breath. "Grenda didn't tell you of her fate."

"Granny hasn't told me much of anything yet."

"Then the hard truth falls to me." Ethan wiped a tear from his eye.

"Ethan, if this is too hard for you, we can talk about it another time. I'm sure my granny will tell me soon enough."

"The strength of your mother is alive inside you, Red Riding."

Red frowned. "From the way you said that, I get the feeling I'm not going to get a chance to meet her."

"I'm afraid you are right, Red. But let us not dwell on such sad thoughts. There is much to rejoice upon today. The Alpha Huntress has returned to Wayward."

"What's this Alpha Huntress business you keep going on about?"

"It's not exactly my place to explain that," said Ethan.

Red snarled in frustration. "Well then whose is it *exactly*?"

Ethan shrugged. "I can't exactly say. Just not me."

"It sounds really important. So why don't you cut the word games and just spill it already."

Ethan belted out a laugh. "If I didn't know better, I would think I was talking to Jenna herself."

"Jenna?"

"That was your mother's name: Jenna Riding."

"Jenna Riding." The name echoed a hundred times over in Red's mind. It was the first time she had ever heard the name of her mother. It was like music to her ears. "So she was just like me?"

"In every way I can see. Though there are hints of your father in you as well."

"You knew my father?"

"That I did. I vowed to him that I would stand by your side and give my life if necessary to assure your safety."

Red looked Ethan in the eyes and had no doubt he was telling the truth. "Please tell me about him."

"I will. But right now there are more important matters to discuss." Ethan pushed open the massive double doors of the temple and gestured for Red to go inside.

"What's in there?" Red couldn't imagine that anything in that old temple was more important than learning about her father.

"You have to trust me, Red. What waits inside is vital to your future."

"This had better be good."

A gust of warm air shot by Red as she took a few cautious steps through the temple doors. A sea of a hundred flickering candles mounted on the walls illuminated the massive stone chamber. On the ceiling high above was a carved image of the Earth encircled by images of the moon in its eight primary phases.

On the wall there was a large wooden clock, counting down from—

5 YEARS / 0 MONTHS / 4 DAYS
2 HOURS / 3 MINUTES / 22 SECONDS

"What is the story with this place?" Red looked back to where Ethan was standing in the open doorway with his feet an inch short of the threshold. His expression made it clear he wasn't taking one more step into the chamber unless he had to. "Hey, Irishman. It's freaking me out that you told me to come in here, but you won't come inside, too."

"Trust me, Red. Nothing bad is going to happen to you."

The honest look in Ethan's eyes told Red that he was telling the truth; not that it made her feel any better about the situation. It took a few calming breaths before she was able to coach herself into venturing further inside.

She soon found herself standing in the center of five marble pedestals, each with a stone sitting upon it. Some were jagged and sharp, while others were rounded and smooth. The colors varied from bright and shiny to scorched and burned. Despite their many differences, the one thing they all had in common was an intense aura of power radiating around them.

Red then noticed that each pedestal had a unique marking carved into the base:

I Alpha
II Skoll & Hati
III Diona
IV Madonna Oriente
V Ragnarok

A strange humming tone rung out nearby. Red whirled, startled, toward a stone altar at the far end of the chamber. Upon it rested a large archway made of some kind of transparent metal. The sight of it consumed her heart with dreadful fear. Still, she felt compelled to walk across the chamber and up the four steps of the altar.

Red stood gazing at her own reflection in the archway. With a trembling hand, she reached out and touched its oddly hot surface. In a flash, an image of the moon blazing in the midnight sky filled her head. Standing before it was a silhouetted figure of a man in a

51

black hooded cloak, extending a bony hand toward Red. She could feel his icy cold breath as he whispered something into her ear. His words were unclear, but their intensions were of pure evil.

"Get away from me." Red leaped backward into the air, startled. She soared ten feet and hit the floor in a battle-ready crouch.

"Red, do not fear," Ethan said. "There is nothing in here that can hurt you."

"What's going on here, Irishman?" Red asked.

"It's difficult to explain. You won't believe me if I do."

"That doesn't mean I don't want you to try. You can start with that metal arch thing there."

Ethan clenched his fist tight enough to cause his knuckles to crack. "Some call it a celestial portal. It connects this world to one hidden deep beneath the lunar surface."

"Are you telling me that thing goes to the moon?"

"It's more like it comes from the moon. I suppose you could use it to go there if you needed to."

"What would be there if I decided to go?"

"I will not utter such terrible things to young ears. All I will say is that it's a place I hope you never have to go."

Red paced around in a whirlwind of frustration. "Is that the best answer you can give me?"

"It is the only answer I will give you about *that* place."

Red stomped toward Ethan. "Listen up, buddy. I'm not some dumb little kid that can't deal with the truth. I want to know what that thing is doing here. And who made it? And what's with all these rocks? And what about that clock counting down? And what about the moon carvings on the ceiling? And so help me, if you say you can't tell me, I am going to kick your butt." Her threat came right as she approached Ethan with an arm extended and a finger pointing at his face.

"Spoken like a true Riding." Ethan nudged Red's hand aside and took a few nervous steps further into the chamber. "This temple was built by the followers of a vile sorcerer called Ragnarok. He was born a man, but through dark spellcraft, he became as powerful as the lunar deities."

"Well that doesn't sound weird."

Ethan took a long breath to clear his thoughts. "It all started two hundred years ago when Ragnarok got the idea that if he could bring part of the moon to Wayward, his followers, mostly made up of werewolves at the time, could have the power to transform at any time, day or night, and not just during the full moon."

"Werewolves that can run around during the day? Well, that's different."

"Red, do you want to hear this or just make a bunch of sarcastic comments?"

"Sorry."

"Using a powerful spellcraft, Ragnarok created a mighty explosion on the moon. It caused thousands of moon rocks to rain down on Wayward and set the forest ablaze."

"So that's what happened," Red muttered.

"You've heard this before?"

Red turned away, not interested in talking about her recent dream. "Just go on with your little story."

"It's not a story, Red. This happened. For three days, all of Wayward was engulfed in smoke and dust from the shattered moon rocks. Fifteen years later, the offspring of those who survived began to develop strange abilities. The most powerful were able to transform into creatures that stood on two legs and looked part human and part wolf. They came to be known as the Children of the Moon."

"You mean werewolves?" Red asked with a nervous crack in her voice.

"Some called them that. A time of great darkness fell upon Wayward. Many children were seduced by Ragnarok to join his clan. They searched the forest far and wide, seeking to find every bit of rock that had fallen from the moon."

"Let me guess, the rocks make werewolves' powers even stronger."

"You're a smart girl, Red. And while that was enough reason to seek them out, what Ragnarok wanted was the means to use the powers beyond the borders of Wayward. It would allow them to go out into the world and conquer the human race."

"But somebody stopped them, right?"

"They did, but not easily. There was a moonstone that was more powerful than all of the others combined. It was known as the Omega Gem. Ragnarok wanted it more than anything. Not to use it. To destroy it. The power it held was the only thing he feared. He knew that in the right hands, it could be used to defeat him."

Red gasped in excitement. "So what happened? I have to know."

"A young woman, the same age as you are now, stood up and fought tirelessly to stop Ragnarok's forces from overrunning the town."

Red took a nervous breath. "Who was this young woman?"

Ethan placed a hand on the stone marked Alpha. "The lunar deities gifted the girl with great power that made her into an unstoppable werewolf. She became far stronger than all the others. Any who dared to face her in battle met their demise. She became known as the Alpha Huntress, the high protector of Wayward. Her quest lasted for five years. In the end, she battled Ragnarok in this room, and forced him back through that gate, into a lunar prison."

"You mean she trapped him inside the moon?" Red looked up at the archway on the altar. The humming emitting from it grew ever louder.

"She did just that. And he has remained there for almost two hundred years, quietly waiting for a chance to return."

Red considered this and then frowned with a grim realization. "That's not the end of the story, is it?"

"I'm afraid not, Red. Just three days shy of fifteen years ago, many children of Wayward began to develop great powers. Dark times have fallen. Ragnarok will soon attempt to use the gate to return to Wayward."

"So why not smash this place to dust?" Red asked.

"If it were that simple, I would have done it myself a long time ago. This place is well protected by powers stronger than anyone can comprehend."

Red frantically paced around. "Then someone has to do something. Ragnarok can't be allowed to come back."

"You have no idea how happy I am to hear you say that." Ethan placed a firm hand on Red's shoulder and looked her in the eyes. "The name of the one who defeated Ragnarok was Red Riding."

"No way." Red nearly stumbled off her feet.

"It's the truth, Red. I would never lie to you about such a thing."

"That can't be, Irishman. There's no way I'm going to become this so-called Alpha Huntress."

"I'm not saying that you're going to become the Alpha. I'm saying you already are. Red Riding's powers live inside you. The only thing you have to decide is if you have the courage to use your gift to become Wayward's new high protector."

Red caught a glimpse of something she had not noticed before: the wall above the entryway featured a painted image of a female werewolf wearing armor and a red cloak. She was in a fierce battle with a deity that Red somehow recognized as Ragnarok.

"You're lying. I won't believe it." Red repeated this over and over as she backed away toward the door.

"You have to trust me, Red Riding. You must take up this calling, or terrible darkness will fall upon Wayward."

"I'm leaving. Don't follow me." Red approached the door. "I'm not her. I never will be."

"Red, it's too dangerous to be out there on your own," Ethan cried out. "You could be killed."

CHAPTER 7

Red walked aimlessly through the dark woods, searching for the path back to Granny's house. Each passing hour, left her feeling all the more hopeless. There was no doubt that she was utterly lost. The chances of her surviving the night were bleak as the temperature dropped to near freezing. She regretted her decision to ditch Ethan at the temple. The glimmer of hope that he might have followed her had long since faded from her thoughts.

As the night progressed, Red considered the things Ethan had told her. The more she thought about it, the more absurd it all seemed. She only saw herself as a poor orphan who had never done a spectacular thing in her life. The idea of becoming some kind of high protector didn't make a bit of sense. She was certain there were others in Wayward far more worthy of such a great gift.

Just when things couldn't get any worse, thunder roared out in the dark sky. A downpour of rain and chilling wind soon followed. Red shivered and shook as she sloshed across the muddy terrain.

She eventually found a hollowed out knot in the trunk of a tree, just big enough for her to fit inside. It was quite uncomfortable and smelled of mold, but she felt fortunate to have shelter from the storm.

It was far too cold to sleep, so she sat awake, watching the rain and listening to all the peculiar sounds of the woods. Some were strange and wonderful, while others were dangerous and even terrifying—trees creaked, insects chirped, and leaves fluttered or crackled from movement nearby and overhead. In the darkest hours of the night, she heard a monstrous roar followed by the terrified screams of a woman on the run. It ended with sounds that Red tried desperately to drown out by pressing her hands over her ears. The ordeal left her with a sinking feeling of shame for not doing anything to help.

By the time dawn broke, the rain had given way to a fine mist. Red hoped to have a better chance of finding her way back home in the light of day. She had not a clue where she was, nor could she even guess a direction to begin her search. The only thing she knew for certain was that hiding inside a hollowed out tree wasn't going to get her anywhere.

Peering out of the tree, Red could see the creatures of the forest starting to emerge. If they felt safe out in the open, then it ought to be safe for her, too. She crawled out onto the wet grass and took a moment to stretch her cramped up muscles.

The crisp morning air was fragrant with wild flowers and other wonderful aromas. It made her empty stomach grumble with hunger, a feeling she knew all too well. She did a quick search around the area, hoping to find some sort of fruit or berries, but there wasn't a sign of anything fit to eat.

A rhythmic thumping like a horse galloping erupted in the near distance. What made it so strange is that it was unclear which direction it was coming from, as if it was everywhere and nowhere at the same time.

As it grew louder, Red considered playing it safe and taking cover back inside the tree. Before she was able to make a decision either way, a large cat dashed out of the bushes and ran right between her legs. Red spun around and watched the three-foot-long spotted feline fleeing across the clearing.

"Where are you off to in such a hurry?" Red asked.

The sound of galloping hooves thundered out right behind Red. She turned around, just as a snow white horse leapt out of the bushes and came right at her.

Reacting on pure instinct, Red executed a dazzling backward handspring, just in time to avoid being trampled. When her senses returned, she saw the horse sprinting off after the cat.

"Out of my way, foolish peasant," said a white-haired teen girl riding atop the horse. She was dressed in formal purple and black riding gear, sitting with perfect posture on a finely crafted leather saddle. From over her shoulder, she pulled a bow and loaded a wooden arrow.

Red watched helplessly as the white-haired girl took aim at the fleeing cat. The arrow soared in the blink of an eye and pierced the creature through the ribs. Crying out, it stumbled and tumbled across the wet ground until it smacked head first into the trunk of a willow tree. Red's heart sank in despair at the sight of the wounded creature groaning in pain, but the hunt wasn't yet over.

With her horse charging forward, the white-haired girl leaped to the ground and dashed in a flash over to the fallen cat. With one hand she grabbed the skin on the back of its neck. With her other, she pulled a long hunting knife from her boot.

"Don't do it," Red shouted.

The white-haired girl looked Red in the eyes. She had ghost white skin and hair that made her look like a walking corpse. Her deep purple eyes glowed in the daylight. She smirked with a malevolent grin and then slit the cat's throat.

"How could you?" Red cried out as she approached the white-haired girl. With tear-soaked eyes, she knelt down by the cat, lying slain at its killer's feet.

"Listen here, peasant girl, I don't know who you are, nor do I care," the white-haired girl said. "What has transpired here is none of your concern."

"It *is* too my business." Red glared up at the white-haired girl. "Who exactly do you think you are?"

"I will not be questioned by a foolish peasant girl." The white-haired girl turned away, dragging the dead cat along behind her.

"Hey. Don't walk away from me." Red raced after her. "What was the point of killing it? You look well off enough not to need it for food."

The white-haired girl responded without bothering to look back at Red. "If I was so poor that I had to eat such vermin to survive, I'd sooner let myself die of starvation."

"Then what will you do with it?"

"Well, peasant girl, if you must know, I'm going to skin it. Twelve or thirteen more, I'll have enough to commission a tailor to make a blanket for my horse."

"Are you mad?" Red watched in disgust as the white-haired girl pulled a cloth sack from the horse's saddlebag and shoved the dead animal inside. "I think you ought to be ashamed for doing such a terrible thing."

"Shame is for the weak." The white-haired girl turned to face Red with a furious glare of irritation. "Crying over the demise of such a disgusting creature is pathetic."

"Maybe you're pathetic for thinking that way."

"How dare you speak to me in that manner, peasant girl." The white-haired girl swung her hand to slap Red in the face. Red's reflexes were so quick that she grabbed the girl's wrist, stopping the strike an inch short of her face. The two girls locked eyes in a dangerous stare-down.

"My, my, peasant girl. You have superior reflexes and a fearlessness that I've scarcely seen. I have surely misjudged you."

Red released the white-haired girl's hand. "Don't let me see you killing any more innocent cats, or you'll answer to me."

"Is that so? And *whom* will I be answering to?"

"My name is Red Riding."

"You mean *the* Red Riding?" The white-haired girl stood up straight to regain her elitist composure. "Now this is indeed unexpected. It's not that I wasn't aware of your return, but I never expected we would meet under such circumstances."

"And who are you?"

"I am so sorry. Where are my manners?" The white-haired girl extended a hand to Red. "My name is Ice of the royal order known to all as the Seether Clan."

"Ice? That's a rather unusual name."

"No less unusual than the name Red, I would presume."

Red shrugged in agreement. "So you're some kind of royalty?"

"Not some kind. The best kind. My family built the entire town of Wayward. Without us, this region would be inhabited by nothing more than uneducated peasants."

"How fortunate for them that you're around, or they might just fall off the face of the world."

"That was sarcasm. I don't care for sarcasm."

Red sighed. "As much as I'm enjoying this little chat, I need to be getting back to my granny's house. Can you point me to the nearest road?"

"I'll do you one better than that, Red Riding. I will take you to old Grenda's home on my horse."

"Oh. You know my granny?"

"Correction. I am aware that such a woman called Grenda Stalk exists in Wayward. We have no personal ties, I can assure you of that."

"Why am I not surprised?"

"You have a sharp tongue, Red. Though I suppose this is to be expected from a woman of the Riding Clan. Not that there are many of you left around."

Red frowned. "That seems to be the case."

"Oh, don't get like that now, Red. It wasn't my intention to be callous. I was merely making a statement of fact."

"In the future, I'll try not to take things you say too seriously, Ice."

Ice cracked an amused grin. "And there you go again with the snappy wit. I have a feeling you and I are going to get along quite smashingly."

Red clenched her fists so tight it made her knuckles crack. "I couldn't agree with your choice of words more, Ice Seether."

"And on that note, it is time for us to ride." With an effortless hop, Ice sprang up onto the back of her horse. She extended a hand to Red. "Shall we?"

Red faked a smile. "It's not necessary. I'll be fine walking."

"Don't be foolish, Red. These woods are treacherous to one who doesn't know her way around. Not to mention that walking would take you well over half the day."

"Oh. I didn't realize I had strayed so far from home." Red concluded that she had no other choice. "I do suppose a ride would be better than walking."

"Now you're talking sensibly. Give me your hand."

Red reached out and accepted Ice's waiting hand. She was startled to discover Ice's skin was chilling cold and as smooth as silk. With one effortless pull, Red hopped up onto the back of the horse and slid into the saddle behind Ice. For the second time since her arrival, a stranger she didn't much care for was giving her a ride home. The irony wasn't lost on her.

"Onward." Ice shouted.

The white horse took off running so lightning fast that it made Red squeal.

"Hang on tight, Red Riding."

Ice gave the horse a kick in the side and it began running even faster. Red experienced a thrill unlike any other as they crossed flowery fields, leaped over a rocky ravine, splashed across a flowing stream, and charged down a steep embankment. The ride lasted for the better part of an hour before they reached a dirt path and Ice let the horse slow to a trot.

"Ice, that was one of the most thrilling experiences of my life. You're a magnificent rider."

"Yes, I know. Now tell me your story, Red Riding."

Red frowned. "I'm afraid there isn't much to tell."

"Nonsense. Even a peasant orphan has a story to be told."

"How do you know I was an orphan?"

"Red, darling, you are far more well-known around Wayward than you're aware of."

"I'm just starting to realize that." Red had a nervous twinge, unsure how to feel about her apparent fame.

"Now come on, Red. I'm sure you have a plethora of interesting tales to share."

Red had no idea what plethora meant, nor did she intend to ask. "My life has always been eventful and filled with complications, but never interesting."

"You'll have to excuse me if I have no ability to relate to such a notion. As a Seether, every day of my fifteen years of life has been nothing less than interesting."

"Why am I not surprised?" Red sighed, wanting nothing more than for this conversation to be over with.

"Don't get me wrong, Red. My path in life has not been without complications. My parents impose expectations upon me that you couldn't begin to comprehend. Not that this isn't to be expected, considering my elevated status."

"I'm sure it's been a terrible struggle for you," Red said.

"I'll ignore the obvious wit intended by your words. Trust me when I say that immense wealth and power does not mean a life free of difficulties," Ice said.

"I suppose you're right, Ice."

"As is *always* the case." Ice pulled the reins, and the horse stopped. "Well then, this is as far as I can take you."

"Thank goodness." Red looked around and was relieved to find they were on the path near Grenda's house. She slid down off the saddle and dropped to the ground. "Ice Seether, I would like to thank you."

"Think nothing of it, Red Riding. The pleasure was mine indeed. It is rare to meet a woman of importance nearly equal to my own."

Red again faked a smile. "As much as I'm enjoying this little chat, I must be going now."

"Before you do, may I ask just one last question?"

"I suppose it depends on the question you want to ask."

"Yes, of course," Ice snarled. "With that qualifier in mind, what is it that has brought you back to Wayward after all these years?"

Red sighed. "Well, I thought it was to find my family, but things have become a bit complicated. Now, I'm not even sure I'll be staying."

"I think it would be sensible if you stayed around for a few more days."

"I didn't mean I was leaving right away. To be quite honest, I haven't decided one way or the other just yet."

"Excellent. That is not a decision to be made in haste. If it were my choice to make, I would certainly take some time to think it over."

Red nodded in agreement. "That's probably what I'll do."

"I'll tell you what, Red. Come to my house tonight. I'm having a little dinner party. Just a few close friends. I'll introduce you to some of the better people of Wayward. Perhaps that will help you decide."

"That's a kind offer, Ice. I'm just not so sure I'm quite up for a party after the night I've had."

"Don't be like that now. I simply won't take no for an answer. I'll even send a driver to pick you up if you're lacking adequate transportation."

"No, that is too much. I couldn't put you out like that."

"Trust me, Red, darling. It's *nothing*."

From the way Ice said it, Red knew it had to be true. There was no doubt Ice had great wealth. "If it really isn't any trouble, then I accept your offer."

"Then it's settled. The driver will arrive at eight. Feel free to bring a date if you can find one on such short notice."

"I'll see if I can work that out," Red said with a shrug of doubt.

"If it's too much of an inconvenience for you at such late notice, I could always arrange an escort. I know several eligible gentlemen who would just jump at the opportunity to accompany you."

"Are you insane?" Just thinking about going on a blind date with somebody Ice picked was nearly enough to make Red's stomach churn inside out.

"You don't have to get like that about it. I wasn't implying that you couldn't get a date on your own accord."

Red felt bad for the harshness of her response. "I'm sorry. That came out all wrong. What I meant to say is that it won't be necessary."

"Then we shall leave it at that." Ice extended a hand. "It has been a pleasure, Red Riding."

"Likewise, Ice Seether."

"Onward." Ice shouted.

The white horse raced off in a flash.

As Red stood watching Ice fade into the distance, she considered that she'd misjudged the girl. She then caught a glimpse of the bag holding the dead animal hanging from the back of the horse. It left Red having no idea what to think of Ice Seether. She figured she would have a better chance to get to know her at the party. That is, if she actually decided to go.

CHAPTER 8

Red was grateful that it was only a short walk to Granny's house from where Ice Seether had dropped her off. Her thighs ached and her legs were a little wobbly from riding on the horse. Not that she had a bit of regret. The high-speed ride across Wayward had been one of the greatest thrills of her life.

When she emerged from the woods into the clearing around Granny's house, she stopped and did a double take. Her little motorcycle was sitting near the porch. Its chrome pipes and faded blue paint glimmered in the afternoon sun.

A smile of joy lit up her face as she dashed over to get a closer look. She was delighted to see her little man had been scrubbed clean and polished to a shine. The broken gas line had even been replaced with brand new chrome tubing.

As she sat on the freshly polished leather seat, she knew that it had to be the work of the mysterious rider. Red considered the idea that she'd misjudged him, but was still suspicious of his motives. Perhaps it was a peace offering. Or maybe it was his way of repaying a debt out of a sense of obligation. She made sure not to forget it was his recklessness that caused the crash to begin with.

"Well, it was mostly his fault," Red mumbled.

A troubling thought came to mind when Red noticed the gas gauge was on the full line. Could this be the rider's way of telling her to leave town? Was he giving her a chance to get away before things got any stranger? The idea not only sounded quite reasonable after all that had happened, but she was seriously considering it. There might never be a better chance to leave Wayward in her memories.

Red only needed to give the key a quick turn to be on her way. She was certain that with enough effort the path leading away from Wayward could be found. Where she would go from there was another question altogether. The point was that it would be far, far away from the weirdness that would surely come her way if she stayed.

Closing her eyes, Red took a deep breath and began turning the key.

"Red Riding! Oh my goodness!" A high-pitched girl's voice squealed out from nearby.

Red snapped her hand away from the key like a kid caught with her hand in the cookie jar. She looked to the front porch, where a rather odd-looking girl was jumping for joy. The girl was wearing the dorkiest glasses Red had ever seen.

"I can't believe you're here." The odd girl spoke with a lisp that was caused by some kind of wire thing in her mouth that may or may not have been a dental retainer.

"Yes, I'm here," Red said.

The odd girl shrieked and dashed toward Red in a frenzy of excitement. She locked her arms around Red, giving her a rather strangling hug. "You have no idea how much I've missed you."

The joy the odd girl had in her eyes was so pure and contagious that Red couldn't help but crack a smile.

"It's good to see you. It's surely been a long time," Red said.

"Almost ten years to the day. That's sixty-six percent of our lives we've been apart."

"Sixty-six?" Red tried to do the math in her head, but just assumed that the odd girl was right. "So we were friends before?"

"The best ever." The odd girl squealed with glee. She then slumped with a nervous gasp. "At least I thought we were?"

Red put on a big smile. "Of course we were. It's just that I've been away for a long time."

"Sixty-six percent of our lives."

Red nodded in agreement. "Right, that long. I've been through a lot, and it's just that I don't entirely remember … well … almost anything at all."

"You forgot me?" The odd girl began pacing in distress. "I'm not the most memorable person in the world, I know that. It's just that we were almost like sisters. Not in the related by blood way, but more in the sisterly best friend sort of way."

"Please don't be upset. It's not that I exactly forgot you." Red recalled the photo she had seen the day before from her third birthday. It was safe to assume that the odd girl was one of the children with her in the photo. She just couldn't remember the name written on it. "You were at my third birthday, right?"

"You do remember me." The odd girl let out a sigh of relief. "That was only the best party ever."

"Unlike any other."

"Oh. You probably don't want to talk about what happened on that day," the odd girl whispered. "I understand if you're not ready."

"Ready?" Red was almost too afraid to ask the odd girl what she was talking about, but it was a chance to learn a bit of her history. "So what did happen?"

"You really don't remember?" The odd girl tapped a finger on the tip of her nose as she pondered this. "Oh, I get it. I've read about this sort of thing. When something real bad happens to somebody, they block out the memory because it's too painful to remember."

"Is that what I've done?" Red considered this odd notion as she stepped off her motorcycle.

"Now don't get all gloomy." The odd girl tried to comfort Red with a hug, but she squeezed so tightly it felt more like an attempt to suffocate her. "And don't worry. When you're ready to talk about it, I will be here for you."

"Honestly, I would be okay talking about it right now."

"Don't be silly. We haven't seen one another in sixty-six percent of our lives. This is a happy day. I would never dream of ruining it with such sadness."

"I guess that makes sense." Red slumped a little. "Maybe another time."

"Any time you're ready."

"Any time but now," Red mumbled. Her face lit up with a smile as the name she was searching for popped into her mind. "Dote. That's who you are."

"You remembered." Dote danced around in a whirlwind of excitement. "I thought you were going to call me Luna, and we both know how much I hate my real name."

"Right, I can see how you would much prefer to be called Dote."

"No joke. I mean it's a little freaky that my mother named me after some nutty old witch that got all mental and ate the souls of a thousand children."

"Yeah, that is a little weird." Red figured Dote had to be talking about an old myth or fairytale. Surely not something that actually happened.

"Right, as if I would ever do something so crazy. Only a witch totally twisted in the head would ever mess with spellcraft that requires using human souls."

"Exactly." Red faked a smile. "And it's not like something that terrible actually happened."

"Oh, *it happened*. It's a messy stain on my family name. We don't talk about it much. Especially on holidays."

Red shuddered with a nervous chill. "I can see why."

"And don't think for a second that I'm not grateful that your family doesn't hold it against us."

"Why would we ever do that?"

"It's just that there are a lot of people who look down on families with such a dark history. Look at the way everybody treats the *Helheim Clan*," Dote said.

"I don't think you have to worry about that around here," said Red.

Dote whispered, "Just because three witches in my family line have been burned at the stake doesn't mean we're all bad."

"Burned at the stake?!" Red yelped.

"Don't get me wrong, Red. Every one of them had it coming. The trouble is that people look at a thing like that and wonder if all the women in the family have some kind of psycho witch gene."

Red faked an awkward smile. "I guess I can see how that might make sense to some people."

Dote frowned. "Oh, I wish I could stay here all day, so we could catch up on old times, but I need to get home soon. You know how mental my mom can get when the sky gets all crazy like it is today."

Red glanced to the perfectly calm blue sky. She decided to just skip asking. "That's okay. There'll be other chances."

"How about I come back tonight? We can have a slumber party. We can stay up all night reading our favorite fairytales to each other, and bake cake, and pie, and eat candy, and draw funny pictures of each other, and make fun of Ash because he's a boy, so he's not allowed to stay over, and it will be wonderful, just like old times."

Red smiled fondly. "That does sound wonderful."

"Then let's do it." Dote wailed out. "Please say 'yes.' Pretty, pretty please?"

"It's not that I don't want to." Red frowned, not wanting to let Dote down. "It's just that I have this party to go to."

"Party? Don't tell me you're going to Ice Seether's party," Dote blurted out with awestruck eyes.

"Well, yes. How do you know about it?"

Dote squealed so loudly it could have shattered the windows. "Everybody knows about it. How did you ever get invited?"

"It's no big deal. I met Ice Seether in the woods earlier today. She said I could come."

"No big deal? It's only like the biggest deal ever!" Dote clutched her heart and twirled around in longing. "Oh, the breaks you get. Sometimes I wish I could be the bloodline descendant of Wayward's high protector."

Red gave Dote an odd look. "You know about that?"

"Well, yeah. My great-great-grandmother only stood by the side of your great, great-great-grandmother in the final battle against Ragnarok."

"Oh," is all Red could manage to say.

"You have forgotten a lot."

"I have, Dote. Would you tell me more?"

"There's so much to tell. It's hard to pick a place to even begin."

"Any little thing you can think of would be fine."

Dote tapped a finger on the tip of her nose. "Wait, I know. Your mom and my mom were best friends as little kids. Then something happened involving some dumb boy when they were our age, and they stopped being friends."

"I'm sorry to hear that."

"Don't be sorry, Red. We weren't even born yet. My mom blames your mom, but I only know the story as my mom tells it, and we know how she exaggerates everything."

"Well, I do hope they worked things out."

"It's more like the problem worked itself out. The boy they were fighting over fell off a bridge and got eaten by a pack of razor rats. Once he was out of the way, they got over it and were friends again."

Red cringed at the thought of this. "Well, I suppose that's good news."

"It really was. If not for that guy dying an awful death, our moms might have just kept on hating each other and we might have never gotten to be friends."

"Or one of them might have ended up with the guy, and then one of us might have never been born," Red said.

Dote held her head in confusion. "I never thought of it that way. I mean if I wasn't born as me, that would be a bummer, but if you weren't born as you …" Dote stopped cold and looked at Red with a rather startling expression.

"Dote, what is it?"

Dote looked away. "Nothing. It's not important."

"You can't leave me wondering like that. What were you going to say?"

"Well, it's just that you're the Alpha. There's no telling who would have ended up with the powers."

"I see. That is an interesting thought," Red said.

"I mean we could almost say that it was fate that made such a thing happen."

Red took a nervous gulp. "Why would we say that?"

Dote giggled. "I'm not saying it happened that way. I'm just saying it could have."

"The idea that a boy had to die to make sure I was born is bad, right?"

"It's not a happy thought, that's for sure. What would be bad is if somebody did something to make sure it happened that way." An odd look overcame Dote's face as she pondered this.

Red took a nervous gulp. "Something like what, Dote?"

"You know, something like …" Dote made a pushing gesture.

"Dote, that's a terrible thing to even suggest."

"Red, I'm not saying *I* would do such a thing."

"I would hope that *nobody* would."

"Oh, there's a bunch of people I can think of who would do it in a heartbeat."

"You're freaking me out here, Dote. Can we move on from this?"

Dote gave Red a warm smile. "You're right. We shouldn't talk about such odd things on this wonderful day."

Red sighed. "I could not agree more."

For a lingering moment, Red and Dote stood in an uncomfortable silence.

Dote finally grabbed Red's hands and looked her in the eyes. "So listen, you have to promise to tell me all about the party. Take notes because I want to know every little detail, all the way down to the color of the napkins."

Red saw the longing in Dote's eyes and could come to only one conclusion. "I've got a better idea. Ice said I could bring a friend. Want to come with me?"

"Are you kidding? You know I would love that more than anything in the whole world." Dote took Red's hand and began to lead her around in a ballroom style dance. "I've been practicing for this for as long as I can remember. I know you know all about that, unless you forgot that too, which is fine with me."

"What are you talking about? Ice said this is just a small party with a few friends."

"Red, don't be silly. Ice Seether doesn't have small parties. This is her birthday ball."

Her birthday ball? Red halfway stumbled off her feet.

Dote continued to lead Red around in the dance. "It's only the biggest event of the summer. Hundreds of people will be there. Thousands, maybe. They come from all over Wayward. Some further than that. Everybody who is anybody will be there. And we are going to be there with them."

"Oh, joy." Red's heart dropped to her feet. She knew nothing of high society, nor did she want to learn. Making it all the worse, there was no way she could get a dress suitable for such an event. As much as she wanted to tell Dote it was a huge mistake, doing so would break her heart into a million pieces. She already knew that Dote would become her greatest friend—for the second time in her life.

"I guess we're going to a ball," Red mumbled.

"Oh, happiness." Dote hugged Red, again just a little tighter than she should have. "Red, you are the best friend ever."

"So are you, Dote." Red sighed. "I guess you'd better hurry home so you can get ready. Be back here by eight o'clock."

"Oh, I will be. You can count on me not to be late to the greatest night of my life. I mean, our life, because we're together again, and nothing is going to ever pull us apart."

Red smiled as she watched Dote dance away in a whirlwind of excitement. When she turned back toward the house, the good feelings faded away. She would now have to deal with Grenda after having stayed out all night without permission. Doing this at an orphanage would have brought with it swift punishment. There was no way of knowing what it would lead to with her granny.

CHAPTER 9

"Granny, are you here?"

As Red peered in through the front door, she was baffled to find that the place looked like an abandoned shack. A thick layer of dust blanketed the room from floor to ceiling. A musky odor hit her senses so hard it made her eyes burn and stomach churn.

She wanted to dash right back outside out of fear of what might be lurking in the house, but that just wasn't an option until she knew for certain that her granny wasn't in danger.

"Granny, if you're in here, please say something."

It was so icy cold that Red could see her breath as she stepped over the threshold. The instant she pushed the door shut, the room transformed to the warm and welcoming home she had come to adore.

All the dust was gone without a trace. A flame ignited in the fireplace, filling the room with comforting warmth. The aroma of fresh baked blueberry muffins filled the air. It was enough to make Red's stomach rumble with hunger and remind her that she hadn't eaten since the previous day.

Curious about the strange phenomenon, Red reached back and pulled the door open. In a flash, the room was again the lifeless tomb she had first seen.

An eight-foot serpent slithered in from the kitchen doorway. It showed Red its venomous fangs and hissed as it raced toward her.

Red screamed and slammed the door. The snake vanished seconds before it would have bitten into her leg.

The room was once again warm, clean, and safe.

"It's a pretty good trick, eh, Red?" said Grenda.

Red's heart skipped a beat as she spun around. She could not have been more relieved to see her granny strutting down the stairs, wearing her furry winter coat and slippers. "Granny, I don't understand how this is possible."

"Nothing to get worked up over. Just a little protection spellcraft I put on the inside of the house. I got worried after you didn't come home last night," Grenda said.

"Spellcraft?"

"You know, crazy concoctions empowered by tongue-twisting incantations," Grenda said.

"Granny, are you saying you can do magic?"

"Couldn't go around calling myself a witch otherwise."

"A Witch?" Red yelped out.

"Don't go getting yourself all in a tizzy over it. I'm not the sinister sort that goes around eating little children or casting curses all willy-nilly."

"I didn't think you were." Red cracked a grin, feeling a little foolish over her startled response. "It's just that I didn't even know there were such things as witches."

"I suppose you wouldn't. There are a lot of things in Wayward you're going to have to get used to," Grenda said.

"No doubt," Red mumbled under her breath. "I hope you were just kidding about there being the sort of witches that eat children and cast curses."

"I wish I was, dear." Grenda reached into a small leather pouch on her belt loop. She pulled out a handful of silver dust and began scattering it around the room.

"What sort of spellcraft are you doing now?" Red asked.

"This is no spellcraft. I'm just spreading a little silver flash powder around to keep away the creepy crawlies."

"I see." Red was quite sure she didn't want to know what creepy crawlies were, so she just assumed her granny meant common household bugs.

Grenda blew handfuls of the powder underneath the furnishings and behind shelves. "There is no shortage of witches who have dabbled around in the dark spellcraft. The problem is that such power is obtained without true discipline. The mystical forces are dangerously seductive, so you have to know how to keep it all in balance. Casting magic for vile purposes can twist a witch's mind up in a hurry. Once things get too far out of control, it's nearly impossible to come back. Those witches usually have to be rounded up and done away with."

"You mean burned at the stake?" Red asked.

Grenda nodded. "Sometimes that's the way it goes. I personally prefer to use methods that are a little less vicious."

Red gasped. "So you've taken part in those hunts?"

"It's dirty work, but somebody has got to do it. Don't go thinking an angry gang of villagers with pitchforks and torches could handle such a dangerous task," Grenda said.

Just the thought of this made Red shudder in fear. "If it's so dangerous, why would anybody want to be a witch?"

Grenda giggled. "Don't go thinking it's all dark and sinister. There are plenty of us who do a lot of good in this world. Not to toot my own horn, but I'm one of the best healers in all of Wayward. Just last week I stopped a plague that could have taken out half the trees in the Tolkien Shire."

"I've never heard of a plague that attacks trees."

Grenda grinned proudly. "And thanks to my crafty solution, you never will. Proof positive that witches aren't so bad to have around."

Red doubtfully shrugged. "I suppose you're right."

"Your friend Luna is my top student. She's one of the most powerful witches around. Or she will be when she grows out of being so dang clumsy."

"Luna?" Red asked. "Oh, you mean Dote. Yes, I just met her outside."

"Dote." Grenda belted out a laugh. "Fifteen years old and still going by that silly nickname you gave her all those years ago."

"I did that?"

Grenda scampered toward the kitchen doorway. "Darn right you did. You had nicknames for most of your friends. Even that imaginary boyfriend you were always going on about."

"Hold on a second. I had an imaginary boyfriend?" Red asked.

"You were hardly a toddler, so don't go making a thing of it. And don't just stand there looking like something the cat dragged in. Get in here and tell me where in Wayward you've been all night." Grenda entered the kitchen.

Red again felt nervous as she recounted the events of the night in her mind. She could only hope that Grenda would understand that most of it wasn't her fault. As she stepped into the kitchen, her head hung low, like a child about to receive a spanking.

"Have a seat." Grenda placed a plate of wonderful fruits and muffins on the table. "You look half-starved."

"Thank you, Granny." Red sat at the table and didn't hesitate to dig right in. Her stomach had been cramping a bit, though she wasn't sure if it was from hunger or the fear of punishment.

"Well, out with it. What sort of mischief did you get yourself into this time?" Grenda asked.

It took Red a moment to gather the courage to speak. "Oh, Granny, I didn't mean to stay out all night. It's just that I got lost and couldn't find my way back. A strange voice called to me. It was a goblin that nearly ate me, but I stabbed him in the chest with a stick and then things got even weirder from there."

"Slow down, Red. You sound like a little tot trying to talk her way out of getting a licking. You're not a child here. Just tell it to me like a grown-up would."

Red's tension drained away. She took a bite of her muffin and savored its wonderful flavor for a moment. "After I slayed the goblin, I blacked out and woke on the steps of a strange temple. I met a woodsman named Ethan who told me I was some kind of alpha hunting werewolf that has to become a high protector and slay some kind of god called Ragnar. Or something like that."

Grenda sat back in her chair and grumbled to herself. "Is that all of it?"

Red frowned. "Well, I also met a girl called Ice who invited me to a ball. I don't much want to go, but I accidentally invited Dote to come along. She was so excited that there's no way out of it, and I don't have a thing to wear."

"That was all one night? Guess that will teach me to leave you home alone."

"Granny, I do hope you're not angry with me."

"Of course I'm not angry, Red. I was darn near shaken out of my shoes when you didn't come home. Wayward has dangers greater than you can even begin to imagine. If something had happened to you, it would have been disastrous."

Red took another bite of her food as she pondered Grenda's words. "I have questions. I need honest answers."

Grenda stood up from the table. "Since the cat's halfway out of the bag, there's no point in dragging it out. Let's go."

Red grabbed another muffin and followed Grenda upstairs. They stopped at a door across from Red's bedroom. Grenda knocked twice, then three times, then twice again. There was the sound of a lock disengaging, and then the door creaked open on its own.

As they entered, Grenda spun around in a circle and waved a hand in the air. Red gasped in amazement as flames ignited in gas lamps mounted on each of the four walls.

"Remind me to teach you that little trick one of these days," Grenda said.

"I surely will." A rush of joy filled Red's heart as she took in the room. "This was my parents' bedroom." She was about to open a finely carved wooden box sitting on top of a dresser, but stopped short.

"Go ahead, dear. It all belongs to you now," Grenda said.

"All of it?"

"Every last trinket."

Red smiled in wonder as she opened a box to discover it contained several pieces of jewelry. None of it was particularly fancy or of high value, but in her eyes it was a trove of priceless treasure.

Next, she opened a drawer and pulled out a green silk scarf. As Red rubbed it against her face, she caught a scent that she assumed belonged to her mother.

She finally opened a large chest at the end of the bed. The sight of its contents was so startling that she slammed it shut in a panic.

"Oh dear. I should have warned you about that." Grenda opened the chest, revealing it held swords, knives, clubs, and battleaxes. "Your parents had many enemies and fought in countless battles." She took out a sword with a three-foot silver blade and placed it into Red's trembling hands. "This belonged to your mother. She used it to slay many attackers."

"No way." The hilt fit perfectly into Red's hand, as if it had been forged just for her. She held it up to the light and gazed into the glimmering blade. In the reflection, she saw her mother thrusting the silver weapon into the heart of a black werewolf with glowing red eyes.

The image was so startling that Red dropped the sword.

Grenda picked up the weapon. "There is no need to fear the sword. It knows who you are. It will proudly serve you as well as it did your mother. Now hold out your thumb."

"What for?" Red took a nervous step backward.

"You have to trust me, Red. Now do as I say."

Red held out a trembling hand. "I hope you're not planning to do what I think you're going to do."

"Relax, my dear. This won't hurt … too much." Grenda flicked Red's thumb across the edge of the sharp blade, cutting into her flesh.

"You call that not too much?" Red pulled her hand away. "I sure hope there was a point to that."

"Look into the blade again, and you will understand," Grenda said.

"If you say so." Red took a nervous breath as she held the sword close to her face. She cringed a bit at the sight of her own blood dripping down the blade. When she gazed into the silver surface, her reflection transformed into a werewolf. Not the hairy dog-faced kind, but her face with wolf-like features. "Granny, is that me?"

When Red lowered the sword, she found herself standing inside the Moon Temple. She was wearing form-fitting battle armor that came down to her knees like a skirt. Claws poked her fingertips. Reddish-brown fur covered her from head to foot. Topping it off, she wore a hooded red cloak that made her look like a superhero.

She looked to the pedestal holding the moonstone marked Alpha. It was illuminated and humming in an eerie low-pitched tone.

She then saw the clock on the wall. It was counting down from—

5 YEARS / 0 MONTHS / 0 DAYS
0 HOURS / 0 MINUTES / 3 SECONDS

The moon gate began swirling with a vortex of mystical energy. Inside was the silhouetted image of a man Red couldn't see, but somehow knew he was Ragnarok. His black armored hand reached out through the vortex.

"Join me, Red Riding," roared a voice of pure evil.

Red's eyes filled with terror as she realized Ragnarok wanted her to pull him through the gate, and even more disturbing, she knew she held the power to do so. "I'll never help you."

"Then everyone in Wayward will die, and it will be your doing," Ragnarok said.

The double doors of the temple exploded open. Red shielded her face as a massive gust of flames blasted in, setting the chamber around her ablaze. A horde of werewolves charged in, growling in rage.

Trembling in fear, Red raised her sword high. A white werewolf with glowing purple eyes lunged at her through a wall of fire. Its mouth was open wide with the intention of crushing her throat. Red wailed out a battle cry and swung her sword with furious intent.

An instant before they collided, Red snapped awake in her parents' room. She leaped backward and swung her sword. The blade sliced through one of the poles holding up a canopy above the bed. The whole thing came plummeting down with a crash and a bang.

"Red, calm down. You're safe," Grenda said.

"Is that what's to come for me, Granny?" Red asked.

Grenda put a comforting hand on Red's shoulder. "What the sword showed you is one possible vision of the future. Never forget that nothing is written in stone."

"How can I face such a terrible ordeal? I'm just an orphan girl that doesn't know anything about fighting in battles or defeating monsters," Red said.

"Of course you can. You're the Alpha Huntress," Grenda proclaimed.

Red sat on the bed. "I am not. I'm nothing."

Grenda gave Red a disapproving glare. "It's a good thing your mother and father aren't around to hear you talk like that. They sacrificed everything to assure that you would live to see this day."

"Are you saying they died for me?"

Grenda sat next to Red. "When it became known that you had received the Alpha Power, there were some who believed they could take it away and give it to another. They planned to invoke a dark spellcraft that would rip the power from you. When the first attackers came that night, your mother fought fearlessly to keep you safe. In the end, she was fatally wounded. Your father refused to leave her side, but when push came to shove, he had no choice. Your mother and I stood together and gave him enough time to take you safely away."

Red struggled to hold back her tears. "So what became of my father?"

Grenda took off her glasses and wiped the lenses clean with her dress. "I am sorry to say that he fell into terrible despair. In one night, he'd lost his beloved wife and had to abandon you to be raised by strangers. He wandered off alone into the woods. I haven't seen a sign of him since."

Red sat clutching her stomach. "It's all so tragic."

Grenda stood and raised her head high. "No. It's a heroic tale that should be remembered as such. To think of it as any less would taint the memory of your parents."

Red considered this and realized it was true. "How can I do this, Granny? How can I stand against such terrible evil?"

"You won't have to face it alone, Red. I'll be with you. Others will make themselves known when the time is right."

Red picked up her mother's sword and stood tall. "You're right. I will honor my parents' sacrifice. I'll fight tooth and nail to make sure Wayward doesn't fall to evil."

"Now that's the Red Riding I've been waiting so long to see."

Red paced in a whirlwind of excitement. "So how do we begin? Do we raise an army? Maybe storm a castle or two?"

Grenda took the sword from Red and put it back into the chest. "When it comes to that, we certainly will. Right now, you have a ball to prepare for."

"Granny, how can I think of such a thing when my destiny is calling?"

"Destiny can wait for tomorrow. Tonight you have other matters that need to be tended to." Grenda opened a wooden wardrobe, revealing it held many dresses.

Red smiled in awe at the wonderful sight. "Did all of these belong to my mother?"

"That they did. She made them with her own hands. It would do her proud for you to wear any one of them." Grenda left the room and closed the door behind her.

Red's heart raced with delight as she browsed through the dresses in the wardrobe. She pulled out a magnificent blue ball gown and held it up to herself. As she looked into a full-length mirror, a dazzling smile overtook her face. She saw herself as the shining image of her mother.

"I'm going to make you proud of me. I promise."

CHAPTER 10

Red paced around on the porch of Granny's house in nervous anticipation. It should have been the most exciting night of her young life, but she was consumed with dreadful anxiety. Her stomach was twisted in knots and the deep breathing Dote had coached her into trying wasn't helping one bit.

Her only comfort was that she was wearing the most beautiful blue ball gown she had ever seen. Grenda had spent the better part of an hour braiding her hair with little flowers and ribbons. Red had never dreamed that she could actually look like a princess, though it was impossible to deny the reality of the moment as she stood there in all her glory.

"At least I'll look good when I faint in front of everybody," Red said.

"Don't be silly," Dote said. "We're about to have the most fun ever."

Dote stood by Red's side wearing the most ridiculous bright orange flower patterned dress anybody had ever seen. Dote's mother had made it for a harvest dance that Dote was to attend, but she never got a chance to wear it because her date had backed out at the last minute.

Red was fairly certain that showing up in that dress would have brought Dote more ridicule than being dumped by her date. Now poor Dote was going to the premier event of Wayward in the same ridiculous dress.

"We both look so pretty," Dote said with a gleaming smile. "I bet everybody at the ball will be staring at us all night."

"Oh, I have no doubt about that."

Red had offered to loan Dote something from her mother's wardrobe, but Dote was set on her orange dress. She insisted that it matched her eyes. This made not a bit of sense, considering that her eyes were hazel.

"Do you think they'll have ice cream?" Dote asked.

"I don't know how balls work, so I can't say either way," Red said.

"I sure hope they'll have chocolate mint cake. That's our favorite."

It felt odd for Red to be with somebody who knew her so well and yet she knew so little about. She hoped that the memories of their time together as children would soon return. Until then, she took comfort in knowing they would have a lifetime to get to know one another again.

"As long as we're together, I don't care what happens," Red said.

"I still can't believe you invited me. I mean considering that my family and the Seethers aren't on the best of terms," Dote said.

"Do I even want to ask why that is?" In Red's haste to invite Dote, she had not considered the idea that it might be a problem.

"It's a long, weird story. Most of it happened before we were even born."

"As long as it doesn't have anything to do with that boy who fell off a cliff."

Dote gave a nervous laugh. "What would make you think such a silly thing like that?"

"Dote, I was only joking. Tell me the boy that our mothers were fighting over wasn't a member of the Seether family."

"Of course he wasn't."

"That's a relief."

"I mean not in a way that anybody could ever prove."

"What exactly does that mean, Dote?"

"It was mostly just rumors, Red, so don't take this too seriously. There were some people who thought maybe the boy, who I think was named Hamelin, was like an unofficial member of the Seether family."

"How can somebody be an unofficial member of a family?" Red asked.

Dote fidgeted, a little nervous. "You know, when somebody who's married to one person goes off and has a baby with another person, but doesn't want anybody to know for whatever reason."

Red nodded in understanding. "Oh, like that kind of unofficial. So he's the reason the Seethers don't like your family?"

"Oh, no. My grandmother once tried to destroy the Seether Clan by casting a spellcraft on them that causes people to go crazy with paranoia," Dote said, quite casually.

Red gasped in disbelief. "Dote, you're only joking, right?"

Dote gave Red a nervous grin.

Just then, in the near distance, the sound of galloping hooves erupted. Red and Dote stood watching in awe as four white horses emerged from the foggy path. They were pulling along a magnificent white carriage with glimmering gold trim. A driver sat atop wearing a formal riding uniform.

"Is that for us, Red?"

"I have no idea, Dote."

The horses pulled the carriage to a stop near the porch. Red and Dote watched in wonder as the driver stepped down and meticulously straightened his uniform. He approached Red and bowed to her, all the while managing to blatantly ignore Dote.

"Your carriage awaits, my lady." The driver spoke with a formal English accent.

It took Red a couple of awestruck seconds to respond. "Thank you."

The driver opened the carriage door and kicked down a wooden step. He turned to Red and extended a white-gloved hand. "My lady."

"After you, Dote," said Red.

The driver looked over Dote a little perplexed. "I was not informed there would be two this evening."

"Ice said I could bring a companion," Red said. "Is it a problem?"

"Of course not," the driver said through clenched teeth.

Dote giggled and took the driver's hand. As he helped her up the step, she lost her balance and fell backward into his arms. Her legs flailed around as the driver fumbled to get her through the carriage door.

Red did her best to contain her laughter as she waited for the frazzled man to regain his composure and straighten his uniform.

He turned to Red and extended a hand. "Shall we?"

"I suppose if we must."

Red took the driver's hand. While stepping up into the carriage, she faked like she was going to tumble backward. The driver gasped in a panic and dashed behind her with his arms extended. Red gave him a devious grin as she stepped inside and sat down on the crushed velvet seat.

"Enjoy your ride, ladies." The driver slammed the carriage door.

"Thank you," said Red and Dote in unison.

The ride to the ball took the better part of an hour. Red and Dote sat mostly in silence. It was all so surreal that neither could come up with much of anything meaningful to say.

Red instead gazed out the window at the lush forest landscape. Even in the dark of the night, Wayward seemed magical to her, like she was living in a fairytale realm of boundless possibilities. Only days ago she was a nameless orphan, and now she was riding in a fancy carriage on her way to a grand ball. It made her feel quite foolish for considering the idea of leaving.

"Dote, if this is a dream, I don't want to ever wake up."

As they rolled up a steep embankment, Red and Dote gasped in astonishment. Thousands of floating lamps that looked like twinkling stars illuminated the night sky. Below was what could best be described as an ivory palace. It towered a hundred feet tall and was many times that in width. There were even guard towers on the two front corners.

"Have you ever seen anything like it in your life, Red?"

"I've never even dreamed that such a thing could exist, Dote."

As they approached the palace, they bypassed a long line of horse-drawn carriages and formally dressed party guests. They rolled to a stop at the front gate. The door opened, and two men wearing formal uniforms stood at attention.

Red gestured for Dote to go ahead, but Dote shook her head to say *no way*. Red sighed and took the lead. As she stepped out, a handsome butler extended a hand and helped her down. He wore a black tuxedo with several medals on his chest.

"Announcing the arrival of the lady Red of the Riding Clan," the butler proclaimed.

Party guests waiting in the line looked curiously at Red. They pointed and whispered things to one another that she couldn't quite hear.

"Thank you, sir," Red said, feeling both flattered and embarrassed by all the attention.

The butler held up his arm to Red. "Would the lady allow me to escort her inside?"

Red giggled. "Oh, that would be wonderful." She took his arm and together they walked toward the main gate.

"Don't forget me." Dote cried out from behind.

Red looked back to see Dote frantically stumbling out of the carriage. "Dote, I'm so sorry. I got so caught up in everything that I nearly forgot you."

Dote's eyes were wide with awe as she took in the sights. The butler let out a prudish sigh and offered his arm to her.

"Are you going to announce her?" Red asked the butler.

"Of course, Miss Riding. I was just about to." The butler looked to Dote. "What is your name, young lady?"

Dote whispered into his ear. The butler grumbled to himself. He then cleared his throat.

"Announcing Miss Dote, of the Shrine family."

Not a single person in the crowd reacted, but Dote smiled and waved just the same. She took the Butler's arm, and the three of them walked through the main gate.

Dote whispered to Red, "I can't believe they didn't make us wait in line."

"Miss Riding is an honored guest," the butler said.

"See, Red? You're totally important," Dote said.

The idea of this seemed strange to Red, but she figured it was best to leave well enough alone and just enjoy the moment.

As they entered the ballroom and approached the top of a grand staircase, Red's and Dote's eyes lit up in amazement. Down below, a full orchestra was playing for countless party guests waltzing on a dance floor. Surrounding them were hundreds of tables, where guests dined on gourmet food and sipped champagne.

"Shall we go down, ladies?"

As the butler led them down the grand staircase, Red felt a surge of excitement that she did not expect.

"Dote, I have a feeling this is going to be a night that we'll never forget," Red said.

"It will be as long as they have mint chocolate cake."

When they neared the bottom of the stairs, Red spotted Ice Seether among the crowd. She was standing with a group of aristocratic gentlemen and their snooty looking wives.

Ice was wearing a long purple gown with a train that dragged for several yards behind her. It was plain to see she had no interest in speaking to the stuffy men and was just waiting for her chance to get away.

The instant Red's feet touched the ballroom floor, Ice looked right to her, as if she sensed her arrival. "Red Riding, thank the goddess!" Ice turned away from the men without a word and dashed over. She greeted Red with a hug, followed by a kiss on each of her cheeks. "I was beginning to worry that you might not come."

"Ice, I can't thank you enough for inviting me. When you said a few friends, I had no idea you meant all this."

"Well, you have to agree that there is nothing too good for our birthday," Ice said.

Red gave Ice a perplexed look. "*Our* birthday?"

"Did you not know, Red, darling? You and I were born on the same day. Within minutes of one another, or so it is to my understanding."

"I didn't know that." Red stood dumbstruck. She had never known the date of her birthday. Making it more confusing, she couldn't figure out how Ice knew, or why she would even care.

"I know it's still three days away. Tonight was far more appropriate for a ball. I hope you don't mind us sharing a party," Ice said.

Red felt quite frazzled. "This is all so unexpected. I don't know what to say."

"Red, tell me I'm not imposing on your own plans. You know how much I hate to be an upstager."

"It's okay. I just got to town, so I hadn't made any plans," Red said.

Dote stepped between Red and Ice. "I'm giving her a slumber party with mint chocolate cake and ice cream."

"What is this that speaks to me?" Ice looked down her nose at Dote as if she were some kind of annoying insect.

Red cleared her throat. "Ice, I would like you to meet my dear friend, Luna Shrine."

Dote extended a hand to Ice. "You can call me Dote, like all my friends do."

Ice blatantly ignored Dote's hand. "This is something different. The last Shrine to step foot in this house departed without her head intact."

Red giggled nervously, unsure if Ice was serious.

Dote held her extended hand right to Ice's face. "Well, I sure don't plan to hold that against you."

Ice gave Dote a stone cold stare.

Red nudged Dote aside. "Dote is here by my invitation. I hope you don't mind. You did say I could bring a guest."

Ice rolled her eyes in irritation. "I distinctly recall using the word *date*, but why not? It is your party as much as it is my own. Enjoy the festivities, little Miss Shrine."

"Dote."

Ice gritted her teeth and turned her back on Dote. She put an arm around Red and ushered her away into the crowd. "So, Red Riding, I know we have discussed this before, but I was hoping you might open up a little more to me. I truly want to know every little thing there is to know about you."

"There isn't much to tell, I'm afraid. Dote probably knows more about me than anybody."

"Yes, of course," Ice snarled. "From what I understand, you disappeared when you were just a child. Excuse my candor. Most people believed that you were dead."

"Honestly, it's not an interesting story," Red said.

"Your apparent resurrection is nothing less than interesting to me. Red, don't leave me wondering a minute longer."

Red sighed. "It's not that I was dead. I was taken away from Wayward and left alone to fend for myself in a city a long way from here. Until a few days ago, I had no memory of this place or anybody in it. I didn't even know my last name and certainly not the date of my own birth."

"That clears up a lot of confusion," Ice muttered.

"I'm sorry I can't tell you more, Ice. In many ways, I'm just as much in the dark as you are."

"Well, none of that matters now. Red Riding is back in Wayward and that is a thing to be celebrated."

Red faked a smile. "If you don't mind my asking, why do you care so much? As far as I can tell, we've never met before this day."

Ice stopped and looked Red in the eyes. "It's not easy to put into words. In Wayward, you're something of a legend. The Alpha Huntress, gifted with powers greater than any in all of the land, born at the exact same moment in time as myself. Among our generation, I am by far the most exceptional of all, save one girl. Red, darling, that is you. In many ways you are my equal. We are connected at a level I can scarcely explain. Having been born so close in time to one another practically makes us twin sisters."

"I suppose so." Red did her best not to cringe at the thought.

"Now, if you don't mind, I need to run off and prepare a little surprise for you."

"For me?"

"I promise not to embarrass you too much. Birthday sister's honor." Ice strutted away into the crowd.

Red found herself standing alone in a sea of strangers she had no interest in talking to, nor would she have a clue what to say if one of them had spoken to her. As she circled the room looking for Dote, she did her best to avoid making eye contact with anybody. It wasn't long before her stomach was churning with anxiety. She began entertaining the notion of slipping out and catching the first carriage back home, though she thought it rude after Ice had gone to so much trouble for her.

Just as she was about to set out in search of a ladies' room to take refuge in, a young man with an English accent spoke from behind her. "May I have this dance, my lady?"

CHAPTER 11

"I said, may I have this dance, my lady?"

A handsome young man with deep blue eyes and long black hair stood before Red with his white-gloved hand extended. He was finely dressed in a tuxedo with a purple cummerbund and a bow tie. A silver-handled rapier sword hung from his belt.

Red couldn't help but swoon a little because he was charming in every way possible. It took her a few seconds to come to her senses enough to speak. "Sorry. I was just looking for my friend."

"I see. Perhaps I can help you to search for him," the handsome man slyly offered.

"Oh, it's not a he, more like a she," Red was quick to note.

"Then you are not here with a gentleman companion?"

"No, not at all."

"Then fortune has indeed smiled upon me, for I am without a lovely lady to join me in this dance."

Red giggled like a giddy schoolgirl. "I don't think that would be a good idea."

"I understand. I am but a mere stranger to you. My manners have escaped me. I have failed to give myself proper introduction. My name is Prince De'Mere."

"You're a prince?"

"Not exactly. My parents were rather ostentatious when they named me."

Red smiled and nodded, having no idea what ostentatious meant. "Well, I'm sure they meant well."

Prince chuckled. "That is an accurate assessment of my parents."

They stood for an awkward moment, both unsure what to say next.

Prince finally cleared his throat. "Now that you know who I am, please bestow on me the sweet melody that is your name."

Red rolled her eyes in amusement. "Okay, I'm liking this prince charming thing you're doing, but that sounded a little silly."

"Me? Silly?"

"A little bit."

"But all I said was …" Prince stopped and considered this. "You're right. It did sound quite ridiculous."

"Totally."

Prince bowed his head. "You have my deepest and most sincere apology."

"And there you go again."

"I'm doing the best I can here, my lady."

"It's endearing."

"I have a suspicion that I'm not going to be able to win with you," Prince said.

"Probably not."

"All I ask is a name and a dance."

"Why didn't you just say so?"

"My lady, I'm quite certain I did."

"Why don't we skip the name game for now and just dance?"

Prince shrugged. "Isn't that what I asked you to do in the first place?"

"You did. Now I'm asking you."

"If that is the way it must be, then I graciously accept your invitation." Prince put an arm around Red's waist and pulled her close. "I will have to insist upon leading."

"I can deal with that." Red gasped as his muscular chest pressed up against her own. She had never danced before, and certainly not under such lavish circumstances. "Shouldn't we move to the dance floor?"

"I only dance in the moment, and the moment is here and now," Prince said.

The orchestra began playing a rather lively symphony. A rush of nervous excitement overcame Red as Prince led her around in a formal waltz. The idea of a fairytale princess being swept off her feet by a handsome prince had always seemed a bit sickening to her, but at the moment, she had to admit that it felt extraordinary.

"The music is getting faster," Prince said.

"Then we'll have to try to keep up," Red said.

As Prince led Red through the crowd, they nudged aside anybody who was in their way. The more it annoyed the other guests, the more amused they both became. It turned into a playful game where they danced their way through the middle of groups involved in conversations. Prince even dipped Red backwards into the lap of an elderly man sitting at a dining table.

By the time the song ended, they had caused quite a scene and held the attention of much of the room.

"Thank you. Thank you." Red gave a playful wave to the crowd as they retreated from the area.

"My lady, I must confess, that was the most fun I've ever had at one of these stuffy balls."

Red blissfully twirled around. "I confess that goes double for me."

"First ball?"

"How'd you guess?"

"You're the only one in the room that doesn't look exceedingly bored," Prince said.

"You don't look bored," Red said.

"I'm not now." Prince gave Red a passionate stare as he moved in for a kiss.

Red turned away. "A dance is about all I can handle tonight."

"Then you will leave me longing?"

"It's looking that way."

Prince sighed. "Then at least give me your name, so I will know who it is I'll be pining over."

Red struck a playfully pretentious pose. "Since you've been such a gentleman, my name is Red Riding."

Prince's eyes lit up with amazement. "Oh, my. This is indeed a most honored occasion." He kneeled down on one knee and bowed his head. "Alpha Huntress, I pledge my life and service to your clan."

"Whoa." Red took a big step back away from Prince. "What are you doing?"

Prince raced to Red's side. "My huntress, please believe that I meant no disrespect with my advances."

"Well, I liked that part. It's just this Alpha Huntress business that's freaking me out."

Prince stood at attention. "You have little to fear with me by your side. The men of my line served as the Alpha's personal guards during the last war against Ragnarok. I came to Wayward to seek you out. I had no idea I would find you here of all places."

A thundering gong rang out.

Red turned to see the crowd was coming to order and looking toward the grand staircase. At the top, a dozen royal knights marched out and formed a line. Two chefs rolled out a towering multi-layered birthday cake with sixteen burning candles, each over a foot in height.

A guard with a trumpet played an ear-piercing song of salute. When he was done, he addressed the crowd. "Now presenting your host for the evening, her Royal Highness, Ice Seether."

The crowd cheered with somewhat fake enthusiasm as Ice marched by the line of knights, waving her arms around and blowing kisses to the crowd. She wore a purple fur robe and a sparkling crown atop her head. In her hand she clutched a gold scepter, studded to the brim with sparkling jewels of every color in the rainbow.

"Thank you. Thank you." Ice said with melodramatic graciousness.

Red rolled her eyes in disbelief. "Is this for real?"

Prince grinned. "Oh, it's only just begun."

Ice raised her scepter, and the crowd again came to order. "Friends, Romans, Countrymen, lend me your ears." Ice chuckled. "Okay, that was just a little joke."

The crowd gave a halfhearted laugh.

Red looked to Prince and stuck her tongue out like she was gagging. Prince snickered, but then did his best to maintain proper composure.

Ice cleared her throat. "Now seriously, I cannot thank you all enough for being so gracious as to share with me, this grand day of all days, my birthday."

The crowd again applauded without much sincerity.

Ice held up a glass of champagne. "I do hope you are all enjoying the food and drink provided to you at no cost by yours very truly."

Red looked to Prince. "Very truly?"

"And she's just getting going."

Ice picked up a finely gift-wrapped box. "Now, I did see the room downstairs overflowing with the plethora of gifts. While I know you would enjoy more than anything to see me open each and every one of them, I'm afraid you would be here watching until my next birthday."

The crowd laughed politely.

"I know, I know. I can be a jokester when I get on a roll." Ice giggled for a long moment. "So, moving on, it is time to get to the occasion at hand. We have a special guest among us tonight. She and I were born on the very same day, only seconds apart, from what I have come to learn. For this reason, I have a deep feeling of sisterhood with her."

Red's face turned ghost-white in a heartbeat.

Ice raised her scepter high. "Join me in welcoming her not only to my home on this night of nights, but in welcoming her foretold return to Wayward. The one that I regard as sister, her royal highness, Red Riding."

Before Red could manage to sneak away, a spotlight blared right onto her face. The entire crowd looked to her and broke into a roar of applause. Prince took Red's arm to steady her as she stumbled, a little off-balance from the shock of it all.

"Come, my sister," Ice said. "Step forward and stand by my side."

Red shook her head in a near panic. "No way. I cannot go up there."

"Do not fear, my Huntress. I will assist you." Prince placed Red's arm on his own and nudged her forward. As they made the long trek through the applauding crowd, Red felt as if the world was spinning around her. By the time they reached the bottom of the staircase, she was nearly hyperventilating. It was far too much attention for her nerves to endure in one night.

Just as she was going to make a break for the nearest exit, Dote approached her with a gushing smile and a big clump of chocolate cake stuck to her dress. "This is the greatest thing to ever happen," Dote said.

A sensation of vertigo overcame Red as she looked up to Ice at the top of the staircase. It was nearly enough to make her throw up right then and there.

"Shall I carry you up?" Prince asked.

Red took a deep breath and held on tight to the polished brass banister. The agonizing climb to the top was only thirty steps, but with the eyes of the crowd glaring on her back, the steps looked as if they stretched into infinity.

She couldn't understand why Ice was making such a big deal over her return to Wayward. Red thought perhaps Ice was so eccentric that she made a big deal over things just for the sake of doing it. With this thought, she realized what Prince meant when he called his parents ostentatious.

"Isn't she just magnificent?" Ice greeted Red at the top of the grand staircase, with a hug and a kiss on each cheek.

"Ice, you shouldn't have done this." Red looked out at the applauding crowd and again had to fight the urge to throw up. She could only hope that whatever Ice was planning would be done and over with as quickly as possible.

"Don't be silly, darling Red. We are royals and deserve to be adored as such." Ice raised her scepter to silence the crowd. "Now, if you would all be so kind as to indulge me for a moment longer. Please join me in singing a birthday salute to my dearest sister."

"Ice, please don't …"

"Dear Red, stop being so modest."

The trumpet player blew a single note. The crowd began singing a birthday salute in Red's honor.

Trembling like a twig in a windstorm, Red looked out over the crowd. Among the finely dressed guests, one face stood out in the very back of the room. He was wearing ripped jeans and a leather jacket. Red was fairly certain it was the mysterious rider. The sound around her faded away as their eyes connected across the crowd.

"You shouldn't be here, Red Riding. You're in major danger," the voice of the mysterious rider spoke out like an echo in the wind.

Ice tapped Red on the back of the shoulder. The sound of the applauding crowd came back like a smack to Red's face. She looked over to see there were sixteen candles burning on the cake. Ice gestured for Red to join her in blowing them out.

Red looked back to the crowd, but the rider was nowhere to be seen. The whole experience was so odd that she wasn't sure it had really happened. As overwhelmed as she was at the moment, it could have been a hallucination.

"Make a wish, birthday sister," Ice said.

When Red joined Ice in blowing out the candles, the only thing she could think to wish for was that she could be anywhere other than there.

Again, the crowd cheered.

Ice picked up a small gift-wrapped box and offered it to Red. "A birthday gift, from one sister to another."

"Ice, this is all too much."

"Red Riding, there is no such thing as too much when it comes to women of our elevated status," Ice said.

Red reluctantly accepted the gift and proceeded to rip away the shiny purple wrapping paper. Underneath was a wooden box with fine carvings of the moon in its eight phases and the Earth in the center. She recalled seeing this same image on the ceiling of the Moon Temple. "Ice, it's beautiful."

"Just wait until you see what's inside, Red Riding."

It occurred to Red that this was the first birthday gift she had ever received, or the first she could remember. The only significant gift she could recall was her beloved motorcycle, which came from a kindly old man that she had befriended during a brief stay in a foster home. He told her that one day she would need it for a special purpose. If he had not insisted she promise never to part with it, she would have traded it away for money to buy food and clothes. She certainly would not have had it to carry her away from the city and into her new life in Wayward.

Ice stepped up behind Red. "Don't make us wait all night."

"Sorry. I'm just trying to savor the moment." Red opened the box, revealing a golden choker with a purple amulet that glimmered in the light. "It's magnificent."

"Isn't it though?" Ice took the choker from the box and proceeded to hook it around Red's throat. "Perfection."

"Ice, I don't know how to thank you."

"It's my deepest pleasure," Ice said. "Now where's my gift?"

Red grimaced as she searched for an answer.

"Just teasing." Ice giggled and hugged Red.

Red faked a grin. "You're too much, Ice Seether."

"You don't have to tell me, birthday sister. Now, if you don't mind, I have some pressing matters to tend to." Ice took off in a dash, again leaving Red standing alone in a crowd of strangers.

The chef approached Red and held out a large knife. "Please honor us by cutting the first piece of cake, your highness."

"If I must." Red took the knife and was about to cut the cake, but stopped short when a thought came that brought a devious grin to her face. She looked down the stairs to where Dote was watching through eyes gushing with pure joy.

Before she could even gesture for her to come up, Dote shrieked and raced up the stairs in a frenzy of excitement. The chef watched with speechless dread as Red placed the knife into Dote's waiting hands.

"Lady Dote, I dub you the royal cutter of my birthday cake," Red said.

Dote didn't hesitate to stab the knife right into the heart of the cake that towered more than twice her height. "Red, you are the best friend ever."

"No, Dote, *you're* the best friend ever."

CHAPTER 12

It took Red the better part of an hour to get away from the grand ballroom. After Ice had made such a big to-do over her, the other party guests just had to meet her. But to Red, they all seemed more interested in making themselves known to her than in knowing her. Most of their questions had to do with how she came to know Ice. Others were curious about any business ventures she might be involved in with the Seether Clan.

Just about the time she couldn't take anymore, Prince intervened and led her away on what he referred to as *"urgent business."* She just wanted to leave Ice's palace in her memories, but Dote was having so much fun serving the cake, it would have been a crime to pull her away.

For the following hour, Red wandered the halls surrounding the ballroom. Most rooms she ventured into held collections of art from various parts of the world. One room was dedicated entirely to weapons, spanning from primitive spears and clubs to medieval swords and crossbows, all the way up to guns.

Through all of it, Red couldn't shake the warning of danger from the mysterious rider. It seemed ridiculous to believe he had spoken to her from across the crowd, but considering the events of the last two days, it was best to keep an open mind to all possibilities. As far as she could tell there wasn't a hint of danger lurking anywhere, but she remained cautious nonetheless.

When Red came upon a door marked *PRIVATE*, she had to resist her mischievous instinct to venture inside. As she turned to walk away, she heard what sounded like a little girl calling out in distress. A quick search of the area didn't reveal anybody who might be in need of help. As far as she could tell, the only place the cries could be coming from was inside the room.

To be certain that there was really something wrong before calling for help and causing a commotion, she pressed an ear against the wooden door marked *PRIVATE*. A girl's cries for help could be heard quite clearly. Had the plea not sounded so deathly urgent, Red would have gone with her original plan of going for help.

The door snapped shut behind Red as she ventured inside. She did a quick search of the wall, but was unable to find a light switch. It was hard to make out the details of the room under the dim lighting. From what she could gather, it was a hall used for fancy banquets, though all the chairs and tables were stacked up in the corner.

"Is anybody in here?" Red spoke just louder than a whisper.

The girl's whimpering cries continued from nearby. Taking a few steps further into the dark room, Red caught a glimpse of a teen girl cowering on her knees. She had long blue-hair, an oversized nose ring, and was as scrawny as a skeleton. What was really odd was that she was wearing a baggy tuxedo that looked like it came from a long-forgotten era.

"Hey there. Are you okay?" Red asked.

"Please help. They're going to kill me," the blue-haired girl screeched.

Red took a couple of cautious steps closer. "Who's going to kill you?"

The blue-haired girl pointed past Red. "They are."

Red sensed something dangerous coming her way, though as far as she could see, there wasn't anybody else in the room. With lightning quick reflexes, she reached up and caught the blunt end of a wooden staff swung at her by an invisible attacker. Even with the extreme force behind the strike, she was able to stop it without a bit of effort.

The invisible attacker tried to pull the staff away, but Red's grip was ironclad. She gave the staff a hard pull, yanking the six-foot-long wooden weapon out of the attacker's hands.

"You'll have to show yourself if you want it back," Red said.

Moving on pure instinct, she swung the staff wide. It was just in time to block a strike from another invisible attacker. The clack of the two weapons colliding told Red it was from a staff of equal size.

A rapid series of unseen strikes came at Red from every side. From what she could figure, there were four invisible attackers in total. She was overcome with an unexpected thrill as she effortlessly fought off their relentless attempts to hit her.

How am I doing this? Red wondered.

It all changed in an instant when a strike got through and smacked Red in the chest. The intense pain consumed Red with a rather dangerous surge of aggression. She unleashed a vicious counterstrike that knocked one of the invisible attackers to the ground with a groan. Judging from the pitch, Red gathered that her attacker was a girl. She was pretty sure that all four of them were.

"Hey, ladies. Why don't we all call a truce before things get out of control here?" Red said.

Red blocked another strike and followed up with a powerful kick to the attacker's gut. This time she saw the silhouetted outline of a girl armed with a wooden staff soaring away.

"Just remember you made me do that," Red said.

Another attack came at Red. She blocked with her forearm and grabbed the attacker's staff. With a powerful yank, she pulled the weapon away, then spun the staff around and cracked the attacker across the face. The attacker's silhouetted image flickered as she crashed to the floor.

"Anybody else want to take a shot at me?" Red's senses were so heightened she could have heard a speck of dust hit the floor. She knew that one attacker remained, and was far more skilled than the others "I know you're there. Come get me, if you dare."

Red heard the final attacker's staff whooshing toward her head. With perfect timing, she dropped down and executed a spinning sweep kick. The blow connected across the back of the invisible attacker's legs, knocking her down.

"You done yet?" Red asked.

The final attacker sprang to her feet and charged Red with a rapid mêlée of staff strikes. Red defended with ease until the attacker executed a downward blow that snapped her staff in half.

The attacker unleashed a powerful series of strikes, forcing Red to block with her forearms. The final swing cracked Red across the ribs, sending a shockwave of pain blasting through her body.

In a flurry of rage, Red began swinging her fists so fast that they made *whooshing* sounds as they cut through the air. She caught her invisible attacker's staff and pulled it away. With a vicious roar, she cracked it in half over her knee and bashed her enemy across the face with the blunt end.

The sound of labored gasping told Red that her attacker was down on her knees, unable to fight. Void of rational thought, Red raised the jagged end of the broken staff and let out a malevolent roar.

"Don't do it." the blue-haired girl yelped out.

Red shot a raging glare at the blue-haired girl then shifted her gaze to the jagged end of her weapon. In an instant, she realized the terrible act she was about to commit. "You four had better get out, or things are going to get messy."

Within seconds, the entrance door swung open. As the light from the hall blared in, Red saw the silhouetted outlines of four teenage girls limping and gasping as they exited the room. They were wearing short skirts and button-down tops similar in style to schoolgirl uniforms. The last attacker to exit looked back at Red and gave a hateful stare, making it clear that this was not over.

"You'd best keep walking," Red said.

After the door slammed shut, Red dropped to her knees and took a breath of relief. Her forearms were throbbing in pain and covered in bruises. She was far more upset to find that the seam of her gown was ripped down one side.

"That was crazy insane." The blue-haired girl stumbled to her feet and walked over to Red. "I thought you were going to off her."

Red shook with a nervous twinge. "Huh?"

"You were a half-second from dusting her. It's a good thing I said something, or we'd have a body to get rid of."

Red gulped in fear when she realized this was true. "Guess I should thank you."

"Nah, you saved my life. I stopped you from taking one. That's what friends are for, Red."

Red took a closer look at the girl. "Do we know each other?"

"Stop messing around. *It's me.* Your best friend in the world."

Red shook her head and shrugged.

The blue-haired girl grumbled. "Oh, you have got to be kidding. You. Me. Dote. The inseparable trio."

Red realized something that didn't make a bit of sense to her. "Are you Ash?"

"Duh. It's about time you recognized me, Red Riding."

"But Ash is a boy."

"Shot to the heart." Ash clutched his chest and gasped in a panic. "You think I'm a girl?"

A feeling of guilt hit Red like a fist in the stomach. It's not like the mistake was entirely her fault. Ash had more girlish features than any boy she had ever seen. After a quick moment of consideration, she resolved that there was only one way that she could undo the damage.

She burst into hysterical laughter.

"Why are you laughing? Nothing about this is funny," Ash whined.

Red stood up and walked toward the door. "You should have seen the look on your face. I had you going there."

"Wait. I get it. You were just messing with my head." Ash took a huge breath of relief. "I should have known. Red Riding, always the prankster."

Red shrugged. "You know me. I just can't help myself."

"Yeah, like the time you convinced me that a gnome ate my cookies, but you'd hid them in my coat pocket. It took me an hour to realize they were there the whole time."

Red giggled. "Or how about that time I hid your extra underwear in granny's icebox?"

Ash slumped in embarrassment. "I totally forgot about that."

"And I remembered it." Red smiled, pleased, as she recounted the memory.

"Those were good times, Red."

"They were, Ash."

Red pushed the door open a crack so she could peer out into the hallway. There wasn't a sign of anybody out there. "So why did you always have an extra pair of underwear in your backpack?"

"Let's just move on from that."

"Fair enough. Now tell me about the girls that were trying to kill you."

"Kill is a strong word. Maim. Disfigure. Humiliate beyond all recognition. That's more like it," Ash said.

Red stepped halfway out into the hallway for a better look. "I don't see anybody around, but that doesn't mean much."

"Nope, those four vanishing babes could be anywhere, and we wouldn't know it," Ash said.

"And how exactly do they do the stealthy thing?"

"Some kind of spellcraft amplified by moonstones embedded into their staffs, I'm guessing. I could ask next time I see them if you really want to know," Ash said.

Red grabbed Ash by the shirt. "Out with it, Dorkus. What's the real story here?"

"Red, you know I hate being called by my given name. It's embarrassing."

"That's right. Your full name is Dorkus Ashley. It's all starting to come back now."

"Of all the things to remember," Ash mumbled.

Red pulled Ash along by the shirt as she started down the hallway. "So speak, boy. Give me all the details. Leave nothing out."

"It's not that complicated. The four girly-girls you just slugged it out with are Ice's prep school pals. They work for her like a gang of personal thugs," Ash said.

"And they were beating you up for *what* reason?"

"They always beat me up. It's a love-hate sort of thing we've got going on. I think their leader Mia has a serious crush on me. Sadly, she's too caught up in her popular girl clique to be able to admit it publicly."

"Okay, now the real reason, Ash."

"I crashed the party."

"How did you pull that one off?"

"Secret entrance through the sewers."

"Yuck. How do you even know about that?"

"When I was a kid, I snuck into this place all the time. I know where all the coolest stuff is hidden," Ash said.

"You'll have to show me around sometime. Now why did those girls attack me?"

"Probably because you walked in on their little game. They tried to bop you on the head, and you gave it to them like a werewolf-powered ninja."

"I got into it with them because you said they were going to kill you," Red shouted.

"Yeah, that was my bad."

"Perfect, now I have to find Ice and explain to her why I beat the brains out of her pet cronies," Red said.

As they were approaching the ballroom entrance, Ash grabbed Red's arm and stopped her. "Have you gone totally cuckoo? Why would you even care what Ice Seether thinks?"

"I don't know. I just feel like I should."

Ash shrugged. "I guess if that's the way it has to be, I won't stop you, but if you're going back inside there, you might want to check yourself in a mirror."

Red looked down at the open seam on the side of her dress. "Give me your jacket."

"Not a chance. These threads are the core of my style."

Red glared at Ash. "I ripped my dress saving your little tail. You're lucky I don't make you swap outfits. And I know this dress will totally fit your scrawniness, so don't mess with me."

Ash grumbled as he pulled off his jacket. Red snatched it away and put it on. It was several sizes too large, causing it to hang on her quite ridiculously.

"Now go home, Ash. And no arguing with me."

Ash was about to protest, but Red held up a hand, warning him to be silent.

"Fine, but if you get even a spot on my jacket, we are going to have some serious words, young lady." Ash slumped a little as he began to walk away.

"Ash."

"Yeah, Red?"

"It's good to see you again."

"You too. Missed you a lot."

Red dashed over to Ash and gave him an affectionate hug. Though she hadn't seen him since she was five years old, or sixty-six percent of their lives as Dote would say, she felt a wonderful bond with him that was unlike any she had ever known.

CHAPTER 13

"Hello? Is anybody here?"

Red stood in the ballroom entryway, baffled to find that there was not a sign of a single party guest or server. The bandstand sat silent and void of musicians. On the upper level, the royal knights were gone. She wondered how the party could have broken up so fast. Not that she was too disappointed. She did feel a little sad that she didn't have a chance to share a piece of chocolate cake with Dote.

Clicking footsteps that sounded like somebody walking in high-heeled shoes came from the upper level. After a tense moment, Ice emerged at the top of the grand staircase. She wore her royal robe and clutched the jeweled scepter.

"Welcome back, Red Riding. I was starting to think you had slipped away," Ice said.

"Ice, something happened I need to tell you about," Red said.

Four girls armed with staffs stepped up behind Ice. They wore white button-down tops and plaid skirts, each with its own unique color. What stood out the most was that they had fresh bruises from a recent beating.

"I know you four have already met," Ice said. "Even so, I would like to formally introduce you to my elite guardians. Not that I need guardians, mind you, but nonetheless, they are Mia the

Neo Edmund

Black, Yuki the Grey, Suki the Yellow, and Naoki the Brown."

Red had no doubt they were the girls she had battled earlier, and couldn't shake the feeling that she had also encountered them somewhere else. "Ice, please understand. It was all a big mistake."

"The only mistake is that my elite guards were so easily defeated." Ice swung a hand back and smacked Mia in the face. "Are you not ashamed, Mia?"

Mia bitterly eyed Ice before she lowered her head. "I am, your highness."

Red took a few steps closer to the staircase. "Ice, if I could just explain."

"Silly Little Red Riding, you just don't know what's going on here," Ice said.

Twenty royal knights rushed in through the ballroom entrance and formed a perimeter around Red. Each pulled a samurai-style sword and stood at attention. Ice held up her scepter. A surge of energy shot out from it and formed a mystical barrier over the entryway.

Red's heart began to race with panic. "What is this?"

"Relax, birthday sister. It's just my way of assuring we're not disturbed," Ice said.

"Ice, you have to believe I didn't mean to make trouble."

"I have no doubt that your intentions when coming here were as pure as mine when I invited you. Sadly, your little scuffle with my girls has proven you are far too dangerous to be allowed to gallivant around unattended."

Red took another step toward the staircase. The knights reacted by raising their swords.

"Ice, if I'm that much trouble, I'll gladly leave," Red said.

"I'm so sorry. It's much too late for friendly departures, my little birthday sister," Ice said.

"Stop calling me that. We are not related," Red said.

"That is most certainly true. There is not a drop of your impure Riding blood in my line. But the circumstances of our births do connect us in a sisterly way."

Red considered this. "This has to do with the Alpha Power."

Ice ground her teeth. "Of course it has to do with the Alpha Power, you foolish peasant girl."

"Now I understand. You think the power should have gone to you," Red said.

Ice screeched, "I don't think it! I know it! The lunar calendar is quite clear that the power was bestowed at the exact moment of my birth. Somehow, by a random blunder of fate, you were born at the exact same moment."

"You think I received your powers by accident?" Red asked.

"It's the only explanation that makes a bit of sense. The idea that the divine power of the lunar deities was bestowed upon a peasant girl is outrageously preposterous," Ice said.

"It's not like I had anything to do with it. I'm not even sure I want it," Red said.

Ice paced in a frantic fit. "It doesn't matter if you want it or not. You simply do not deserve to have it. The power was to be mine, and I want it this instant."

"I thought the power came to me because I'm a descendant of the last Alpha," Red said.

"No, no, no," Ice ranted. "That's not how this works at all. The power of the Alpha doesn't get passed down through generations. It is bestowed to the most powerful werewolf in all of the land."

"So then you're a werewolf, too?" Red asked.

"Well, duh. This is precisely the problem. Even with the Alpha Power, your little peasant mind can't see that everybody in this room is a werewolf," Ice said.

Red trembled with fear as she looked to the knights surrounding her. In the blink of an eye, it all became clear to her. Nothing about them changed physically; their smell confirmed it. Each knight had a distinct scent that revealed to Red a bounty of insight into their character. The most important revelation was that she could tell who was the strongest and who were weakest.

"I can smell your fear." Red then snapped a look toward Mia, Suki, Yuki, and Naoki. "Yours too."

In a flash, Red was back in the forest clearing where the Omega Gem sat atop a stone pedestal. Five wolves were slowly moving in on her to attack. They were white, black, grey, brown, and yellow.

The white wolf spoke with Ice's voice, "Well, well, well. It looks like our little huntress has had an awakening."

Red blinked and was again in the ballroom. Her ears had a faint ringing in them. Beads of sweat formed on her head as her body temperature spiked. She held out her trembling hands to discover that talons were piercing through the tips of her fingers.

Ice snickered. "Watch out, boys, I think the claws are about to come out."

The royal knights grew nervous and tightened their grips on their swords.

Red could feel her anger rising. "Ice Seether, what are you trying to do here?"

"All will be revealed soon enough, Little Red Riding," Ice said. "Knights, attack the Alpha."

"Ice, please don't do this." Red spun around and saw that the royal knights were transforming into hairy wolf-men with razor-sharp claws and incisor fangs.

Ice grinned. "This is going to be quite entertaining."

Red's blood burned to a boil as the knights began to advance. She snapped a look at the knight who was clearly the leader. While he stood the furthest back, there was no question that he was by far the most dangerous. She suspected that taking him down would send the others scattering like frightened children.

"We don't have to do this," Red said.

The first knight raised his sword and swung downward. Red could smell his nervous apprehension as she sidestepped the attack. His blade went straight down and clunked into the floor. She threw a powerful punch into his gut, doubling him over with a groan.

"Just so we're clear, you made me do that." Red let Ash's jacket fall to the floor and took a fighting stance. "Don't say I didn't warn you, boys."

A knight swung his sword at Red from behind.

Hearing the blade cutting through the air, she dodged clear. She kicked back right into the knight's chest, sending him stumbling to the floor. "Anybody else?"

Two knights dashed at Red. One swung his sword high, while the other swung his low. Red executed a perfect back handspring, passing between their blades. As soon as she landed, another knight grabbed her from behind. She reached back, gripped his coat, and with a mighty heave, flung him over her shoulder. His arms flailed as he soared through the air and slammed into the two knights who had just attacked Red. The three men crashed to the floor with painful thuds and grunts.

Red took a quick look around the room and spotted the lead knight about twenty feet away. The world around her went into slow motion as she began to charge toward him. A knight jumped into her path and swung his sword. Red leaped high and soared over his blade. On her descent she kicked him in the head, sending him crashing down.

Another knight jumped into Red's path and thrust his sword at her. Red dropped down onto her back and slid between his legs. She popped up to her feet behind him. With a powerful shove, she sent him crashing face-first into a nearby pillar.

"Are you guys even trying to get me?"

The lead knight flipped the blade of his sword into his hand and javelined it at Red's chest. Dodging to the side, she grabbed the sword out of the air. She then leaped forward and swung the blade wide. The man never saw the lightning-fast strike that slashed deep into his chest.

As his dead body hit the floor, Red spun around and faced the remaining knights. "Surrender, or you're all going down just like him."

The knights exchanged nervous looks, unsure what to do.

"Now." Red shouted.

A knight dropped his blade and raised his hands. Red pointed her sword at the others, and they got the message. One after another they put down their weapons and surrendered.

"Cowards!" Ice screamed. "I did not give you permission to surrender. Pick up your weapons and continue attacking."

The knights stood firm, refusing to obey her command.

Ice raised her scepter. It began to glow with purple energy. "Well, if you're too afraid to fight, then I have no choice but to discharge you from my service."

The knights broke into an outright panic and dashed for the entryway, but the mystical barrier blocked their escape. They began to clutch at their throats and gagged for breath. It wasn't long before they all collapsed and their lives faded away.

"How could you?" Red stood trembling and clutching her sword.

"How could I?" Ice gave a wicked laugh. "How could you?"

Red looked down and saw the lifeless body of the knight she had slain. A feeling of panic overcame her. She dropped her weapon and stumbled backward. "No. I couldn't have. I would never do that."

"Take a good look, birthday sister. As the Alpha, this will be your future path."

Red paced in a panic. "They were trying to kill me. I had no choice."

"You'd better get used to it. As long as you possess that power, you will always be under attack. To survive you will have to slay many more like him," Ice said.

Red looked at the fallen knight. He was transforming back from his werewolf form into a man. She shook her head in desperate denial. "No, I won't do that."

Ice began to descend the staircase. "Don't be naïve. I did this to prove to you how powerless you are to control the rage once the big bad wolf takes over. I know you did not want to do this, yet the tragic reality lies right before you. And you will do it again, and again, and again."

"I'll learn to control it," Red said.

"Red Riding, the power inside you is raw and primal. It can't be beaten into submission like a caged beast," Ice said.

"I didn't ask for this." Red dropped to her knees and broke into tears.

"There is nothing to fear. Nobody will ever have to know of the terrible act you committed tonight," Ice said.

"What are you saying?"

"You've taken a life. A thing like that doesn't just go away on its own."

"I was defending myself. That is no crime."

"I know that just as well as you do." Ice reached the bottom of the staircase and continued strutting toward Red. "You have my word that together we will make sure nobody gets the misguided notion that it's anything more."

Red noticed a spot of blood on her hand and knew it was not her own. She frantically wiped it away onto the floor.

Ice stood over her. "See what the power has done to you, my dear sister. It's truly tragic that you have been afflicted this way. Let me help you be rid of this curse."

"Rid of it?" Red gave Ice a curious glare. "Is that even possible?"

Ice placed a comforting hand on Red's shoulder. "It's not only possible, I know how to do it."

Red looked over to the dead knights near the entryway. "How would you do that?"

Ice kneeled down next to her. "It's rather complicated. Simply put, it requires a powerful spellcraft that only a witch as skilled as I can pull off."

"So you're both a werewolf and a witch?" Red asked.

Ice placed her hands on Red's face. "Red, darling, you're straying from the point. I only want to free you from this suffering. I do care so deeply for you."

Red looked Ice in the eyes. "What would happen to the power if I gave it up?"

"I suppose it would go to another. One equipped to handle it adequately," Ice said.

"Would that one be you?"

"Perhaps, if the deities deem me worthy."

"And what would happen if they didn't?"

"As far as I can tell, they already had, before the power was mistakenly thrust upon you."

"I think I understand now." Red wiped the tears from her eyes.

"I knew you would come to your senses, dear sister."

Red stood up. "I understand that you are not my sister."

Ice frowned. "Red, don't say such things. You'll hurt my feelings."

Red pointed to the fallen knights near the door. "You would use the power to do terrible things."

Ice clenched her teeth. "That is simply not true."

"I killed tonight in self-defense. You killed those men in cold blood," Red said.

"Don't push me," Ice warned, eyes narrowing.

"You're a monster. That makes you my enemy," Red said.

"I am so sorry to hear you say that, Red."

"I'm not sorry that I said it, Ice."

"I was going to let you live after I took the power from you."

"I wouldn't let you have it if my life depended on it."

"The bad news for you is that your life does depend on it, Red Riding."

Red took a fighting stance. "Then bring it on, Ice Seether."

CHAPTER 14

I'm waiting, Ice Seether. Show me what you've got."

In the center of the ballroom floor, Red and Ice stood face-to-face in a chilling stare-down. An intense mystical force flowed through Red's body that she both loved and feared, empowering her. There was nothing more she wanted than to knock the smug expression right off Ice's face. She held no delusions that battling Ice would be easy, but something inside told her that she could win this fight.

"Do you take me for a fool, Red Riding?" Ice raised her scepter high. It began glowing with mystical energy. "I'm not going to lower myself to such primal tactics."

"Oh, no." Red looked down and saw that the choker Ice had given her was now illuminated with a pulsing purple glow. It was clear why Ice had made such a scene over her at the party. "It was all just a trick to get this thing around my neck."

"Don't be getting all egocentric now. The party was also to celebrate my rise as the new Alpha Huntress of Wayward," Ice said.

"There's no way that's going to happen." Red said.

"If you won't give over the power willingly, I will rip it out of you."

Red flopped to the floor, limp "Hey, how did you do that?" she protested as she struggled to stand.

"Dear Red, if you want to stand, all you have to do is ask." Ice waved her scepter.

A mystical force pulled Red to her feet like a puppet on strings. With her body dangling, she strained with all her will but was unable to control her own movements. "Let me go, you freaking psycho witch."

"That's not a nice way to speak to your hostess." Ice again waved her scepter. "Perhaps you would like to dance for my amusement."

Red's limbs flailed around in a creepy dance. She strained with all her might, but could not control her own body. "You're starting to get on my last nerve, Ice Seether."

"Now, Red, don't go hurting yourself. We're just getting started." Ice lowered her scepter, causing Red to fall limp to the floor.

"Ice, when I get this thing off my neck, you are so going down."

"Give it up. I always win." Ice strutted toward the stairs and called, "Now bring me the dodo bird."

"Oh, no. Dote." Red said.

At the top of the stairs, Mia and her three sidekicks were dragging Dote in from another room. They had her arms bound behind her back with rope.

"Let go of me," Dote demanded. "I'll have you know, I'm an honored guest."

Red *growled*. "You leave her out of this, Ice."

"Believe me, there is nothing I would like better than to get this dodo bird out of my palace. For the record, it is your fault she's here to begin with," Ice said.

"Red, don't worry about me," Dote said. "I know what she wants. You can't give it to her."

"What are you trying to pull here, Ice?" Red asked.

"This is my way of giving you one last chance to make this easy on yourself. Play nice, so I won't have to hurt your little dodo pet. And don't think for a second I wouldn't get great pleasure out of squeezing the life out of a member of the Shrine Clan," Ice said.

"What would I have to do?" Red asked.

"Just a harmless little ritual. You probably won't feel a thing," Ice said.

"How about you let Dote go, and I'll consider it."

"How about I have my girls shove the little dodo bird headfirst down the stairs."

Mia pushed Dote right to the edge of the stairs. Red could hear Dote whimper in fear.

"Wait, don't hurt her," Red cried out.

"Then agree to do exactly as I tell you," Ice said.

Red gave Ice a suspicious glare. "Why are you trying so hard to get me to agree to play along?"

"I already told you. I'm trying to make this easy on you."

"I think you're lying. If you could just take the power, you would have done it already. I think you need me to willingly give it over," Red said.

Mia held Dote closer to the edge.

Ice giggled. "Are you prepared to gamble your little pet's life?"

Dote shook her head, urging Red not to do it.

"I don't have to," Red said. "If you hurt her, I'll never give you what you want."

Ice grabbed Red and glared into her eyes. "This has gone on long enough. I want the Alpha Power. You are going to give it to me, or you're both going to die."

"Not gonna happen. If you could take it by killing me, I'm betting I'd be belly up already," Red said.

"That's where you're wrong, Red Riding. I'm going to win this one way or another. I will have the Alpha Power, or nobody will."

Ice waved her scepter. Red's arms wrapped around her own body and began squeezing. The force was so strong she couldn't get a single breath.

"*NO!*" Dote shouted.

Dote's eyes began to glow bright white. Her hands radiated mystical energy that caused the ropes binding her to burn to dust. She held out her palm toward Mia and blasted her away with a vortex of energy.

Naoki lunged at Dote, but Dote blasted her away with another burst. Dote turned to Suki and Yuki and gave them a dangerous glare. The two girls didn't hesitate to leap over the railing and drop onto the ballroom floor.

Dote stomped down the staircase. Her eyes were swirling with mystical energy. "Ice Seether, you will release my friend, or you will be destroyed." Her voice had an eerie tone that echoed throughout the ballroom.

Grinning with amusement, Ice looked to Red. "The little dodo bird has got some of the Shrine family spunk in her. Just wait until the day she snaps and goes off like a cuckoo clock."

Ice aimed her scepter at Dote and fired a blast of purple energy. Dote raised her hands and put up a protective mystical barrier, deflecting the shot. She countered by firing a vortex from her hands.

The force knocked Ice down and caused her to drop her scepter. As Ice reached for it, Dote fired another energy vortex, knocking it away. The scepter slid into the wall, hitting hard enough to shatter one of its glowing gems.

Red fell limp to the floor and gasped to get air into her lungs.

The energy vortex blocking the entry door faded away.

Dote stumbled to her knees, gasping in exhaustion.

"I will make you suffer for this insolence." Ice raised her arms and transformed into a werewolf with bleached-white fur and glowing purple eyes.

Mia, Naoki, Suki, and Yuki, raced down the stairs and joined Ice. They too transformed into their werewolf forms.

"Now, let's see where this goes," Ice said.

Red stumbled to her feet and limped over to Dote. "We have to get out of here."

Dote was still gasping from exhaustion. "I'm sorry I can't help more. Using such powerful spellcraft is exhausting."

"You did great. We'll figure something out," Red said.

Ice and her four elite guards advanced on Red and Dote.

"It was a valiant effort," Ice said. "But your path ends here, Red Riding."

"Dote, stand behind me," Red said as they backed away toward the entry door.

Dote took up position behind Red. She squeezed her hands together, trying to conjure more mystical power, but she didn't have a bit of energy left.

"Last chance, Red," said Ice. "Speak now, or forever rest in peace."

"Red, don't give in to her," Dote said. "It will be much worse if she gets what she wants."

Ice rolled her eyes in irritation and looked to Mia. "Let's do away with the little dodo witch and let Red watch her beg for mercy."

"So help me, Ice, if you hurt her." Red dashed toward Ice, but Mia and her three counterparts tackled her all at once, each subduing one of her limbs, and then pinning her to the floor.

Ice stalked toward Dote with a malicious grin. "I do hope you enjoyed the party, little miss Shrine."

"Stay away from me, Ice Seether." Dote raised her hands to fire a vortex. Still nothing came.

Ice giggled. "All out of bling, little witch? That's too bad. I would have enjoyed a bit more struggle." She grabbed Dote with one hand and raised her clawed hand to slash down.

"Unhand her, you foul beast." a valiant male voice called out.

Red looked over to see Prince standing in the entryway with his rapier at the ready.

Ice sighed in irritation. "Prince De'Mere. What could you possibly be doing here?"

Dote gasped in awe. "He sure is pretty."

Prince advanced toward Ice. "I am a bloodline member of the royal order known far and wide as the Knights of the Alpha. We stand as the proud protectors of the Alpha Huntress."

"Prince, get out of here!" Red shouted. "It's too dangerous!"

"Nonsense, my Huntress. I would never abandon you in your hour of need." Prince pointed his rapier toward Ice. "Ice of the Seether Clan, prepare to feel the cold steel of my blade."

"You have got to be kidding yourself," Ice said. "I know full well that the Knights of the Alpha were hunted down and put to death as punishment for crimes against our lord and master, Ragnarok."

Prince straightened, tall and proud. "You say that, yet here I stand, one of many who have carried on the loyal traditions of our sacred order."

"That will be corrected shortly, starting with you." Ice looked to her four elite guards. "Will one of you get rid of him already?"

"This has to be a dream." Red tried to comprehend the circumstances that had led her from being a lonely orphan girl to this moment only days later. It felt silly to think of such a thing in an hour of great peril, but she couldn't get the thought out of her mind.

Prince fearlessly stood his ground as Mia dashed toward him. He stood unmoving as she leaped high and slashed a claw at him. At the last second, he sidestepped and swung his sword in a flash, hacking Mia's hand off at the wrist.

Mia screamed in rage and collapsed to her knees, clutching her wounded arm. Her three companions were so furious that they dropped Red and advanced on Prince.

"You are so going to die for that." Ice shoved Dote aside.

Prince raised his weapon, showing no fear. "Which of you is next?"

"I am," a masculine voice called out.

Without looking, Red knew who it belonged to. The mysterious rider strutted down the grand staircase. He was wearing ripped jeans and a leather jacket without a shirt underneath, surely with the intention of showing off his rippled abs.

"What the holy heck is *he* doing here?" Dote said.

"You mean you know who he is?" Red asked.

"Everybody in Wayward knows who *he* is," Dote said.

Ice snarled in rage. "Wolfgang Helheim, I distinctly recall warning you of the grave consequences you would face if I was ever forced to lay eyes on you again."

Wolfgang approached Ice with a smug grin. "Ice, now don't go getting like that. I know you miss me. I see the manic desire flickering in those crazed purple eyes."

"Your name is Wolfgang?" Red belted this out like it was the weirdest thing she had ever heard.

Wolfgang shrugged. "Now you see why I didn't tell you before."

"I see you two have met already," Ice said.

Dote looked to Red. "You met him already? Why didn't you tell me?"

"It's a long story, Dote."

Prince held his sword up high. "Declare your allegiance, Wolfgang of the Helheim Clan. Friend or foe?"

"None of the above to you, pretty boy. I'm only here to bail the redhead out of her little jam," Wolfgang said.

"Then for now that we are comrades-in-arms," Prince said.

Wolfgang shrugged. "Whatever makes you feel better about it."

Ice screeched out. "This is getting irritating. Anybody else want to crash my party?"

"Excuse me." At the entryway, Ash peered into the room. "Hate to interrupt. Anyone looking for a way out of here had best follow me."

Red looked to Ash. "Didn't I tell you to go home?"

Prince called to Wolfgang. "Get the Alpha Huntress to safety. I will hold them off."

"Sounds good to me," Wolfgang said.

Red flailed her arms in irritation. "Don't I have a say in this?"

Prince raised his rapier and charged at Naoki, Suki, and Yuki. He unleashed a rapid series of attacks that forced them to retreat in haste. "I will smite thee in the name of the Alpha Huntress."

Red and Dote held one another up as they limped toward the entryway.

"We need to get out of this nuthouse," Red said.

"I had a feeling coming here was going to lead to something like this," Dote said.

"Nice, Dote. Glad you decided to wait until now to tell me that." Red glanced back to see Wolfgang and Ice were circling each other in a stone cold stare down.

Ice snarled. "I warned you to never come here again, Wolfgang Helheim."

"Get over it, princess. You're too high and mighty to be playing the jaded ex routine. I think a rematch is in order."

"Quite overdue."

Wolfgang raised his fists and transformed into a werewolf. He howled and gestured for Ice to attack. Ice roared and lunged at him. The two exchanged a mêlée of powerful grappling blows.

Red could hardly believe her eyes. "Is there anybody in this town who isn't a werewolf?"

"I'm not," Dote said. "Ash sure as heck isn't, either."

Ash grumbled. "Dote, you don't have to keep rubbing that in all the time."

"Sorry."

Red looked back and saw that Prince had Naoki, Suki, and Yuki well under control.

"Red, you could have grabbed my jacket," Ash whined.

"We'll buy you a new one," Dote said.

"Sure. It's just a family heirloom," Ash muttered.

"One last thing before we go." Dote grabbed the amulet around Red's neck and closed her eyes. *"Release."* A flash of mystical energy sparked out as she pulled it off Red. She dropped the amulet and slumped in exhaustion.

Red took a deep breath. "Thanks, Dote, I needed that."

"Just promise not to put on any more strange amulets until I check them out first," Dote said.

"Will do. Alpha's honor."

"We need to get out of here," Ash said. "It's now or never."

"What about Wolfgang?" Red looked back and saw Ice and Wolfgang exchanging a mêlée of punches and kicks with a trio guards. He effortlessly blocked and countered their every strike with impressive skill.

Ash bitterly clenched his teeth. "Trust me. That guy can hold his own in a fight."

With one arm around Ash and the other around Dote, the three friends fled from the grand ballroom. As much as Red wanted to make sure Wolfgang was going to be okay, she had to get Ash and Dote to safety. She knew there wasn't much chance of protecting them if anybody else showed up to pick a fight.

CHAPTER 15

We've gotta get out of here sooner than later, or we're totally doomed," Ash said.

Red, Ash, and Dote dashed down the long corridor leading away from Ice's grand ballroom. The wounds Red had taken during the battle were starting to throb and ache. Her ribs were going to be sore for some time after the crushing they took at the hands of Ice's vile spellcraft.

At the moment, her only concern was getting Ash and Dote safely out of the palace. She just could not endure the thought of something bad happening to them.

"Ash, didn't I tell you to go home?" Red said.

"Consider yourself darn fortunate that I never listen to a thing you tell me, or you would never have gotten out of this mess."

"So what happens now?" Dote asked.

"We make a break for the sewers and hope they don't catch us before we get there," Ash said.

The sewers? Red and Dote said in unison.

"Yes, the sewers. Unless you know a better way," Ash said.

For the next few minutes, Ash led Red and Dote through a series of hallways and doorways that only one totally familiar with the layout of the house could follow. Along the way, they snuck by several guard posts and even maneuvered around a couple of hidden ones.

"I can't believe anybody could have such a massive house," Red said.

"It's over a half-mile from end to end and has hundreds of rooms," Ash said.

"And from the look of it, enough priceless junk to fill a museum," Dote said.

Ash led Red and Dote down a hidden staircase that the servants used to get in and out of the house. He explained, "The Seethers designed the palace so their servants can come and go without ever being seen. Not that many of them ever leave. In the basement there's a huge living area. The estate even has a greenhouse and cattle stable to assure that outside food is never needed."

"Ash, you sound like a tour guide," Red said.

"You did say I should show you around sometime."

"So what about Ice's parents?" Dote asked.

"From what I hear, they're always off traveling," Ash said. "I don't know anybody who has ever seen them. I'm not even sure what they look like."

Ash led them to a huge metal door in the darkest corner of the servants' area. He pulled and heaved with his scrawny arms, forcing the door open. The harsh stench that came from the darkness inside made Red and Dote recoil in disgust. Making it worse, the sound of a clanging bell erupted in the near distance.

"That's a bad sound, right?" Red asked.

"Yep, opening this door sets off the alarm," Ash said. "If they're not already looking for us, they will be now."

Red grabbed Ash by the shirt. "Are you trying to get us caught?"

"Trust me, Red. I've got it covered."

Red let out a sigh of doubt and released Ash. "Just so you know, it would be good to avoid getting caught. I'm not exactly in shape for a fight at the moment."

As they entered a pitch-dark stone chamber, Red could hear water flowing down below. One at a time, they carefully made their way across a creaky metal bridge.

At the far end, Ash opened the rusty cover over an air duct. "After you, ladies."

Red and Dote exchanged reluctant shrugs. As soon as they were all inside, Ash slid the cover shut. The smell was worse than it was on the bridge, surely the result of clumps of wet mildew and roaches crawling around the inner walls.

"How is this helping us?" Red asked.

Ash gestured for Red and Dote to be silent. Seconds later, several guards entered through the metal doorway and dashed across the bridge. Red watched through the vent cover as they passed by and headed down a long staircase.

Ash whispered, "We have to wait a couple of minutes for the guards to search the basement. Once they've cleared it, we'll be good to go."

Red did her best not to look at the cockroaches scurrying around their feet. "I sure hope Wolfgang is okay."

"In all my life, I would have never guessed he would come to our rescue," Dote said.

"Stop kidding yourselves," Ash said. "Whatever reason that guy showed up, it had nothing to do with saving Red's tail. Not unless doing it can help him get whatever it is he's after."

Red shrugged. "All I know is he covered our tails while we got away, so he's got a friend in me."

"I sure hope you don't live to regret that," Ash said. "Now quiet. They'll be back any second."

As soon as the words left Ash's mouth, the guards raced back up the stairs. There was soon the sound of a metal door slamming shut. Ash slid the vent cover open and peered out to make sure it was clear. "Okay, let's move."

Red, Ash, and Dote crawled out of the vent and headed down the metal staircase into the darkness below. The further down they went, the worse the smell got.

Red shuddered at the sounds of what she assumed were rodents scurrying all around them. "This place is a major creep show."

"Don't worry, I've been down here a hundred times," Ash said.

When they reached the bottom of the stairs, the sound of flowing water became thundering loud.

Red pressed a hand over her nose. "When you said sewers, I had no idea you meant this."

"How about a little less complaining and a lot more *thanks for saving our lives?*" Ash reached into a gap in a cracked brick wall and pulled out a small lantern. A few hard shakes caused it to illuminate.

Red took a closer look at the lantern. Inside a glass sphere, dozens of tiny glowing creatures were flying around. They were quite furious over being disturbed. "Whoa, are those fire flies?"

"More like teeny tiny fire fairies," Ash said.

"Just hope you never encounter their people-sized cousins," Dote said. "They'll burn down your house if you get on their bad side."

"These little ones are mostly harmless," Ash said. "You just have to remember to feed them every so often, and they'll pretty much live forever."

Red looked at the fairies banging against the glass. "They don't look harmless to me."

"They are as long as they don't get out." Ash approached a rusty metal gate and shined the light through the bars, illuminating a brick waterway on the other side. "This is our way out."

Dote whimpered. "Are you sure this is the only way? It stinks like something died down there."

"Lots of things die down there," Ash said. "Unless you want to be one of them, we'd better get moving."

"Just open it up already," Red said.

The gate's rusty hinges squeaked and screeched as Ash pulled it open. Red and Dote cringed, both sure that the noise would alert the guards.

"Don't worry," Ash said. "I've done this a hundred times. The guards won't give the noise a second thought."

On the final push, one of the rusty hinges sheared in half under the gate's weight. The entire thing crashed down, causing a metallic banging and screeching. It was so loud, Red, Ash and Dote had to press their hands over their ears.

The three friends exchanged nervous looks.

"Oops." Ash said.

"Let's move. You can't tell me they didn't hear *that*," Red said.

Ash was quick to squeeze through the jagged metal debris left in the wake of the fallen gate. Once he got into the waterway he reached back to help Dote as she fumbled to get through. From the top of the stairs came the sound of a door opening, followed by the shuffling of booted feet dashing down the steps.

"They're coming," Red whispered. "We've gotta hurry."

"Distract them for a few seconds. Dote's foot is stuck on something," Ash said.

"Sorry," Dote said with a whimper.

"What am I supposed to do?" Red asked.

"You're the Alpha. Come up with something," Ash said.

The guards emerged at the bottom of the stairs and stopped cold when they saw Red.

The lead guard pulled his sword and pointed it at her. "Hold it right there, little girl!"

"Little girl? I'll have you know, I'm the Alpha Huntress."

The guards began to advance. Having no energy to fight, Red did the only thing she could think of. She grabbed Ash's lantern and flung it at their feet.

The glass sphere shattered to bits, freeing the fire fairies inside. An ear-piercing buzz erupted as the tiny creatures swarmed all around. The guards broke into a panic of swatting and swinging their swords at the attacking fairies.

"Red, we actually needed that," Ash said.

"You said to improvise." As Red squeezed through the jagged debris, she heard fabric shredding. A glance down revealed a shard of metal had ripped her dress down the side. "I have *soo* had enough of my clothes getting trashed."

"I'll buy you a new one," Ash said.

Red hopped into the waterway and landed in ankle-deep water. She glanced back to see the guards were advancing and several more were emerging at the bottom of the stairs.

"Ash, don't let us down now," Red said.

"I sure hope I can find the way in the dark."

The three friends began a long trek down the slippery tunnel. Dote and Red pressed their hands over their noses to block out the foul stench. Red couldn't believe that the odor wasn't bothering Ash in the least. She wondered if it was because he was just used to it, or if it had something to do with his being a boy.

From behind, sounds of metallic screeching erupted.

"The guards are coming," Dote said.

"We need to move faster," Red said.

"This would be a lot easier if you hadn't trashed my lantern," Ash said.

They pressed on through the darkness for another hundred yards or so.

"Red, is it just me, or is it odd that Ash knows his way around these tunnels so well?" Dote asked.

"It is a little weird. I'm strongly considering having a talk with him when we get to granny's house," Red said.

"How about you two stop talking about me like I'm not here," Ash said.

"Ash, you have to admit it is a little weird," Red said.

"Can we just focus on staying alive?" Ash said. "Even if we escape the palace, we've got a long journey across Wayward ahead of us."

"Sorry." Red and Dote said in unison.

They came to a point where the waterway forked off into two different directions.

"Which way now?" Red asked.

Ash looked to one tunnel and then to the other. "Left. No. I mean right."

The sound of the guard's shuffling boots could be heard not far behind them.

"Are you *totally* certain?" Dote asked.

"Remember? Smashed lantern? I'm going on instinct here," Ash said.

"Ash, you have to make a choice right now," Red said.

Ash closed his eyes and thought for a few seconds. "It's right. I'm sure of it."

"That's good enough for me." Red ripped some fabric off her dress. She hooked it onto a shard of metal sticking out of the wall of the waterway that forked to the left.

"Red, that's a clever idea," Dote said.

"Let's just hope they buy it," Red said.

The three friends forked off to the right and headed deeper into the darkness of the waterway. The ground was so slippery that they had to hold each other's hands to keep their balance.

Red could hear the guards approaching from behind. What was truly strange is that she could smell their sweat, and the fragrance told her that they were growing angrier by the minute.

"Which way did they go?" a guard's voice echoed out.

"Look sir, it's a piece of the girl's dress." another guard said.

"We have them now."

The sound of the guard's voices soon faded away.

"It worked, Red. You're a genius," Dote said.

They continued for another minute or two, taking several turns along the way and hopping down a few drop-off points. They rounded a corner and could see the moonlight illuminating the open end of the tunnel.

"You did it, Ash. We're home free," Dote said.

Ash took a nervous gulp. "Yeah. We made it somewhere."

The three friends dashed the final twenty yards to the end of the tunnel. Peering over the edge, they all gasped at an alarming sight. The waterway was on the side of a cliff, with a drop off a hundred feet straight down.

"This was your big escape plan?" Red asked.

Ash whimpered. "I guess we were supposed to go left."

Dote began twitching in a panic. "We can't go back. They'll find us for sure."

"You're right. We can't." Red looked over the edge and saw a small lake below, though it was impossible to know how deep it was. With no other choice, she nodded her head in a calm resolve. "We have to make a jump for it."

Dote took a frantic step backward. "No way. We'll go major splatter."

Ash shook his head in outright refusal. "We have to double back and hope they don't find us."

Red looked to Ash and Dote with fearless eyes. "There's no time to debate it. Now take my hands."

Dote took Red's hand and squeezed it. Ash trembled as he took her other hand. Red feared their chances of surviving the drop weren't great, but it was still better than risking a fight with the guards in her weakened state.

"We go on my count," Red said.

"I so wish I had said left," Ash muttered.

Red took a deep breath. *"1 ... 2 ... 3 ..."*

Hand in hand, the three friends jumped from the ledge and began free-falling toward the water below. In that brief instant, Red thought of her life before she came to Wayward.

She recalled the countless nights lying in bed, feeling sad and alone, wondering if she would ever have a family to love and call her own—or friends that would stand by her side through thick and thin—or if her life would ever have a true purpose.

As the surface of the water rushed closer, Red realized that in just two days, all of these things had come to pass. "I'm not afraid."

Red's mind went blank when they hit the icy cold water. The darkness that surrounded her brought a feeling of tranquility that she would have never thought possible. For the first time, she was truly free from a lifetime of cares and concerns. The moment was so perfect that she wished it would never end.

"Wake up, Red Riding."

A woman's hand reached down into the dark abyss and locked on to Red's arm. Red somehow knew the voice belonged to the Alpha Huntress who came before her.

"The time has come to rise as the new high protector of Wayward."

"What if I fail? I'm not strong enough to face this," Red said.

"Victory can be achieved if you believe in the great power that lives inside you."

A sudden surge of energy shot through Red's body. The feeling was so intense it felt like her heart was going to explode. It was the power of the Alpha in its purest form.

"I can feel it."

Red's eyes snapped open. All of her senses awoke in a heartbeat. There wasn't a bit of air in her lungs as she sank deeper into darkness. She could see a faint flickering of moonlight on the surface of the water far above. For most anybody, drowning would have been a certainty, but Red refused to let this be her end.

With a strength that came from a place deep within, she began kicking her legs with furious intent. It took mere seconds before her head broke the surface of the lake and she was able to take in a gasping breath of air.

Red experienced an astonishing new connection to the world around her. Every tree, every bush, every flower, even every blade of grass had its own distinct fragrance. She could hear the voices of the trees and the creatures that dwelled within them speaking out in the wind.

When she finally found the energy to swim toward the shore, she spotted Ash and Dote wading out to her. She smiled at her friends as they pulled her out of the water.

"Easy, Red. We've got you," Ash assured.

"You're going to be okay now," Dote rejoiced.

Ash and Dote held Red in their arms as she kneeled on the shore, gasping for air and coughing up water. It took only a brief moment before her strength began returning.

She looked up to the sky and saw that the moon was now glowing crimson red and looming directly overhead. The voices of the lunar deities whispered into her ears, telling her things that only one gifted with the Alpha Power could ever understand.

"I hear you."

Ash and Dote backed away in awe, as if they knew what was about to come.

"Red, don't be afraid," Dote said.

"We're here with you," Ash said.

Red broke into a sweat as her blood nearly boiled in her veins. Razor-sharp claws tore through the skin of her fingertips— brownish-red fur grew from her skin, covering her from head to toe—her muscles became empowered with immense strength— canine ears even poked out the sides of her head.

"Rise up, Alpha Huntress."

Red's transformation into a werewolf was complete. The power of the Alpha surging through her body felt like pure awesomeness. She gazed at her reflection in the lake's surface, expecting to see a dog-faced girl. It was a huge relief to see her feminine form was well intact. "With the right outfit, I could make myself a smoking hot, werewolf-powered hero."

A thumping sound of heavy footsteps rushing their way broke the silence. Red turned to see a dozen of Ice's guards emerging from the trees, wearing heavy armor and carrying broadswords.

"They've found us," Dote cried out. "We have to run."

Ash grabbed Dote's hand. "Our girl has got this one."

With fearless eyes, Red charged flat out at the men. The first guard swung his sword at her with a powerful grunt. Red caught his arm and took his weapon without effort. She then kicked him in the stomach, sending him crashing to his knees.

The next guard swung his blade at Red from behind. Red spun around and blocked his attack with the sword she had just claimed. She followed up with a counterstrike that was so powerful it hacked the guard's blade clean in half. The exchange ended with a punch to the jaw that put the man on his knees.

The other guards attempted to engage Red with attacks that were futile against her superior power. She took each of them down with effortless speed and precision, spinning and kicking, punching and ducking, darting and striking, her motions lightning fast.

When the last guard crashed to the ground, Red dropped her sword and dashed back over to Ash and Dote. The three friends stood under the moonlight, looking at one another in silence for a lingering moment. Red wasn't sure what to say, fearing that they were thinking she was some kind of freak.

Ash finally lowered his head and dropped down to one knee. "Alpha Huntress, I pledge my loyalty and ask that you accept me into your clan."

Dote kneeled down and lowered her head. "My grandmother from many generations ago stood by the side of the Alpha Huntress through the darkest of times. I now ask that you allow me to stand by yours."

Red looked down at her two greatest friends in the world. "I'm honored by your pledge of loyalty and gratefully accept you as the first two members of my clan. You two are my trusted friends. I know with you by my side, nothing on this earth will stand in my way."

Red pulled Ash and Dote to their feet and hugged them tightly. It was certain her road ahead would be paved with unknown perils. While her mission wasn't at all clear, she knew a great evil was coming their way. It was now her duty to face it head on, and if she failed, Wayward would surely fall into darkness.

Ash finally broke the silence. "So anybody know what we're supposed to do now?"

PART TWO

CHAPTER 16

With Ash leading the way, the three friends hiked through the dark woods. It took nearly two hours before Red felt they had cleared enough distance from Ice's palace to take a short rest. They would have continued on, but Ash insisted that they should stay put and make camp. The region ahead just wasn't safe to venture into during the night.

"Tree gnomes are nocturnal creatures that viciously attack anybody who dares to enter their territory." Ash went on to recount a rather unsavory tale of a time he came across a pair of them mating in the woods. He couldn't decide which scars were worse, those spanning the length of his back, or those from the horrific images that had forever stained his memory.

"Fine, we'll set up camp," Red said. "But as soon as dawn breaks, we're moving on." She had a moment of panic when she tried to turn back into her human form. Without anybody to guide her, she feared being stuck as a werewolf for the rest of her life.

Ash's and Dote's attempts to coach her through a visualization exercise only made the situation more frustrating.

"Imagine looking at yourself in a mirror, and you're in human form," Dote said.

"Tell yourself over and over that's the way you're supposed to be," Ash said.

It wasn't that Red didn't appreciate their help, but it only caused more frustration when it didn't work. The change finally came when she got a moment of silence to calm her mind. Like a child realizing she could stand and walk, it required an instinctual understanding that could never be put into words.

Gazing into the star-sprinkled sky, Red tried to imagine what her future would be like. She couldn't deny that the idea of rising up as a werewolf-powered hero was really cool. Venturing out into the woods at night to fight monsters, protecting the helpless, and building a clan of loyal followers. It was all so surreal that she kept expecting to wake up in her bed back in the orphanage.

If it was all just a crazy dream conjured up by her imagination, Red would rather just stay asleep forever.

"We should put that fire out," Ash said.

Dote was sleeping soundly in a big pile of sweet grass. Red felt a bit envious because Dote slept like she didn't have a care or concern in the world. She certainly didn't look like a witch who could conjure energy vortexes from her hands.

Watching Dote got Red to wondering what she looked like while asleep. It was safe to guess that it wasn't a sight of blissful slumber. From what the other kids in the orphanages told her, she tended to toss and turn and talk about strange things in the night.

"Did you hear what I said about the fire?" Ash asked.

Red wondered how Ash would fit into her clan. He was as loyal as a cocker spaniel, and his oddly in-depth knowledge of Ice's palace might also one day come in handy. It was just hard to get past the memory of him cowering in fear at the hands of Mia and her cronies. He was crying like a baby, even knowing they weren't going to kill him. There's no telling what he would do in the heat of a dangerous battle.

"I'm telling you, we need to put out that fire," Ash said.

The real problem Red had is that she'd just reunited with Ash and Dote after being away for so long. In such a short while, she had grown quite attached to both of them. If something bad were to happen, there was just no telling how she would deal with it.

"If we don't put out that fire right now, somebody is going to find us out here," Ash insisted.

"Then put it out if you want to. I'm not even cold," Dote said without opening her eyes.

"You don't see me stopping you," Red said.

Ash dashed over and doused their tiny campfire with clumps of dirt until it went dark. "Now we can only hope nobody saw it."

"Easy, boy. I don't think there's anybody around here for miles," Red said.

"Excuse me for not agreeing with your Alphaness," Ash said. "I know these woods as well as anybody. I can say for sure that there's always somebody or something hanging around. A campfire at night is like ringing a dinner bell for a pack of hungry dogs."

"Why didn't you say so before?" Red asked.

"I did say so before. Nobody was listening," Ash said.

"Next time you have something important to say, speak up just a little louder," Dote said.

"I would have if not for the fact that speaking up might attract things that are out looking for dinner right about now," Ash said.

While Ash and Dote continued a rather spirited discussion on the subject, Red reflected on the events of the night. Of all the things that went through her mind, there was one troubling thought that she could not shake. "I sure hope Wolfgang got out okay," she said.

"What is your hang-up over that guy?" Ash asked.

"I don't have a hang-up over him," Red said. "He helped save our lives tonight."

"He totally risked his life so that we could escape," Dote said.

"I admit he was somewhat helpful getting us out," Ash said. "I'm saying that he did it because he's after something."

"How do you know that?" Red asked.

"I just do. Trust me on this one," Ash said.

"Maybe Wolfgang has a hang-up over Red," Dote said.

"Don't be ridiculous," Ash blurted out.

Red gave Ash a glare. "Why is that ridiculous? I may not be a beauty queen, but I don't think I'm so hard on the eyes either. Am I?"

"You're major hotness," Dote said. "I'm so envious."

"See? Dote thinks I'm worthy of a boy getting hung up over me," Red said.

Ash was starting to look frazzled. "I didn't say you weren't worthy of some major ogling."

"Oh. So you think Red is ogling hot?" Dote said.

"Ash, do you think I'm hot?" Red asked.

Ash flailed his arms in frustration. "Hey, I didn't say I think you're hot."

"Then you don't think she's hot?" Dote asked.

"What do you think of me, Ash?" Red asked.

"Yeah, Dorkus Ashley. Do tell," Dote said.

Ash leaped up and paced around in a frantic fit. "I think you're my best friend. I am not supposed to think of you that way. Just drop it already, so we can all get on with our lives."

"I thought I was your best friend," Dote said.

"You're both my best friends, so don't even get started on the *who do I like better* thing you girls always pull on me," Ash shouted.

"Sorry." Red and Dote said in unison.

Ash flopped down and took a deep breath to calm himself. It wasn't long before he cracked a smile. "If Red had never left Wayward, this is how every day would have been."

"That's for sure," Dote said.

"Totally," Red said.

Ash frowned. "We missed out on a lot of fun times."

Red slid over and put a comforting arm around Ash. "Hey, don't go getting all Mr. Gloomypants now."

Ash laughed a little. "I used to hate it when you called me that."

Red smiled. "I remember. It's all starting to come back to me now. I can't believe I could have ever forgotten about you two."

"It makes sense with you living so far away," Dote said.

"How was it out there?" Ash asked. "I've never been beyond the borders of Wayward."

"I'm not even sure I know where the borders are," Dote said.

"It's completely different from here," Red said. "As far as I know, there's no magical witches or werewolves. There are creatures that act like goblins, but none of them have giant mouths that can swallow you whole."

"Sounds boring," Dote said.

"No place I ever want to go," Ash said.

"Some people were happy there. I sure wasn't one of them, though," Red said.

Dote crawled over and squeezed between Red and Ash. "Well, now you're back with your best two friends in the world, and we're all about to set out on an amazing adventure together."

"With us by your side, it's going to be pure awesomeness from this day on," Ash said.

"And if you kids don't keep your voices down, you won't live long enough to go on that little adventure," a male voice called out from the darkness.

Ash and Dote yelped out.

Without making the slightest sound, Red jumped to her feet and dashed away into the shadows. She could hear the crackling sound of footsteps nearby. In a single breath, she was able to catch the scent of every living thing around her. It was startling when she realized how many creatures were lurking so near their campsite.

Among all of them, one stood out from of the rest.

"Wolfgang," Red said.

Wolfgang leaped out of a tree and landed right in front of Ash and Dote. *"Boo!"*

"Ahhhhhh." Ash and Dote wailed.

"What happened to Red?" Wolfgang asked.

"Right behind you, Wolf Boy."

Red soared out of the bushes and kicked Wolfgang to the ground. He rolled to his feet and charged at her. They broke into a rapid exchange of punches and kicks.

"I can't tell if they're fighting or flirting," Dote said.

Red got a grip on Wolfgang's wrist and flipped him onto his back. His attempt to break her grip was futile as she pinned him to the ground.

"You're finished." Red said.

Ash raised his arms in victory. "You go, girl. Knock the daylights out of him."

Wolfgang struggled to get up. "Get off me, Alpha girl."

Red pressed her forearm against his throat. "Why don't you make me, Wolf Boy?"

"Maybe I'll just lie here and enjoy the view."

"Maybe you're just saying that because you can't get up."

"Maybe I'm okay with that."

"Maybe I am, too."

Dote shyly covered her eyes. "Maybe we should leave you two alone to work it out."

"Maybe you two should cut it out," Ash said. "This little moment you two are having is going to make me hurl."

Red glared into Wolfgang's eyes. "One wrong move and you'll be walking with a limp for the rest of your miserable life."

"Promises, promises," Wolfgang said.

Red stepped back and offered Wolfgang a hand up. When he took it, she pulled him to his feet and locked a hand around his throat. "Friend or foe, werewolf?"

"We're on the same side of the line, Alpha Huntress."

"Guess I'll have to accept that for now."

Red released Wolfgang and shoved him onto the ground. He did his best to look cool as he got to his feet.

"So why were you stalking us, Wolf Boy?" Ash asked.

Wolfgang gave Ash a hard stare down. "I know you. Dorkus Ashley, right?"

"Ash will do just fine."

"Well listen up, Ashley. I don't answer to little girls. And I won't bother to say what's going to happen if you call me 'Wolf Boy' even one more time."

Ash wailed in frustration. "Red, we need to ditch this guy, like yesterday."

"As much noise as you were all making, you couldn't ditch a deaf cave sloth," Wolfgang said.

Ash looked to Dote. "You know the deal with this guy. Tell Red what you really think of him."

Dote gave a nervous shrug. "I guess he has a seedy history."

Wolfgang grinned. "Don't sell me short, Dote. I'm a well-known delinquent. An antisocial misfit. A big, bad wolf."

Ash pointed an accusing finger at Wolfgang. "You see? He doesn't even try to deny it. If you let him hang around, he's going to turn on us."

"You'll be first on my list, girly boy," Wolfgang said.

Red knew that telling Wolfgang to get lost was the sensible choice. If trouble could have a smell, he was reeking of it. She told herself that her decision should have nothing to do with the way he made her blood boil, nor should it have anything to do with his rugged good looks, long hair, and rock-hard abs.

"Letting this guy hang around us comes with major risk," Ash said.

Ash's words reminded Red of the night she arrived in Wayward. The spirits of the forest had told her that only one brave enough to risk everything will gain anything in this world. Her decision to believe in that got her through the great tree. She now felt that she had to believe in that idea once again.

Before Red could do that, there was one question that demanded an answer. "How did you get away from Ice's palace?"

"She let me go," Wolfgang said, with a casual shrug.

"You see? He *is* on the side of the enemy," Ash said.

"Why would Ice do that?" Red asked.

"Ice and I have a complicated history," Wolfgang said. "A couple of years ago, we had a thing going, but I had to drop her because it turns out she's flipping insane."

"I won't argue with that," Ash said.

"The truth is she's whacked-out obsessed with me," Wolfgang said. "I'm not making that up either. It's total love-to-hate craziness with her."

Red skeptically eyed Wolfgang. "So that's why she just let you go? Even after you helped me get away?"

"She let me walk right out the front door even though she totally wanted to kill me. Ice just can't bring herself to do it. Not yet, at least," Wolfgang said.

Ash gave Wolfgang a hard glare. "I find this story to be highly suspicious."

"I'll buy it," Dote said. "Girls can do crazy things when it comes to boys. Especially pretty ones."

"Why, thank you, Dote," Wolfgang gave her a flirtatious smile.

Dote giggled like a giddy little girl. "Oh, you cut that out right now, mister."

Ash raised his arms in defeat. "And with that, I'm out. This guy is a top-notch troublemaker. I know he's going to turn on us when we least expect it, and when that happens, I'll be able to say I told you so, but it won't matter because it will be way past too late to say it." He stomped away and sat on a log at the far end of their campsite.

Wolfgang grinned. "The little girly boy's got spunk. I'll give her that."

"Enough trash-talking my friend," Red said. "Any more and you'll answer to my fist in your face."

"As you command, your Alpha highness," Wolfgang said.

Red carefully considered the situation and came to the only decision she could live with. "Okay, this is the deal, Wolf Boy. We're camping here tonight. You're free to stay if you want to. Tomorrow I'll figure out if you can travel with us. If I decide you need to go away, then you take a hike, no questions asked. Agreed?"

"You're the one in charge here," Wolfgang said.

"Then it's settled. You all get some sleep. I'll take first watch," Red said.

"I'll sleep with one eye open," Ash said.

"Ash, that's enough," Red said.

"Whatever." Ash flopped back and continued to pout.

Dote laid down in her pile of sweet grass. "Wolfgang, can I ask one more question?"

Wolfgang leaned back against a fallen log. "Ask away, Doteness."

"What happened to the prince who helped us escape?"

"If you mean the guy who hacked Mia's paw off, I have no idea. If Ice got her claws on him, I can tell you it's not good." Wolfgang turned on his side and closed his eyes.

"That's too bad. He was brave. And so pretty. I do hope he's okay." Dote then fell right to sleep.

Red sat on a tree stump and watched Wolfgang as he dozed off. As much as it annoyed her, it was impossible to deny that she had strong feelings for him. She knew things between them were about to get complicated, an idea that she loved and feared. "I guess bad boys really do make a girl's heart beat faster," she muttered under her breath. "I am so doomed."

CHAPTER 17

I couldn't have been asleep more than a minute or two." The instant Red's eyes snapped open, there was no doubt they were in serious trouble. The foul stench of something dangerous was lurking in the air. Just from its odor, she could tell that it was huge and headed in their direction.

Red knew it would have been smart to wake Ash or Dote to take second watch, but they were both sleeping so soundly, and dawn was only a couple of hours away. Making things worse, Wolfgang was no longer in the spot where he had been sleeping only minutes ago.

Sniffing the air, she couldn't find any sign of his scent. She knew Ash would say he'd ditched them at the first hint of trouble. That was unlikely considering how Wolfgang had saved them at Ice's palace. Of course, Ash would then argue that Wolfgang knew by his own admission that Ice wouldn't harm him, so technically the situation didn't hold any legitimate risk on his part.

"Ash. Dote. Wake up," Red whispered.

They were both only a few feet away, deep in sleep. Waking them should have been easy enough, if not for Red's fear that the slightest sound could reveal their presence to the beast headed their way and getting closer by the second. Something had to be done soon or they were going to end up in a battle she was unsure they could survive.

"Will you two wake up?" Red spoke a little louder than before.

Both remained in blissful slumber without a care in the world. Left with no choice, Red gathered up a few pebbles from the dirt. One by one, she began to fling them at Ash. The first few hit him in the chest and stomach. After this failed to get the slightest reaction, Red decided to stop playing nice and aimed right at his head. On the third or fourth attempt, she scored a shot right between his eyes.

"Dorkus Ashley, you wake up this instant."

Ash opened his eyes with a grunt of irritation. "Red, stop messing around. I'm trying to get a little sleepy time here."

"Keep quiet," Red whispered. "Something's coming."

"Define *something*."

"I'm not sure. It's smells big and hairy and dripping with sweat, and its breath smells like dead stuff."

Ash leaped up to his feet. "It's a bridge troll. We're totally doomed."

"A bridge troll?" Red felt ridiculous just saying it.

"You know, they live under bridges and lure unsuspecting travelers to their untimely demise."

Red rolled her eyes. "I should have known that's what you meant."

"It's been wandering aimlessly since Rowling's bridge got trashed by a couple of crazy old wizards that were wand dueling on it."

"That makes total sense," Red muttered.

"How far away is it?"

Red sniffed the air. "Twenty, maybe thirty yards, at the most."

"Which is it, twenty or thirty?"

"I don't know. What difference does it make?"

"None if it smells us." Ash began to rip handfuls of sweet grass from the ground and rubbed the roots all over his face and arms.

Red was about to ask what he was doing when Dote opened her eyes and sat up. "What did I miss?"

Ash shoved clumps of sweet grass and dirt into his shirt and down his pants. "Bridge troll, coming our way."

Dote screeched. "What do we do, Red?"

"How should I know? I've never even seen a bridge troll."

"I have," Ash said. "They're big and ugly and have a hankering for the taste of human flesh." He began to rub his face in the grass.

"And how will whatever you're doing help our cause?" Red asked.

"Bridge trolls are meat eaters. They hate the taste of vegetation. I'm making myself smell like a garden salad," Ash said.

Dote shook her head in disagreement. "That's just an old wives' tale. It *never* works."

Ash rolled in the grass. "Unless you've got a better idea, I'm following the teachings of the old wives club."

"What happened to Wolfgang?" Dote asked.

"I don't know. I guess he took off," Red said.

"Why am I not surprised that he ran off at the first hint of trouble?" Ash said.

"Why am I not surprised you were going to say that?" Red mumbled.

"Maybe the troll ate him and got a stomachache," Ash said.

Dote smacked Ash in the back of the head. "That's a mean thing to say, Dorkus Ashley."

Ash rubbed his head. "Dote. That hurt."

"You deserved it for saying such mean things," Dote said.

"Quiet down. The troll is getting closer," Red said.

Dote gasped and started shoving sweet grass down her shirt.

Red gave her a look of disbelief. "You just said that wouldn't work."

"With a bridge troll coming our way, those old wives are starting to sound pretty smart right about now," Dote said.

"We could just make a run for it," Red said.

"Don't you know anything about bridge trolls?" Ash asked. "Running only gets them more worked up."

Dote whimpered. "Well, it's going to be here in about a minute, so we'd better be ready to deal with it, however the holy heck we're going to deal with it."

Red sighed. "Fine. Give me some of that stuff." She began to wipe sweet grass all over herself and shoved several clumps down her dress. "I might be making this up, but this reminds me of the time we all got into a mud fight with some weird boys."

Ash cracked a smile. "Of all the things to remember. You got us in a mess of trouble with that little scuffle."

"How was it my fault?" Red asked.

"It wasn't totally your fault," Dote said. "Those creepy Gruff Brothers were a mean little trio."

"Serious bullies, more like it," Ash said. "They took Dote's snake, Mister Squiggly, and wouldn't give him back."

"You had a pet snake, Dote?" Red asked.

"Thanks to you, I still do. You whacked those mean Gruffs around with a big stick and sent them running like a bunch of little babies," Dote said.

"The next day you decided to get them back by ambushing them with mud clods from a tree outside their house," Ash said.

"I did that?" Red asked.

Dote nodded. "You were a seriously tough toddler."

Red cracked a grin. It was hard to imagine that they had done such things at age five, and even harder to believe she was once a rough and tough girl. In the orphanages, the other kids often pushed her around. She had always considered herself to be a serious weakling. It was nice to learn that it wasn't always the case.

"Everybody quiet, I think I hear it," Dote whispered.

The three friends stopped cold and held their breath. The thumping of massive footsteps could be heard, getting closer and louder with each passing second. Red put a hand over Dote's mouth to silence her whimpering. Soon the branches of a nearby tree began to shudder. The troll's heavy breathing erupted nearby. It was seconds from discovering them.

"This is it," Red whispered.

Tree branches snapped and sheared as the bridge troll forced its way into their campsite. With a massive fist, it knocked a tree out of its way with a single bash. The beast's giant head was the first thing they saw. Its mouth was big enough to swallow a person whole.

Ash screeched like a baby and curled up in the fetal position on the ground. Red grumbled in disbelief. She was now certain that he was going to be a liability in battle, but this didn't mean she wouldn't fight tooth and nail to protect him.

"You both get behind me." Red said.

Dote didn't hesitate to follow Red's instruction. Ash was too busy whimpering to hear her. When the troll came into full view, a surge of crippling fear overtook Red. The beast was covered from head to toe in grungy wet fur and stood twenty feet tall. It stepped close to Red and gave a furious roar. The raunchy stink of its breath flooded her lungs, making her dizzy.

"Red, isn't it time to go all Alpha on this thing?" Dote asked.

Ash spoke without looking up, "Dote, you should know better than that. The smell of hot werewolf blood can make bridge trolls go psycho with hunger. If Red transforms, that thing will rip the forest apart to get at her."

"Why in the world would I ever know a thing like that?" Dote asked.

Red took a nervous gulp. "Good safety tip, Ash. Let's just hope your theory about the smell of veggies is just as good." She pulled a clump of sweet grass from her dress and waved it around at the bridge troll. "Take a good sniff. This is what we taste like."

The bridge troll grunted in disgust from the smell and backed off a bit. Red flung the sweet grass at the troll, causing some to stick in its wet fur. The beast roared as it reached up to pull the grass off. Its fingers were so massive that it couldn't get a grip. The troll got so angry that it clubbed itself in the chest with its own fist.

"I see you don't like this stuff," Red said.

She pulled more clumps of grass from her dress and flung them at the troll. The beast became frantic as it tried to get the grass off of its fur. The harder it tried, the more damage it inflicted on itself.

"Major good plan," Dote said.

"Just making it up as I go along here," Red said. "I could use a bit of help."

"Helping out is what I do best." Dote gathered clumps of sweet grass and piled them near Red's feet. "I'll gather, you fling."

Ash looked up just as the troll clubbed itself in the face. "Are we winning?"

"We just might do that if you'd man up and help," Red said.

"Hey, go easy on me. I had a bad experience with one of these guys that I'm still a little shaken over." Ash finally got up and grabbed a clump of grass. He flung it at the troll, hitting it right in the face. The troll responded by bashing itself, this time hard enough to make it stumble backward, off balance.

"Red, you're a genius," Ash said.

"I couldn't have come up with the idea without you," Red said.

Red and Ash continued flinging sweet grass, driving the troll into a frantic frenzy.

"Why you hitting yourself, mister troll?" Ash taunted.

The final clump of sweet grass that Red threw went right up the troll's nose. The beast wailed out in agony and began thrashing around. It swung a fist wide and smashed the trunk of a massive oak tree. The three friends watched in awe as the tree fell, crashing down on top of the troll. The beast twitched and trembled for a few seconds before it finally went lifeless.

"Is it, you know?" Dote asked.

"Totally." Red said.

Ash cheered and danced around. "Take that, you stinking troll. That'll teach you to knock my house over."

"When did a troll knock your house over?" Dote asked.

"It was a tree house. I worked really hard on it," Ash said.

Dote glared at Ash. "You had a tree house and never told me?"

"I had just finished building it. I was going to surprise you on your birthday," Ash said.

"Oh, Ash. You are the best friend ever." Dote gave Ash a smothering hug.

"Save the mushy stuff for later," Red said. "We need to get moving, double-time."

"You're right," Ash said. "The scavengers will soon come looking for a free breakfast."

Red cringed at the thought. "That's not the reason I was thinking, but it is a good point."

Just as they were about to start walking, Red stopped cold and sniffed the air. "You have got to be kidding me."

Ash gasped in a panic. "What is it now? It's too close to dawn for tree gnomes. Is it road snakes? Tell me it's not road snakes."

Red would have asked him what road snakes were if she weren't too annoyed for the words to come out. All she could say was "Wolfgang." She turned around right as the wolf boy was emerging from the bushes.

"And we were just starting to have fun," Ash said.

"Whoa. Is that the troll from Rowling's bridge?" Wolfgang asked.

Red gave him a hard stare. "Where'd you run off to, Wolf Boy?"

"I had some personal business to take care of," Wolfgang said.

Ash stepped up to Wolfgang and gave him a tough glare. "Is that your secret way of saying you had to find a bridge troll to sic on us?"

"It means I had to go potty. Number two, if you want the dirty details," Wolfgang said.

"You are so lying," Ash said.

Wolfgang gave Ash a dangerous stare. "Listen up, Ashley. I don't like being called a liar. If you want to see the evidence, I'll be happy to bring it to you."

Red stepped in between Wolfgang and Ash and nudged them away from each other. "It seems convenient that you took off right before the troll showed up, and then came back right after we finished it off."

Wolfgang *growled*. "I didn't want to give away our location so I hiked out a full mile to do my thing."

"Lies, lies, and more lies," Ash said.

"It makes sense," Dote said. "The smell of our ... you know ... stuff ... can attract razor-rats."

Wolfgang clenched his fist tight. "Not to mention it's a dead giveaway to a skilled tracker. Ice only hires the best of the worst to do her dirty work."

Red shrugged. "It all makes perfect sense."

"You've got that right," Wolfgang said.

"I wasn't done," Red said. "It makes perfect sense. I'm just not so sure I believe it."

"Finally." Ash said.

Wolfgang's face twitched with anger. "So you think I'm lying, Alpha?"

"I don't know enough about you to know what to think." Red turned her back on Wolfgang and started walking away. Ash and Dote followed closely behind.

"So is it cool if I come along, or what?" Wolfgang asked.

"If I say no, you'll probably just do it anyway," Red said.

Wolfgang bashed a fist into a tree, busting a hole through the thick bark. "I'm going to make you trust me, Red Riding."

"Not if I have anything to say about it," Ash said.

Red looked back and saw Wolfgang bashing his fists into the tree. The intense rage in his eyes was both disturbing and tragic. It almost made her feel sorry for him, though she knew that thinking this way had too much to do with the strange attraction she felt for him. Telling him not to follow would be the most sensible choice, but that was a decision Red just couldn't bring herself to make.

CHAPTER 18

"T his has a major risk factor," Ash whispered to Red and Dote. "I say we hang back and wait for Granny to give us a sign that it's all clear."

The three friends had been hiding in the bushes across the clearing from Grenda's house for well over an hour. Red knew something was out of sorts as soon as she set eyes on the place. It now looked like a dump that had sat abandoned for years.

"Granny put a protection spellcraft on the *inside* of the house," Red whispered. "Is it possible she could have expanded the spellcraft to cover the outside, too?"

Dote was tapping a nervous finger on the tip of her nose. "The enchantments feel like Grenda's. The problem is a skilled witch could do a pretty good job of faking them, if she knows the nature of the spellcraft Grenda uses."

Red sighed. "So what you're saying is that there is no way of knowing for sure."

"I'm sorry, Red, if I was a better witch, maybe I could. I mean, I'm pretty good, but not *that* good," Dote said.

Ash was lying on his stomach in the dirt, trying to get a clear look at the house. "We know Ice knows that Red lives here. There's a good chance her cronies are hiding out, just waiting for us to show up."

Dote whimpered. "Grenda could be in major danger. She could be in hiding, or hurt, or something way worse."

Red had never felt so tired in her life. Her body was aching from the events of the previous night. It didn't help that the sweet grass she had stuffed down her dress earlier was causing an itch that would not quit. The thought of sitting in a nice hot bath was almost enough to risk stepping out into the open.

Complicating the situation, Wolfgang was lingering somewhere nearby. No matter how hard Red tried to avoid thinking about him, it had become physically impossible not to. Her heightened sense of smell was locked on to his distinct scent and would not let go.

Trust was the major issue Red had when it came to him. His reasons for helping them escape from Ice's palace didn't quite add up for her. It made it hard to ignore Ash's claim that Wolfgang had a secret motive. At the same time, she could sense good in him, so it was hard to blow him off entirely.

Red again turned her attention to Grenda's house. "We need to make a decision right now. So tell me what you're thinking here."

Dote took a deep breath to center herself. "We've been here for an hour now and I haven't sensed the presence of any dark spellcraft. I think we should go for it."

Ash crawled up from the bushes. "But if you're wrong, there could be a dozen of Ice's goons standing right on the front porch."

"Anybody wanna know what I think?" Wolfgang asked.

Red, Ash, and Dote *screamed*. They snapped a look back to find Wolfgang standing right behind them.

"Why, Wolfgang, what amazing stealth skills you have," Red said.

"The better to sneak up on you, Little Red."

Dote looked at Red and Wolfgang with a perplexed glare. "Something about the way you two said that felt odd."

Red and Wolfgang looked at one another and shrugged.

"What we need to do is put a bell on you," Ash said.

Wolfgang grinned. "Then maybe you could go around and put bells on all of Ice's cronies, just in case they try to sneak up on you."

"Do you think that any of them are hanging around waiting to ambush us?" Red asked.

"Nope." Wolfgang said.

"What makes you so certain?" Dote asked.

"Because with all the noise you kids have been making, they would have found you already."

Red grimaced. "He's got a point."

"I remain skeptical," Ash said.

"I'll prove it to you." Wolfgang leaped from the bushes and out into the clearing.

"Wolfgang, you get back here this minute," Red whispered.

Wolfgang walked across the clearing and straight on up to the porch. "Come and get me, Ice Seether. I'm right here."

Red watched Wolfgang for a tense moment, but nothing happened.

"That doesn't prove anything," Ash said. "They're not after him. They're after you, Red. And what if he's on their side and he's trying to trick you out into the open."

"That's dumb," Dote said. "If he wanted to get us, he could have done it already."

"I agree," Red said. "I've had enough of this." Without another thought or hesitation, she stepped out into the clearing.

"Right behind you." Dote dashed after Red.

They were halfway across the clearing before Ash raced out after them. "Hey, wait for me."

Red's senses were on edge as they walked the fifty feet from the bushes to the house. From what she could tell, there wasn't a hint of danger anywhere around them. After a tense moment, they reached the front door, where Wolfgang was waiting with a smug grin.

"You see. Nobody's waiting around to ambush us."

No sooner had Wolfgang said this, then Ethan the woodsman leaped out from behind a pile of logs. He grabbed Wolfgang by the throat and picked him up off the ground with one hand while clutching his massive battle-axe in the other. Wolfgang's legs flailed around as he struggled to get away.

"Helheim, I warned you to stay away from here!" Ethan shouted.

With a vicious roar, Wolfgang transformed into a werewolf. He planted his feet on Ethan's chest and pushed with furious force, breaking Ethan's grip. When his feet hit the ground, he kicked

Ethan in the gut, knocking him back several feet.

"And I warned *you* to stay away from me, old man!" Wolfgang growled.

The two warriors circled one another in an intense stare-down. Wolfgang had his claws raised. Ethan gripped his axe, ready to strike.

"Hold up a minute," Red said. "What is going on here?"

Ethan swung his axe with deadly intent. Wolfgang leaped over it and followed up with a kick to Ethan's chest, knocking him back.

Red turned to Ash and Dote. "Do either of you know what this is all about?"

"It's an old grudge," Dote said. "The woodsman has a major issue with Wolfgang's family."

"*Everybody* in Wayward has a serious issue with the Helheim Clan," Ash said. "Hack him to bits, Ethan!"

Ethan repeatedly swung his axe at Wolfgang, time and again missing by only a hair. Wolfgang unleashed counterstrikes, but Ethan was too big and powerful for him to stop.

Red knew that if one of Ethan's strikes connected, it would be over for Wolfgang. She had no idea how to stop the fight, or if she even should.

"What has his family done that's so bad?" Red asked.

"Where to begin?" Ash said. "How about a total disregard for every law ever written? Stealing. Lying. Cheating. Backstabbing anybody who ever trusted them. Oh, and they started a riot that ended with them burning down half of Wayward Village."

"That is true," Dote said. "But most of that happened a long time ago, before Wolfgang was even born."

Ethan swung his axe at Wolfgang's head. Wolfgang dodged and countered with a furious slash of his claws across Ethan's wrist. Ethan grunted and lost his grip on his axe.

"So most of the stuff people hold against Wolfgang wasn't even his fault?" Red asked.

"*He's a Helheim.* Everybody knows they're all major defects," Ash said.

Ethan swung a fist and pummeled Wolfgang in the jaw. Wolfgang was so dazed that he couldn't defend himself when Ethan followed up with a series of brutal punches. He ended the brawl with a massive uppercut that sent Wolfgang soaring. Red winced as she watched.

"The worst part is that the Helheims had an alliance with Ragnarok when he was on Earth," Dote said. "They were granted powers that they used to terrorize the people of Wayward."

"And they were mortal enemies of the first Red Riding," Ash said.

Wolfgang tried to claw to his feet, but he was much too dizzy.

Ethan picked up his axe. "Your path of tyranny ends here, Wolfgang of the Helheim Clan."

Red watched in terror as Ethan strutted over to Wolfgang. "But all that stuff was done by his family. What has Wolfgang actually done that's so bad?"

"Want me to make a list?" Ash said. "How about he's a major jerk who rides around on his motorcycle acting all cool and treating everybody like total crap."

Dote covered her eyes, unable to watch what was happening. "As far as I know, he's never done anything truly terrible."

Ethan raised his axe to strike. Wolfgang looked up at him with dreadful fear in his eyes.

"This feels wrong," Red said.

As Ethan thrust his axe downward, Red dashed forward and took her werewolf form. She grabbed Ethan's arm and stopped his attack an inch short of Wolfgang's head.

"That's far enough, woodsman," Red said.

Ethan quickly pulled away and lowered his weapon. "Red, have you gone mad? You could have been killed."

Wolfgang looked at Red in disbelief. "You saved me."

Red gave Ethan a stone cold stare. "I'm not going to let you kill him unless you can give me a good reason for it."

"His clan has committed unspeakable crimes," Ethan said.

"What crimes has *he* committed?" Red asked. "Tell me what he deserves to die for."

Ethan's face twitched with hatred. "*He's a Helheim.* That's more than enough reason for me."

"If that's all you've got, then you'll have to go through me to do it," Red said, stiffening as she took up a ready stance, prepared to defend the biker.

"Red, you must understand," Ethan said.

"My mind is made up. Stand down or attack."

Ethan stared at Red in such disbelief he was unable to speak.

Wolfgang stumbled to his feet. "Red, you don't have to do this for me."

"I'm not doing it for you. I'm doing it because it's right. If I'm really this high protector you all keep talking about, I figure it's my right to make that decision."

"Okay, time out." Ash rushed over and stepped right in between Red and Ethan. "This has gotten way out of control here. We're all supposed to be on the same side."

"Ash, stay out of this," Red said.

"No. No way. Not a chance," Ash said. "This is the last thing we need right now. Ice and her cronies could show up at any time and attack us."

Ethan tightened his grip on his axe. "Why is Ice of the Seether Clan hunting you?"

"She's a major power hungry psycho, and I've got something she wants," Red said.

"I'm betting you mean the Alpha Power," Ethan said.

"Why am I not surprised you know that?" Red muttered.

"Ash is right," Dote said. "It would be good if we all got inside. Standing out here in the open is dangerous."

Red looked Ethan in the eyes. "We're going inside. I'm taking Wolfgang with me. Are you going to try and stop me or step aside?"

"You're making a dangerous mistake," Ethan said. "But you are the Alpha, so it's your mistake to make."

"You're welcome to come inside with us," Red said. "I could use your help right about now."

"I'm not stepping foot inside *that* house." Ethan turned and walked away toward the woods. "Just call my name if you need me."

Wolfgang approached Red, his eyes softening. "I don't know what to say. Nobody has ever done anything like that for me."

"Just don't make me regret it, Wolf Boy." Red turned her back on him and entered the house.

"Granny, are you here?" Red called out as she stepped into the living room, followed by Wolfgang, Ash, and Dote. With the protection spellcraft active, it looked dusty and abandoned, just as Red had expected.

"I love what Grenda's done with the place," Wolfgang said.

What Red didn't expect to find was Prince floating inside a mystical bubble, frozen and lifeless like a statue. "What happened to him?"

"Looks like granny got herself a cool new knickknack," Ash said.

Dote pushed her way past the others and approached Prince. Red and Ash exchanged grins when they noticed how she was swooning at the sight of him.

"Even trapped in enchanted limbo, he's still the prettiest man I've ever seen," Dote said.

"Cut it out before you make me hurl," Wolfgang said.

"I think it's cute," Red said.

"Our little Dote is in l-o-v-e," Ash said.

"I am not in l-o-v-e!" Dote shouted.

Wolfgang slammed the door. The room changed into its true clean and cozy form with a warm fire crackling in the fireplace. In the same instant, Prince vanished from sight.

"Don't close the door, you dummy," Dote said. "We have to get him out of there."

Wolfgang grumbled and opened the door. Prince reappeared, and the room returned to its dusty and deserted state. Intrigued by the phenomenon, Wolfgang opened and closed the door several times, causing the room to shift back and forth. A strange *humming* rang out, making the walls and windows rattle. It was as if he was causing the protection spellcraft to overload.

"Cut it out, already." Dote said. "You keep that up, you'll blow the house to bits and all of us with it."

Wolfgang finally stopped, leaving the door slightly cracked open. "My bad."

Dote put her hands against the bubble holding Prince. A spark of mystical energy forced her to step away in haste. "Granny sure knows how to cast an enchanted prison. There's no way I can get him out without knowing which spellcraft she used."

"Sucks to be him right now," Wolfgang said.

Ash grinned. "I'd rather be stuck in an enchanted bubble than you on your best day."

Wolfgang gave Ash a hard glare. "Keep talking like that, I might forget that Red is making me play nice with you."

"I just might forget, too," Red said. "Give it a rest, Ash."

Ash grumbled in frustration. "Fine. So what do we do about Dote's boyfriend there?"

Dote snarled. "He's not my boyfriend, and I'm not in l-o-v-e with him."

"Not much, you're not," Ash said.

White energy ignited in Dote's eyes. "Dorkus Ashley, so help me, if you don't cut that out this instant ..."

Red stepped in between Ash and Dote. "You both cut it out. I think Prince is going to have to stay there until we find Granny."

Wolfgang pushed the door shut, causing Prince to vanish and the room to shift again. Dote whimpered like a sad kitty cat.

Red then headed upstairs. When she reached the top, she stopped cold, feeling quite perplexed. There were now three doors in a hallway that she distinctly recalled having had four. The doors leading into her bedroom, her parents' bedroom, and the bathroom still remained, but the fourth door that Red assumed led to Granny's bedroom was gone. In its place hung a full-length mirror in a glossy black metallic frame. Each step she took toward the mirror came with an unsettling feeling that somebody was watching her. When she finally stood before the hazy glass, the sight was quite startling. The reflection that stared back was not exactly her own. Her mirrored version wore a short skirt, a tight tank top, and knee-high leather boots, which were all as black as her hair. If not for the eyes being entirely void of color, Red might have liked this alternative image of herself.

A careful examination of her hair assured her that it was still red, and a quick glance down confirmed she still wore her mother's tattered blue ball gown. She waved a hand around and saw that the reflection matched her moves, just as one would expect. To be certain, she lifted a foot, spun in a circle, and jumped around in random directions. Her reflected self precisely matched each movement.

As Red looked away, the reflection snarled at her. It was so quick that she wasn't entirely sure it actually happened. There was no doubt that it would be most sensible to stay clear of the mirror, but it was far too intriguing to resist. Her hand trembled a bit as she placed it on the glass. The surface felt oddly warm. A strange static barrier made Red's skin tingle. She looked into the eyes of her reflection and made a snarky expression.

In response, her reflection gave a sinister glare. It then reached a hand right through the glass and locked onto Red's wrist. "Declare yourself."

CHAPTER 19

Red was overcome with a paralyzing rush of fear as her arm was pulled through the black mirror by her own reflection. With her face pressed against the glass, she couldn't call for help. Her desperate attempt to pull away proved to be a futile effort. She could only watch as the reflection closely inspected her palm. A disturbing tingling sensation rushed through her body. It felt as if her reflection's black eyes were peering right into her soul.

"Your linage has been confirmed, granddaughter of Grenda Stalk," Red's reflected self said.

The mirror vanished from sight, leaving Red standing with her arm awkwardly extended. The missing door then appeared. Red stood frozen, trying to calm her shaken nerves. The ordeal was so strange that she had to fight the urge to dash down the stairs and right out the front door.

"What's got you so rattled?" Grenda said from behind Red.

Deathly startled, Red spun around just as Grenda stepped out of the bathroom door. She wore a fuzzy bathrobe and had a towel wrapped around her head.

"Granny, you gotta stop startling me like that."

"You gotta stop startling me by staying out all night." Grenda opened her bedroom door and stepped inside. "Now get in here and tell me what happened this time."

The door swung shut with a slam right after Red stepped through it, leaving her friends waiting out in the hallway. Grenda began rummaging through a dresser drawer, carelessly tossing clothes aside.

Her Granny's bedroom wasn't at all what Red expected. Unlike the rest of the house, it was a cluttered mess with piles of dirty laundry. The shelves were overflowing with random trinkets, strange knickknacks, and disorganized stacks of books.

"So, out with it, Red. From the look of you, it must have been one thrill of a night," Grenda said.

"Things got out of control at the ball." Red frowned as she looked at her tattered dress. "Ice Seether tried to force me to give her the Alpha Power."

"*Ha!* I had a feeling that girl was up to mischief," Grenda said.

"You knew that could have happen and let me go anyway?"

"Well, you're not going to learn how to deal with these sorts of things if I go coddling you all the time."

Red gasped. "Granny, we barely escaped with our lives."

"Don't mean to sound harsh, Red. It's just that you'd best get used to things like that if you're going to take up this Alpha calling. Now turn around, unless you want to see a mighty frightful sight."

Red spun around just as she heard Grenda drop her robe to the floor. "Could Ice have taken the powers from me?"

"Not on her own, she couldn't have. That girl uses what us real witches call borrowed power. It comes from mystical jewels and other trinkets she probably bought or stole."

Red recalled how Ice was dominating the battle until she lost her jeweled scepter. "What if I had willingly agreed? Then could she have taken it?"

"It's possible, if she really had the resources to pull off such a thing. It would take a mighty powerful spellcraft that would send you straight to your maker. It's a good thing you would never do something so foolish."

Red sat on the edge of Grenda's bed. "I ask because I'm afraid she could use my friends against me. I don't know if I could overcome that sort of thing."

Now wearing a loose-fitting flowered dress, Grenda sat down next to Red. "That's always going to be a risk. Not just with somebody trying to force you to give up your powers. Every time you lead folks into a fight, you're putting their lives in danger."

Red wiped a tear from her eye. "How can I ask my friends to do that? It's not right that they should have to risk so much for my sake."

"This isn't about you, Red Riding. It's about all the people and creatures of Wayward that will suffer if you don't do what has to be done. If your friends don't understand that, you have to make it good and clear. If they still decide to follow you, all you can do is be the best leader you can be for them."

"What if I fail, Granny?"

"Then we all go down fighting together."

Red looked to Grenda, a little surprised. "All of us?"

"That's right, Red. You're the Alpha. That makes you our leader. Even I must abide by your decisions." Grenda put a comforting arm around Red. "It's okay to be afraid. When the time is right, you'll know what to do, and you will do it courageously. Never forget that the blood and the spirit of the one who faced this before lives inside you. She will not abandon you, even in the darkest hours. And neither will I."

"Thank you, Granny. I love you so much."

"I love you, too, my dear."

Red recalled the things Ice had told her during their battle. The one that stuck out above all was Ice's claim that the lunar deities decide who gets the Alpha Power, and that it isn't passed down through her family line. "Granny, there's something important I need to ask you about."

Grenda stood up. "You'll have to ask later. I need to get dinner on the stove."

"But it will only take a minute."

The door swung open as Grenda approached. "There's no such thing as important questions that only take a minute."

"I suppose not."

"Don't fret, Red. All things will be revealed in their proper time." Grenda stepped out into the hallway. "And the next time you come across a strange mirror, it would be best not to go touching it."

The door slammed shut.

For the next few minutes, Red sat alone, thinking about all the things her Granny had said. It was scary enough to think that the fate of Wayward was in her hands. The idea that something bad could happen to her friends was more than she could endure.

It occurred to Red that she might never have a better chance to snoop around her Granny's room. The prospect was quite intriguing, but it felt best to venture down that road another time. After the strange encounter with the mirror, she wasn't sure her nerves could deal with anything bizarre that would surely be found.

As Red stepped into the hallway, the door slammed itself shut and locked with a click. It was a startling thrill to see, as it was likely the result of a spellcraft. For all of Red's life, magic existed only in her dreams and fantasies. On many occasions, she had tried without success to move things with her mind.

Red heard the muffled laughs of Ash and Dote coming from behind her bedroom door. They were joking about a time when the three of them had gotten into Granny's potion cabinet and unleashed some serious mischief.

As much as Red wanted to listen to all the wonderful memories, the idea of getting some rest was a bit more appealing at the moment. She figured there would be plenty of time to hear all the funny stories of her childhood when things finally settled down.

With Wolfgang still hanging around downstairs, there was only one place to avoid being disturbed. Taking a nervous breath, she nudged open the door of her parents' bedroom and stepped inside. It felt a little odd being in their room because in many ways they were strangers to her. She hoped that surrounding herself with their worldly possessions would bring back memories of their time together.

Every object in the room told Red many things about her parents. She first deduced that her mother was most fond of the color green. It was also quite clear that she preferred to wear dresses and skirts over pants and shorts.

Judging by the size of her father's clothes, he was a large man. Red figured he must have been the rugged type because his pants and shirts were all mended and patched in numerous places.

Red began to create stories of how her parents came to possess the various trinkets around the room. She picked up a pearl necklace and decided that her father had made it himself, after diving deep into the sea to collect oysters. It was a special gift that he had given to her mother on perhaps a birthday or anniversary.

Under the bed, Red found a wooden box filled with an odd assortment of colorful rocks. She decided that her parents had collected them during long hikes in the woods. Each was from a different place where they had stopped to rest.

She then went on to decide that a rather bizarre set of masks that hung on the wall were once worn by her parents to a big costume party.

Flopping down on the bed, she sank several inches into the soft mattress. Her mind was abuzz with so many thoughts that there wasn't much chance of falling asleep. She picked up a book from the nightstand and blew the dust away from the cover. It was titled *The Very Strange Tales from the Distant Land of Your Own Imagination*. She tried to make out the author's name, but it was too faded to read.

The brittle spine cracked a bit as Red opened the cover. On the first page was an inscription handwritten in black ink that read: *Let it be known that the tales contained within this book may cause dreams that will awake you with a fright.*

The yellowed pages were so frail that Red had to be extra careful not to rip any as she flipped through them. It was hard picking a place to begin because the titles of the tales were all quite strange and intriguing. She stopped upon coming to a page that was dog-eared in the corner. It was on the first page of a story titled *The Boy Called Lie.*

The story told of a young man who always told the truth and yet, no matter how hard he tried, nobody ever believed a word he said. Things got so bad that people began calling him "Lie." The elders eventually shoved Lie down a well and sealed it shut, knowing full well that he would die. Through many strange happenings that followed, Lie survived and grew to be a man with great power and a terrible desire for vengeance. He ultimately burned the town to the ground, assuring that all who lived within its walls would perish.

The grim tale annoyed Red so much that she flung the old book at a wall. The fairy tales she had known ended with a simple moral and people living happily ever after. It made her angry that somebody would write a story that had an outcome so tragic that it could make people feel hopeless and sad.

Refusing to give it another thought, she closed her eyes and soon drifted off to sleep. No more than a minute or two passed before the sound of the door creaking open awoke her. Assuming it was her granny, Red didn't bother to open her eyes.

"I'm just going to take a short nap. I hope that's okay," Red said.

"Take all the time you want, Little Red," said Wolfgang. "Not like you're being hunted by a psycho chick that wants your powers."

Fuming with irritation, Red quickly sat up as Wolfgang began rummaging through the chest of weapons at the end of the bed.

"Get out." Red demanded. "You are never, ever allowed to come in here."

Wolfgang strained to hold up a rather large spiked mace. "I wonder how many werewolf skulls your old man bashed open with this thing?"

"What part of *you are not welcome here* did you not understand?" Red leaped up and grabbed the mace from Wolfgang's hands, nearly collapsing under its great weight. "Whoa, my father must have been really strong to have used this."

"The guy was killer in battle. Remind me to tell you the gory stories I've heard," Wolfgang said.

Red gave Wolfgang a shove. "Maybe you missed the part when I told you to get out, so I will tell you again. Get out of here this instant."

"What's your issue with me?"

"Should I make a list?" Red dropped the mace into the chest and slammed the top shut.

"You don't know anything about me, but you seem to hate my guts. You push me away and then save my life. These mixed signals are getting a little annoying."

"I'm so not in the mood for this," Red muttered.

Wolfgang sat down on the bed. "I guess it's the stigma of being a Helheim. People just assume the worst. Nobody ever believes a word I say. Some people even call me a born liar."

Wolfgang's words made Red shudder as she reflected on the story about Lie. For a brief instant, she wondered if the tale might have meaning, but dismissed it as nothing more than a coincidence. She was certain that the story could not possibly be about him, though it was a little odd that she had read it only minutes before their conversation.

"Listen up, Wolf Boy. This girl's not buying your little routine here, so don't even get started."

"What routine is that, Little Red?"

"The one where you play the tragically misunderstood boy from the wrong side of the woods, and I'm supposed to feel *soooo* bad for you because underneath that rough and tough exterior beats a heart of pure gold," Red said.

Wolfgang laughed. "Is that what I was doing?"

"You tell me, Wolf Boy."

"Fine. You got me. It's not like most of that terrible stuff isn't true. So do you feel bad for me?" Wolfgang gave Red a flirtatious smile.

"Devastated. I must swoon into your arms and try to mend your bad boy ways through my understanding and compassionate girly nature."

Wolfgang cracked a grin. "Why did you come back to Wayward?"

"It sure wasn't to hang out in my parents' bedroom with you, Wolf Boy."

"I'm serious." Wolfgang flopped back on the bed and looked Red in the eyes. "I want to know more about you."

Red paced around in frustration. "You're so lucky my father's mace is too heavy for me to use."

"I just love your witty sense of humor."

"Do I look like I'm trying to be funny here?"

"When I saw you the other night, I knew we were destined to be the best of friends," Wolfgang said.

"When I saw you, I thought you were going to kill me. You almost did when you sped at me like a maniac."

"For those here who have been keeping score, you sped right back at me."

"A momentary lapse in judgment. Don't count on me having another one in my parents' bedroom."

"I'm not trying to make a move on you, so just calm down," Wolfgang said.

Red's face tightened with anger. "Don't you tell me to calm down, Wolf Boy. This is *my* house. You're here uninvited. *I* decide when and if I calm down, or when and if I lose my mind and do something crazy."

"Don't hold back. Go crazy."

Red clenched her teeth. "Maybe I will."

"Then do it, Little Red. I can smell your blood boiling."

Red knew he was right. Beads of sweat were forming on her forehead. The feeling was causing her to lose control, and she wasn't sure if she liked it or hated it.

"Don't push me, Wolf Boy."

"Take your best shot, Little Red."

"Why are you doing this to me?"

"Because it's what you want."

"All I want is for you to get out."

"Then prove it. Make me leave."

"This is your last chance."

"I can see that. The claws are coming out."

Red could feel her claws protruding from her fingertips. She now knew with certainty that Wolfgang held far too much power over her. "I want you to go away right now."

Wolfgang stood up and got into Red's face. "I think you want me to stay."

Red turned away. "No, you want me to want you to stay."

"Why are you trying so hard to shut me out?"

"Why are you trying so hard to get in?"

"Because I care about you, Red Riding."

"You don't even know me, Wolfgang Helheim."

"I know so much more than you even realize," Wolfgang said.

His words gave Red a strange shiver. "What does that even mean?"

"Maybe the answer will come when you *calm down*," Wolfgang said.

"Stop telling me to calm down." Without a rational thought, Red slugged Wolfgang in the arm so hard it made him recoil in pain.

"I'm sorry. I had that coming," Wolfgang said. "I just hope that was enough to make you calm down."

"Does this look like me calmed down?" Red slugged Wolfgang in the stomach, so hard it doubled him over.

"I guess you've still got some angst left to get out. Too bad you still hit like a little girl," Wolfgang said.

Red punched Wolfgang in the face, knocking him into the wall and off his feet.

"Now that was a good one," Wolfgang said, rubbing his jaw as he looked up at her.

"What is your malfunction?" Red grunted.

"I was just going to ask the same of you. Want to try for a knockout this time?"

"I'm not playing your game anymore." Red grabbed Wolfgang by the jacket and pulled him to his feet. You're leaving right now."

"But we're just starting to have fun. Round two is looking to get a lot more interesting," Wolfgang said.

Red gave Wolfgang a spiteful glare. "Now I can see why the woodsman attacked you."

"The man hates me because of my family name."

"Maybe he's right to feel that way. You're dangerous, Helheim."

"Don't treat me like that."

"Don't treat me like this."

"What am I doing that's so bad?"

"You're being a guy."

"So tell me how you want me to be."

"I don't want anything from you."

"If that was true, you wouldn't be getting so worked up."

"Get out, Helheim."

"You're not getting rid of me so easy, Riding."

"I said get out." Red shoved Wolfgang toward the door.

"I won't ever give up on you."

"Then you'll be waiting for a long time."

"I can live with that, because I know you and I are meant to be."

"That's impossible." As Red gazed into Wolfgang's copper red eyes, she realized that it was true. The connection between them was a lot more complicated than she could yet understand. She just knew that her feelings for him ran deeper than a simple attraction.

Putting all rational thoughts aside, she moved in toward his lips. The instant before they met, she was overcome with a feeling so cold and dark that it made her dizzy.

"Wolfgang, I have a feeling something bad is about to happen."

"It's just a kiss. Nothing to be afraid of."

"No, I mean something even worse than that."

"If you two kids don't break it up, I'll give you both something to be afraid of," Grenda said.

Chapter 20

"Why, Granny, this isn't what it looks like." Red said. Grenda stood in the open doorway, giving Red and Wolfgang a harsh glare of disapproval. Her eyes were shimmering with mystical energy. The sight was so startling that Red was nearly trembling out of her shoes.

Wolfgang casually wiped a drop of blood away from his nose. "Or maybe this is exactly what it looks like, depending on what you're thinking."

Red slugged Wolfgang in the arm. "Nobody asked you to speak, wolf boy."

The glowing energy in Grenda's eyes flickered. "Wolf Boy? Now that is an interesting little nickname."

Red eyed Grenda a little oddly. "What does that mean?"

Grenda nudged past Red and headed to the weapons chest. "I'll say it once and never again, so you both best listen good. If there's any funny business going on between you two, it had best not happen in this house."

Red gave Wolfgang a shove. "This is all your fault."

"You might as well get used to people thinking the worst if you're going to insist on hanging around me," Wolfgang said.

Red was so irritated that the only responses she could get out were incoherent grunts and grumbles.

From the weapons chest, Grenda pulled out the sword that once belonged to Red's mother.

Wolfgang took a nervous step back. "Let's not get crazy now. I never touched her. Tell her, Red."

"It's true. Unless you count my fist in his face as touching," Red said.

Grenda pointed the sword toward Wolfgang. "Helheim, I'll deal with you later. Now get lost."

"Okay, okay. Don't go getting all psycho witch on me." Wolfgang dashed out the door and slammed it behind him.

"Granny, you have to believe me. Nothing happened," Red said.

"Forget about the pretty boy for half a second. We've got a mighty serious problem to deal with," Grenda said.

"So then it's true. Something evil *is* coming our way."

Grenda held out the sword. "Red Riding, the time has come for you to make a choice. Are you ready to become Wayward's high protector?"

Red gazed at the glimmering blade, knowing that once she accepted it there would be no going back. "Do I have a choice? If I refuse, Wayward could fall into darkness."

"Those are the hard knocks of being chosen to stand as the hero. So what's it going to be? We're running out of time." Grenda asked.

Red took a calming breath. "I'm ready."

Grenda placed the sword into Red's hands. "This was once carried by the Red Riding that came before you. It possesses great power intended for the Alpha Huntress."

Red looked at the glimmering blade. In the reflection, she was in her werewolf form, wearing battle armor. "I can feel the power inside me."

Grenda bowed to Red. "From this moment on, you are in command. I will act according to your orders."

Red stepped out of her parents' bedroom and dashed down the stairs. Grenda followed close behind her. In the living room, Dote and Wolfgang were peering out the window. They had expressions of grave concern.

Ash was cowering in the corner. "Not fire orcs. Anything but fire orcs."

"What's Ash going on about?" Red asked.

"There's a bunch of yucky fire orcs outside," Dote said.

"I count ten," Wolfgang said. "But there could be a lot more of them hanging around. I wouldn't be surprised if Ice sent them."

Grenda peered out the window. "They may have been sent by Ice Seether, but fire orcs are servants of Ragnarok. They would only be here to serve his dark purpose."

Red had a nervous twinge. "And what does that mean, exactly?"

"It means we're totally doomed," Ash said. "They'll burn half these woods down if that's what it takes to get us."

"You mean to get *me*," Red said.

Dote was trembling in fear. "Red, what do we do?"

Red shrugged. "How should I know? I've never even seen a fire orc."

Ash began pacing frantically. "They're big. They're scary. They shoot fire from their mouth and burn stuff."

Red turned to Grenda. "You gotta tell me what to do."

"You're the Alpha Huntress," Grenda replied. "You tell us what to do."

"How should I know? I'm a little new at this stuff."

"Just calm yourself down and think it through."

Wolfgang again peered out the window. "Better think quickly. They're lighting up the trees."

Red closed her eyes and took a deep breath. "Okay, if they make fire, then we need water. A lot of water. Anybody know a rain spellcraft?"

"I do." Dote said. "It takes a long time. Sometimes an entire day."

Red pressed her hands over her face, feeling both frustrated and afraid. "There's got to be some way to get a lot of water."

"Such as?" Wolfgang asked.

Red peered out the window. She saw something that made her eyes light up with an idea. "Wait a minute. Maybe we could use the well."

Grenda nodded. "Now you're thinking. How can we use it?"

Red groaned. "Cut me a little slack here. I don't know much about what spellcraft can and can't do."

"So then you're seeking the counsel of your clan?" Granny asked.

Red flailed her arms in irritation. "Yes. Somebody please tell me what we can do with the water from the well."

Dote's eyes were overcome with excitement. "We might be able to make the well go all geyser-like. Granny and I would have to do it together, for sure. That's an awfully big spellcraft."

"Fine, then we do it," Red said.

"Then what?" Wolfgang asked. "Even if we take their fire away, these guys are way tough. We could take maybe four or five, but no way we can beat ten."

"You'd better decide soon because the protection spellcraft won't hold for much longer," Dote said.

"The protection spellcraft. I almost forgot." Red walked over and inched open the front door. The room transformed into its desolate appearance. Prince reemerged, still trapped inside the energy bubble.

Granny grinned. "It looks like my trap caught a rat."

"He's not a rat," Red said. "He's a loyal member of my clan. I need you to release him, Granny."

"You're in charge here." Grenda approached the mystical bubble. She looked back at Dote. "Luna, you should take this one. It will be good practice."

"But I don't know the spellcraft you used."

Grenda whispered into Dote's ear.

Dote giggled. "Oh, so that's how you did it." She held up her hands to the bubble and closed her eyes to focus her mind. *"Be free."*

The mystical barrier vanished and Prince snapped back to life. He stood awkwardly looking at Red with a perplexed expression. "Alpha Huntress, praise the deities. I was waiting here alone, hoping you would return, and then in a flash, you appeared. How can this be?"

Dote gave Prince an adoring smile. "It's a long story. The important thing is you're safe now, my pretty man."

Prince looked at Dote oddly. "Pretty man?"

Red pushed the door closed, causing the room to transform back to normal.

"Vile witches." Prince pulled his rapier and snapped into a fighting stance. "Behind me, Alpha Huntress. I will protect you."

Red approached Prince and nudged his blade aside. "Easy there. All the witches here are on my side."

"Those who deal in spellcraft are on nobody's side but their own," Prince said.

Dote snarled. "That is not a nice thing to say, mister."

Red cleared her throat. "We don't have time for this. There are fire orcs outside, too many for me to deal with on my own. Prince, will you help me fight them off?"

Prince kneeled before Red. "Alpha Huntress, you need never ask for my assistance in the face of evil. As a Knight of the Alpha, I have vowed to stand with you to the end."

Dote swooned. "He's so heroic."

"Then it's settled. We blow the well and attack with all we've got," Red said.

Wolfgang shook his head in disagreement. "Even with me, you, and the pretty prince here, our chances are not so good. Fire orcs have thick skin. Your blades won't do much. My claws won't either."

"Don't worry. I've got an ace up my sleeve," Red said.

"I sure hope that involves clearing a path for Luna and I to get close to that well," Grenda said.

Red pulled her sword. "I'll go first and distract them. Once it's clear, you two get out there and do your thing as quickly as you can."

"I'll be right behind you," Wolfgang said.

Prince raised his rapier. "As will I."

Ash stepped up. "What about me? What do I do?"

Red put a hand on Ash's shoulder. "I need you to stay out of this. It's way too dangerous."

"But I want to help. There must be something I can do."

"Not this time, Ash. Please do as I say."

"Fine, you're the big, powerful Alpha." Ash swung a fist in frustration and stomped away sulking.

Red's shoulders sank as she called after him, "Ash, I'm sorry. Come back."

Grenda put a hand on Red's shoulder. "Red, you can deal with that later. It's now or never."

Red gripped her sword tightly. "Let's do this."

Red and Wolfgang transformed into werewolves and dashed out the front door. Prince wailed out a battle cry and followed.

The trees surrounding Grenda's house were ablaze. Red choked on the thick black smoke that filled the air as she charged across the clearing. An intense surge of energy began to pulse through her body when she caught a glimpse of a fire orc.

The beast stood eight feet tall and had flaming red eyes. Its thick, blubbery skin hung loose and was dripping with some kind of gooey liquid, which protected it from being burned by its own flames.

"Just keep them distracted for now," Red called out to Wolfgang and Prince.

A fire orc opened its mouth wide and blasted a searing white flame at Red. She could feel the intense heat on her face as she jumped high into the air, just clearing the blast. Upon landing, she looked back and saw Wolfgang and Prince drawing the orcs' fire by dodging and leaping clear of their flames.

"Granny! Dote! Work fast!" Red shouted.

Grenda and Dote already stood near the well with their eyes closed and hands joined. They were chanting in a strange language that Red had never heard before. For several minutes, she and the others struggled to keep the fire orcs distracted. Just about the time Red thought the plan was going to fail, the ground began quaking.

"This might just work out," Red said.

"Red, behind you!" Wolfgang shouted from the far end of the clearing.

Red spun around to see a fire orc running straight for the well. Dote and Grenda had their eyes closed and were too deep in concentration to know what was coming.

"Granny! Dote! Look out!" With her sword held high, Red charged toward the orc. Her feet were moving so fast that they began to lose traction on the dirt. With ten yards to go, there was no chance she'd make it in time.

The orc opened its mouth wide to unleash its fire at Dote and Grenda. Ash, armed with a pitchfork, lunged out from behind the well. With a mighty heave, he javelined the weapon into the orc's mouth.

"Suck on that, lava breath," Ash said.

The orc cried out in agony and retreated toward the forest.

"Ash, I'm sorry I ever doubted you," Red said.

Ash raised his arms in victory. "You should know I've always got your back, Red Riding."

A sound like thunder rumbled out. Red looked over and saw water sloshing up over the sides of the old stone well. Grenda and Dote were already backing away in haste.

"You all might want to take cover," Grenda warned.

A massive geyser exploded from the well, spraying water hundreds of feet into the sky. The water rained down, soaking the ground and trees, extinguishing the flames. An orc tried to blast a mouthful of fire at Red, but the flame puffed out.

"This is your chance," Grenda said. "Best make it count."

Before Red could react, she saw Prince unleash a series of hacks and slashes at a fire orc. The beast was more irritated than injured by the assault. It responded by bashing Prince with a fist, knocking him back at least ten feet. He hit the ground with a thud and a grunt of pain.

Dote dashed over to Prince and took him into her arms. "Are you hurt, my brave and pretty man?"

Prince clutched his throbbing head. "Why do you keep calling me 'pretty'?"

Red soared into the air and slashed an orc's throat. Her blade only cut through its outer skin. It wasn't nearly enough damage to take the beast down.

Wolfgang was nearby, clawing and slashing at a fire orc with the same hopeless result. "Now would be a good time to play that ace, Alpha."

Red knew Wolfgang was right. There was no way they would be able to win this day without some major help. She looked toward the forest and shouted, "Woodsman, if you're out there, I could use your help!"

Ethan charged out of the forest with his battle-axe at the ready. "I was wondering if you were going to call on me."

"Next time, feel free to just jump right into the action," Red said.

Ethan dashed toward the nearest fire orc; the beast didn't look half as menacing next to the woodman's buffed-out stature. The orc swung its huge fist, but Ethan blocked the attack with his powerful arm. He countered with a mighty swing of his axe. The remains of the fallen orc fell to the ground in two separate pieces.

A pair of fire orcs rushed Ethan. The first tried to grab him, but lost its leg when Ethan spun around with his axe swinging in a wide arc. He followed up with a downward bash that crushed the beast. Without hesitation, he again spun around and executed another downward strike, taking out the other orc with a single blow.

Wolfgang stepped up behind Red. "Do we help him?"

"You want to get in the way of that?" Red said.

Ethan continued his brutal assault, bashing and hacking the other orcs to pieces. When only one remained, he strutted over and stood face-to-face with the blubbery beast.

"Let this be a lesson to your wretched kind. Stay away from my family," Ethan said.

Red was overcome with a sensation of dizziness as she looked to Wolfgang. "Family? Why did he just say that?"

"Because he's your old man," Wolfgang said.

"You mean, like my father?"

"You didn't know?

Red almost stumbled off her feet. "Why didn't he tell me?"

Ethan swung his axe at the orc. The beast blocked the attack and smacked his weapon away. It pulled out a jagged knife and stabbed Ethan in the chest. The strike was so fast that it took a moment before Ethan realized it had happened. Red watched petrified with fear as her father dropped to his knees. The orc picked up Ethan's axe and gripped it tight.

"No!" Without a beat of hesitation, Red took off running and sprang into the air. The blade of her sword ignited with a blazing red glow. Seconds later, it was over. The beast's head hit the ground long before the rest of its body crashed down.

By the time Red landed, Grenda and Dote were already dashing to Ethan's side. In a flurry of panic, Red tried to run toward her father, but Ash and Wolfgang stepped in her way.

"Let me go. I have to see him."

Wolfgang held Red tight. "Not like this. You have to trust me, Red."

"He's right," Ash said. "You gotta let Granny do her thing."

Red broke into tears and fell into Ash's arms. "Why didn't anybody tell me?"

Grenda cried out, "We need some muscle over here to get him inside."

"You stay with her," Wolfgang said to Ash. He then dashed over to help Grenda.

Ash put a comforting arm around Red. "Granny's gonna take great care of him. She's the best healer around."

Red dropped to her knees and broke into a terrible fit of sobbing. She watched through tear-soaked eyes as Wolfgang and Prince picked up Ethan and strained to carry him into the house. The instant before the front door swung shut, she saw Grenda looking back with a dreadfully grim look in her eyes.

CHAPTER 21

Red was deep below the surface of an icy pond, blissfully at peace and sinking deeper and deeper into the dark abyss, just as she had been after the escape from Ice's palace. She thought of how easy it would be to drift off into sleep forever, and never again have to concern herself with the duties of being an Alpha Huntress—or having to ask her friends to risk their lives in battle—or face the coming of an evil lunar god plotting to bring eternal night.

The moment of tranquility came to a startling end when an image of Ragnarok invaded her mind. His eyes were blazing with fire as he reached for her through the Moon Temple's gate.

"Set me free, Alpha Huntress."

Drifting further into darkness, Red saw herself as a werewolf wearing sleek battle armor. She stood before her friends and family atop a hill in the dark forest. They were waiting in silence for her to command them into action.

In the sky above, the moon looked like a flaming ball of fire. A shower of blazing moonrocks was raining down. Red could only watch in paralyzed fear as they slammed into the earth and consumed her loved ones in a blazing inferno.

"It's not like you could ever have saved them," Wolfgang said.

Red looked over to see Wolfgang was standing at her side, glaring at her through eyes glowing red with pure evil. The good she had once sensed buried deep in his heart was gone. Only hate and rage remained. He had become an agent of darkness who would bring chaos and destruction in his wake.

"Alpha Huntress, we are now one." The voice that came from Wolfgang was not his own; it belonged to Ragnarok.

Red tried to speak, but the words didn't come out. Instead, she snapped back to the realization that she was still submerged in bone-chilling water, out of breath, and seconds from drowning.

"Is this really how it's going to end for me?"

The voice of the first Red Riding spoke softly in her mind. *If you are to survive what is to come you must believe that the power of the Alpha is yours to command.*

"I don't know how. Please, show me."

In mere seconds, Red's body temperature spiked to near burning as the Alpha Power began to course through her veins. She started kicking her legs so fast and hard that it took only seconds to reach the surface of the pond.

When her head emerged from the water, Red took in a gasping breath. The air was thick with smoke and blazing soot that burned in her lungs. She looked around to see that the lake was deep in the heart of the forest. Towering flames engulfed the trees and illuminated the midnight sky.

Red swam to the shore and clawed up onto the land. The heat from the flames was so intense that she couldn't wait around to recover. She was soon dashing aimlessly down a rocky path. It didn't matter how far she went, it was impossible to escape the inferno. All of Wayward Woods would burn to the ground, and nothing could be done to stop it. The idea that her failure to rise to her calling would lead to such destruction consumed her heart with rage.

"Why me? Why do I have to be the one to do this?"

With the trees ablaze all around, Red had to push through a thick patch of bushes overgrowing the path. The sting of the thorns scratching and cutting into her skin brought back the memory of the dream she had on the first night at Granny's house.

Just as before, she emerged into a clearing where the Omega Gem sat atop a stone pedestal. A quick glance around the area and a sniff of the air assured her that the wolves that had attacked her last time she was there were not around.

"Come forward, Red Riding," whispered a woman's voice.

With each step closer to the Omega Gem, Red felt a growing tingling sensation throughout her body. She could only describe the feeling as godlike. A voice with a sinister tone spoke out in her mind. It told her that with the gem, she could have power without limits. Her thoughts began to swirl with ideas that were both thrilling and disturbing.

Red saw herself as a tyrant queen sitting upon a throne constructed of colorless moonstone. Her iron fortress towered high atop a hill, built on the burned remains of Ice Seether's palace. Looking out a window, she gazed out onto the charred remains of a once great metropolis. She then looked down to see she clutched a golden scepter, studded with the Omega Gem. She knew that it had given her the power to become the supreme goddess who ruled over everyone and everything in Wayward.

"I won't allow myself to become that," Red said.

"That is why you, and none other, must wield the Alpha Power." A beautiful woman emerged from the forest wearing a red cloak over a flowing green dress. Her braided red hair was adorned with ribbons and white wildflowers.

"I know you." Red somehow recognized this woman to be the one that had come before her, the first Red Riding.

"You carry much fear in your heart, young Alpha Huntress. You must bury it down deep if you are to face the darkness that is upon us," the first Red Riding said.

Red looked away in fear. "I'm not ready for this. There has to be somebody better to take up this quest. Someone that knows how to lead people into battle and isn't afraid to ask them to risk their lives."

The first Red Riding held a hand near the Omega Gem. "There is another who can command the power, but would use it for great evil."

"I know all about it. Ice tried to take the power from me," Red said.

"Ice Seether's quest for the Alpha Power is a futile effort. On the night she was born, her parents employed a vile spellcraft to steal the power. The lunar deities rejected Ice because of her impure bloodline. Even she does not know that her ancient ancestors used dark enchantments to gain the power to become werewolves."

Red considered this, coming to an unexpected revelation. "When the Alpha Power rejected her, she was left with hair and skin as white as ice. How do I know that?"

The first Red Riding smiled at Red. "Because I know it. The strength of all the Alphas that came before you resides in your memory. They will guide you along the way, if you allow yourself to listen."

Red looked into the eyes of her predecessor and realized that there had not been just one previous Alpha. Six had come before her. As their faces appeared to her, both men and women alike, she was overcome with a troubling thought.

"None of them are from the same bloodline. The Alpha Power chose them. How is it that this time the power came to me, your descendant?" Red asked.

"The reason for this is not mine to reveal."

Red snarled. "Why not? What are you not telling me?"

"You will soon discover that truth on your own. Do not let it cause you to lose sight of what needs to be done."

"What needs to be done?" Red shouted. "Tell me. I've had all I can take of these half-truths."

"In three days, the Alpha Stone in the Moon Temple will illuminate. For seven minutes, the moon gate will open. Ragnarok will try to use it to enter this world, but only the Alpha can bring him through."

"Then there's nothing to worry about. I would never do that," Red said.

"Don't allow yourself to believe it will be so simple. Ragnarok has vast influence in Wayward. He will stop at nothing to force you to help him. Or find another to do it in your place."

Red raised a fist. "Then I'll have to make sure he can't do that."

"To put a final end to Ragnarok, you will need the Omega Gem. Finding it will be a long and difficult quest. Be warned that there are many others seeking it. They will commit the darkest of deeds to possess it."

"But won't using it turn me into a tyrant?"

The first Red Riding placed a hand on Red's shoulder and looked her in the eyes. "Not if you stay strong and remain true to what you know is right."

Red glared at the Omega Gem. "What could happen that would turn me into something so terrible?"

"I cannot answer that for you. Search your heart and you will find the truth."

Red sighed. "You're not being helpful here."

The first Red Riding turned and walked toward the trees. As Red watched her go, she realized something she had not considered. "Wait! You said there is another who can carry the power. If it isn't Ice Seether, then who is it?"

"Wake up, Red Riding," another voice said.

Red snapped awake and was looking up at Wolfgang's face. He was shouting in her face, though his voice was distant and distorted. She was flat on her back in the mud outside Granny's house. The fire orc that had stabbed Ethan was lying slain only a few feet away. Its eyes were wide-open and looking right at her.

"Red, wake up!" Wolfgang shouted at the top of his lungs. This time his voice came through like a siren blasting in her ears.

Red sat up, holding tight to her aching head. "What did you do to me?"

"What did *I* do?" Wolfgang grunted. "Grenda asked me to bring you inside. I came out here and found you taking a nap in the mud. Are you okay?"

Red stumbled to her feet and started walking toward the house. "I was trying to find out who else could get the Alpha Power, and you had to go and wake me up."

Wolfgang dashed after Red. "What did you just say about the Alpha Power?"

Red opened the front door of the house and stepped inside. "Forget it. None of it has anything to do with you anyway." She slammed the door in Wolfgang's face, leaving him outside.

In the living room, Ash and Dote were sitting on the couch with tears in their eyes.

"Red, I'm so sorry," Dote said.

"We didn't know he was your father," Ash said. "It feels like we should have."

"Why are you two crying? Where is he?" Red asked.

Dote whimpered and pointed to the stairs.

Red was so overwhelmed with mixed up emotions that she couldn't find the words to ask if her father was still alive. With each step up the stairs, her concern for his well-being faded away and turned into anger. It didn't make a bit of sense that he had hidden the truth from her when they had first met. All the deceptions that she'd been dealing with had about pushed her to the limit.

"If I find out one more person has been holding back on me, there's going to be serious trouble."

Red's anger faded as soon as she reached the door to her parents' bedroom. For a tense moment she stood petrified, holding out a hand an inch short of the doorknob. There was no way she could have prepared herself for what might await on the other side. If her father was no longer among the living, it would be the first time she ever had to endure the loss of death.

When she finally found the courage to open the door, she was startled to find Grenda standing on the other side. Her complexion was ghost white, and she was so groggy with exhaustion that she could hardly stand up straight.

"Is he …?" Red couldn't get the rest of the words out.

Grenda took off her glasses and wiped the lenses clean with her dress. "Your father is still with us. It took a mighty powerful spellcraft to undo the damage. I was just able to drag his tail back to the world of the living."

Red took a deep breath of relief. "Then why do you look so grim, Granny?"

Grenda stepped into the hallway and closed the door. "Your father blames himself for your mother's death. He feels if he had been a stronger warrior, he could have saved her life and not been forced to abandon you to be raised by strangers. He believes he failed you, Red."

Red nodded in understanding. "I would like to talk with him, if I can."

"That will be fine. Just know that his grip on this world is not strong right now. If you hold any grievances against him, this is not the time to voice them. If he's pushed too far, he could slip away, and I won't be able to bring him back again." Grenda stumbled away and entered her own room.

As Red stepped into her parents' room, she saw her father lying on the bed with his eyes closed. A strange blue aura emanated from bandages wrapped around his massive chest. Each breath he took sounded like it came from a snoring grizzly bear. For a lingering moment, Red tried to find the words to speak, but couldn't come up with a thing to say.

"Red Riding, I know you're there. Step closer, so I can see your eyes." Ethan's voice was frail and distant.

Red took another step into the room. She was startled to see Ethan had pasty white skin and eyes that were hollow and lifeless. She took a deep breath. "Granny told me about what happened with my mother and the choice you had to make to save my life."

Ethan looked away in shame. "I'm so sorry, Red. If I had been stronger, she would still be here with us."

Red sat on the edge of the bed. "You don't know that. If you had stayed, we might all be dead. I don't think we can know one way or the other."

Ethan strained to pull himself up to a sitting position. He gazed at Red with great pride. "You look so much like your mother. If she could see you now, she would be glowing with joy over the young woman you've become."

Red shamefully frowned. "She might not think that if she knew how much trouble I've been. I'm not always the most agreeable person. I get into a lot of mischief."

"If you told me any different, I wouldn't believe you were a true Riding." Ethan let out a belting laugh. It made him cough from the pain it caused in his chest.

Red began to weep a little. "It's been so hard not knowing where I came from. Until a few days ago, I had no idea if I had any family, or if my parents were alive or dead, or that my last name was Riding."

"Red, you have to understand, I didn't want to have to leave you. I didn't know what else I could do. I had to get you as far away from this place as possible. Everything had to be left behind. Not just your name; your memories would also have put you in danger."

"My memories were taken from me?" Red asked.

"Not taken away. Buried down real deep. There are forms of spellcraft so vile that we can be hunted down through our feelings. Specters called Soul Hunters will search the world over for you. All they need to know is what you love the most, hate the strongest, or fear more than anything. They'll hunt for years if it takes that long, but they will find you."

Red shivered in fear. "Is that why you erased all signs of yourself in this house?"

Ethan's face tightened as he recalled the painful memories. "I used a spellcraft far more dangerous than the one we used on you. I had to purge myself of all my feelings, not just those for you and your mother. I was hollowed to my core. If I felt even the smallest emotion, they would have found me and done wicked things to force me to reveal what became of you."

"So that's why you didn't tell me who you were when we met?"

"Believe me, Red, it was not easy to keep that to myself. A few days ago, all the old feelings started coming back. At first I feared the spellcraft had worn off. It wasn't until I found you lying outside the Moon Temple that I realized it was because you had returned to Wayward."

Red thought about how hard it must have been for her father to make such an awful choice to ensure her safety. Though her life was terribly lonely, Ethan had had to live void of even a single emotion for ten years. It was a fate so grim that she couldn't begin to imagine what it must have been like. It was certain that without his sacrifice, there was little chance she would have lived to see that day.

Ethan finally broke the tense silence. "I've lived far too long without you, Red. All those years of knowing you were out there but not being able to feel anything has broken me. Is there any way you can ever forgive me?"

Red stood up and looked her father in the eyes. "No, I *can't* forgive you. There's no need for it. You only did what had to be done. I have no more right to feel angry than you have a right to feel guilty. Let's put it all behind us and start over."

Ethan's eyes lit up with joy as Red threw her arms around his massive arm. A flood of lost memories filled Red's heart and mind, reminding her that they were once a happy family with great love for one another. It had all changed for the worse on the night the werewolves had come to take her away.

The terror she had felt came rushing back as she recalled a pack of black werewolves storming into Granny's living room. The image that stuck out above all was a werewolf with glowing red eyes stabbing her mother through the chest. Red could hear the terrible screams of her mother as Ethan carried her away from the house.

"Father, I have a question. I need you to tell me the truth, no matter how much you think it will hurt me."

"I am done keeping the truth from you, Red Riding. Ask me anything."

"Who killed my mother?"

"You mean Grenda didn't tell you?"

Red's face twitched with anger. "Don't answer my question with a question. Just tell me who it was."

"Now I understand why you stopped me from killing *him*." Ethan looked Red in the eyes. "The Helheim Clan attacked us that night. The werewolf who fatally wounded your mother was Wolfgang's father. Or he was until I took his head off."

Red's heart filled with rage darker than any she had ever known. "Does Wolfgang know about this?"

"Of course he does. They had planned to kill you so they could steal the Alpha Power and give it to him."

CHAPTER 22

Minutes after Red's troubling conversation with her father, she was wearing a pair of her mother's old denim pants, a tank top, and a light jacket. Over her shoulder hung a sheath made of old cloth and rope, which concealed her sword inside. Her hair had been brushed back into a sloppy ponytail, and she had wiped her face clean, though she still felt quite dirty. Not that it mattered to her in the least; there were far more pressing concerns on her mind.

"Wolfgang and I need to have a little chat," she said aloud.

Red spotted him on the far end of the clearing, crouched down next to her motorcycle. Without making the faintest sound, she walked up behind him. From what she could tell, he was making some sort of mechanical adjustment to the engine.

"So is he running, or what?" Red asked.

Deathly startled, Wolfgang spun around. "I see you've been working on those stealth skills."

"Yeah, it's totally impressive. Now is my little man good to go, or not?"

Wolfgang bit down on his lip, frustrated with the harshness of her tone. "I was just checking the intake valve, but yes, your boy is primed and ready to roll."

"See, giving me a straight answer wasn't so hard. Try making a habit of it." Red grabbed the handlebars of her motorcycle and rolled it toward the outskirts of the clearing.

Wolfgang raced after her. "You're welcome, by the way."

"For what exactly?"

"What do you mean for what? Do you think the little guy there fixed himself?"

"Where are my manners? Thanks for breaking my bike and then fixing it." Red reached the path leading off into the woods and sat on the seat of her motorcycle.

"You going somewhere?" Wolfgang asked.

"No, *we* are." Red hit the kick-starter. Her motorcycle started up with a roar.

Wolfgang smiled with pride. "Now that's what a well-tuned motor sounds like."

"You getting on, or what?" Red glanced back to the house and saw Ash and Dote were stepping out onto the front porch. She revved the throttle a few times. "I don't got all night, Wolf Boy."

"Whatever." Wolfgang climbed onto the back of the seat. There was hardly enough space for both of them.

Red squeezed the throttle, and they sped off into the dark forest, kicking up a blast of mud in their wake.

"It feels weird riding on the back. It's usually the other way around when I'm cruising with a lady," Wolfgang said.

"That is *soooo* interesting." Red bit down on her lip and glared straight ahead.

"You're a little intense tonight. Things work out okay with your old man?" Wolfgang asked.

Red squeezed the throttle, pushing her little motorcycle even faster. "The Omega Gem. Tell me what you know about it."

"From what I hear, it's a moonstone that's supposed to give the Alpha some major butt-kicking powers. Most people say it's just a myth," Wolfgang said.

"So then you wouldn't have any idea where to find it, would you?"

"Why would I?"

"That was a question. I asked for an answer." Red made a hard turn into a curve. It was so fast the she had to plant a foot on the ground to keep the wheels from losing traction on the wet dirt.

Wolfgang tightened his grip around Red's waist to avoid falling off the back. "Going a little hard there tonight. I gotta admit I'm liking it."

Red gritted her teeth. "You still haven't answered my question."

"You mean about the Omega Gem?"

"Of course I mean the Omega Gem." Red pushed into another hard turn. She cut away from the safety of the path and headed off into the dark woods. Without letting up on the throttle, she maneuvered over the bumpy terrain and around the massive trees.

"Red, I don't know what's going on with you tonight, but you need to calm down a whole lot," Wolfgang said.

"Maybe I'll calm down when you answer my question. Do you know where the Omega Gem is?"

"Why do you want to know so much?"

"Why won't you just answer my question?"

"Maybe you need to start asking a lot nicer, Miss Riding."

"Maybe you need to start telling me the truth about some things, Mister Helheim."

"I've never lied to you about anything."

"Oh, that is *it*."

Red thrust her elbow into Wolfgang's chest, knocking him off the back of her motorcycle. In the rearview mirror, she saw him slamming back first into the hard ground. She hit the brakes and skidded for several yards before coming to a stop.

"I'll show you how I calm down."

Red jumped off her motorcycle and let it fall into the mud. In a flash she pulled her sword and turned into her werewolf form. Before Wolfgang could catch his breath, she grabbed him by the throat, slammed his back up against a large oak tree, and jammed the blade of her sword up to his neck.

"Red, what is your issue?"

"Your endless lies are my issue."

"If you're still talking about the Omega Gem, I don't know where it is."

"Fine, then let's forget about that and flash back to the night when your father killed my mother." Red slammed Wolfgang into the tree.

A look of guilt filled Wolfgang's eyes. "So that's what this is about. The big lug told you."

"So you do know. Why did you keep it from me?" Red again bashed Wolfgang into the tree.

Wolfgang groaned. "It's not like we've had a lot of time for meaningful conversation since you got to town."

Red's eyes swelled with tears. "How can you look me in the eye knowing what your family did to me?"

"Hey, it's not like my old man didn't get it for what he did. Your dad lobbed his head clean off, so maybe we can call it even."

"My father didn't bust into your home with the intention of killing your family. Of killing me." Red said.

"If you think taking me out will make you feel better about it, then go ahead. I won't even fight back."

Red looked Wolfgang in the eyes as she pushed her blade tighter against his throat.

True to his word, he didn't move a muscle. "Go ahead, Red. You deserve justice."

"I don't want justice. I want my family back."

"I would give you that if I could, but I can't change what my family did to yours. The best I can offer you is my life."

Red's heart swelled with rage. She wanted nothing more than to unleash her desire for vengeance onto Wolfgang. He had been only a child when it all happened, so it didn't feel right to hold him responsible. She lowered the blade from his throat and then bashed him across the face with the hilt.

"That's for not telling me you knew about this before." Red then kicked him in the shin, knocking him to his knees. "And that's because I just felt like doing it."

Wolfgang gasped to catch his breath. "You're disappointing me, Riding. Don't hold back now. I don't deserve your pity, and I don't want it."

Red paced around in a frantic fit. "The worst part of it is, I actually thought I felt something for you. How could I have been so stupid?"

Wolfgang cracked a grin. "You felt something for me?"

"It was only for one second, and it was a major mistake. Don't go getting any crazy ideas in that big dumb head of yours, Wolf Boy."

"Why do you keep calling me that?"

"Because that's what you are. A pathetic little Wolf Boy."

Wolfgang clutched a hand over his head. "There's more to it than that. When you say it, I see you, but it's not you. It's more like you, when we were …"

A rather unsettling feeling overcame Red. "Time out. Back up. It was more like me when I was what?"

"Little Red." Wolfgang squinted in pain.

"Little Red?" Red gasped nervously.

Wolfgang again shook his head in pain. "I can't think straight. It's all mixed up." He grabbed Red and looked her in the eyes. "Red, listen to me, you need to get out of here, right now. She must be nearby. You have to hurry."

"Who is this *she* you're talking about?" He didn't answer. "Wolfgang, tell me what's going on here!" she demanded.

Wolfgang dashed over to Red's motorcycle and picked it up out of the mud. "Ash was right about me."

Red looked Wolfgang in the eyes. "You mean the part where you saved me from Ice for some secret selfish reason?"

"That's right. Only I was totally wrong. Now you need to get out of here before things get worse," Wolfgang said.

Red held the tip of her sword to Wolfgang's throat. "I already know how they were going to kill me so they could give you the Alpha Power."

"It's true. Just like Ice, I was also born at the exact same time as you. The thing is, with you and me it's a lot more complicated," Wolfgang said.

Red lowered her sword as she considered this curious notion. "How do you mean?"

Wolfgang hit the kick-starter on Red's motorcycle, firing up the engine. "I promise to explain later, but for now you need to go." He whispered, "She's coming for you."

Red shivered as the temperature dropped, so much so she could see her own breath in the air. There was no doubt something evil was approaching from behind her. She turned around and gasped in horror.

A middle-aged woman with glowing red eyes was emerging from the trees. She had ratty black hair and skin that looked as rough as sandpaper. From her waist stemmed six arachnid legs.

"Hello there, little Alpha Huntress," the arachnid-woman said with a wicked, high-pitched voice.

Wolfgang was overcome with a look of guilt. "I'm sorry, Red. I was wrong about you."

"Nothing to be sorry about, Wolfgang," the arachnid-woman said. "You did the right thing, leading me to the Alpha."

Red's eyes filled with rage. "Wolfgang, you set me up?"

"It's not like that, Red. She put a spellcraft on me. But that was before I got to know you."

Red got onto her motorcycle and hit the throttle. "Stay away from me, Helheim. You're a monster."

Wolfgang slumped over, devastated by her words.

"Leaving so soon, Alpha?" The arachnid-woman fired webs from her fingertips, binding the back wheel of Red's motorcycle.

Wolfgang jumped between Red and the arachnid-woman. "Mother, please don't do this."

"I'll deal with you later." The arachnid-woman shoved Wolfgang into a tree and fired her webs, binding him to the trunk.

"That thing is your mother?" Red's eyes filled with furious rage. She let off the throttle and leaped off her motorcycle.

"That's right, little Alpha. Your mother knew me as Eyona. You have her eyes. I will enjoy plucking them from your head."

Red raised her sword. "If you want them, come and get them."

"You have to run, Red." Wolfgang said. "You can't win this."

"Silence, my precious boy." Eyona fired her webs at Wolfgang's mouth, sealing it shut. "Well, well, Alpha Huntress, you've seduced my son to your favor."

"I have no idea how a freak like you could be Wolfgang's mother, and I don't care." Red tightened her grip on her sword as Eyona advanced on her. "Your little boy is dead to me. I'll deal with him just as soon as I'm done dealing with you."

Eyona gave a wicked laugh. "You may be the Alpha, but you're not yet strong enough to begin dealing with me."

"We'll just see about that." Red swung her sword at one of Eyona's six legs.

"Foolish child." Eyona fired a web, catching Red's blade before it connected. With a powerful yank, she pulled the sword out of

Red's hands and flipped it into her own. "This was the sword your mother used to defend you on the night of her death. How fitting that you would carry it on the night of yours."

"I'm not finished yet."

Red charged at Eyona, swinging her claws in a furious mêlée. Eyona blocked each strike with ease while delivering powerful counterstrikes. It wasn't long before Red knew that Wolfgang was right when he had said there was no way she could win this fight.

"I do hope you are almost done dealing with me," Eyona said. "I so eagerly look forward to *dealing* with you."

As much as Red hated admitting defeat, her only hope was to turn tail and make a run for it. She dashed for the nearest tree and tried to make a quick climb to safety.

Eyona fired her webs, binding Red's legs. With only the use of her arms, Red jammed her claws into the brittle bark and began to work her way up the side.

"Don't give up now, Alpha. The higher you get, the more hopeful you will become that you can escape my grasp," Eyona said.

Every inch Red climbed became more exhausting than the last as Eyona tried to pull her back down. When Red at last reached a limb strong enough to support her weight, she was able to slash her way free of the webbing.

For a moment she through that she was going to be okay. This changed in an instant when she saw that Eyona was climbing up the tree and would soon reach her.

"Don't give up now," Eyona said. "I want you to truly believe you can escape me."

As far as Red could figure, her last chance to escape was to make a jump for a nearby tree. She locked eyes on a suitable branch over twenty feet away and struggled to get her balance as she stood up on the narrow branch. Using it to get a running start without falling would require agility she was unsure she had.

"You'd better hurry or I'm going to get you." Eyona said.

Putting her fears aside, she dashed forward for about ten feet and lunged off the branch with all of her might. Red felt like the world was moving in slow motion as she soared through the air.

It overwhelmed her with a mix of excitement and outright terror. There was no doubt that she had enough forward momentum to make it all the way, but just as fast as hope came, it was stolen away. Eyona fired her webs and hooked Red around the waist.

The jolt that stopped Red in mid-flight was so hard it knocked the breath right out of her. The next thing she knew, she was dangling upside down from the tree she had jumped from. Eyona descended on a web and hung in front of her. It sickened Red to see the witch grinning with such malicious delight.

"Now, the real fun begins," Eyona said.

Eyona's hands moved at lightning speed as she weaved a cocoon around Red's body. The webs squeezed so tightly that it was impossible to move even a muscle. Without hope of escape or rescue, Red could only await her unknown fate.

A tear came to her eye as she realized her journey could end in such a meaningless way. There were so many things she would never discover about her destiny in the mysterious world known as Wayward Woods.

CHAPTER 23

"P lease let me wake up safe at home."

Robbed of her external senses inside Eyona's cocoon of webs, Red could do nothing but focus her efforts on getting air into her lungs. With her chest unable to expand, the tiny breaths she was able to take were just enough to stay alive. It was her inability to move even a finger that made the ordeal truly maddening. The webs sensed any bit of movement and responded by squeezing tighter.

As Red passed in and out of consciousness, it became difficult to know how much time had gone by. It felt like days, though she suspected that only hours had passed. She wasn't having the sort of stomach cramps one gets from going for a long time without food, which was something she had experienced more than once in her life.

With nothing to do but await her fate, her mind drifted off to times long ago. The spellcraft that had hidden her memories was no longer affecting her. The images that filled her mind were vague because she had been so young when the events took place, but the feelings that came with them were quite real.

Red recalled festive family holidays—the smiling faces of her mother and father, the silly antics of her granny, and playing and laughing with Ash and Dote. She found comfort in knowing that if she was truly about to face death, it would come with a mind overflowing with fond memories and a heart full of love.

An oddly familiar image of a young boy with the face of a wolf entered Red's mind. She recalled that before her departure from Wayward, he came to visit her every day. They played games and told each other their deepest secrets. The boy was her best friend in the world, and she loved him above all others.

What was truly odd is that only Red could see the boy. Grenda and her mother believed he was merely an imaginary friend. Ethan refused to accept the boy as a mere childhood fantasy, even though Grenda insisted that no dark forces were involved. A rush of panic hit Red when she heard the voice of her father speak in her memory, insisting she no longer play with the invisible child that she called *Wolf Boy*.

Red had no doubt that the invisible boy had to be Wolfgang. This sent her mind spinning into a flurry of confusion as she tried to figure out how he could have been around in such a peculiar way. She recalled how Wolfgang told her that they were born on the same day and the connection between them was complicated. This revelation awoke a renewed need to survive in Red's heart. If she didn't escape from the cocoon, the truth would never be discovered.

Red cleared her mind and focused her thoughts onto the Alpha Power dwelling within. She knew little of what the power could do, but if it was as great as everybody claimed, she should be able to break free from the cocoon.

Red pushed her arms and legs outward with every bit of strength she could conjure. The webs reacted by squeezing tighter and tighter, but this time she refused to give in. A surge of primal energy empowered Red's mind and senses. The harder the webs fought against her efforts to escape, the stronger the energy inside her became. It was so intense that she soon felt as if she would explode if she didn't break free.

Red called out to the Alphas who had held the power before her, asking them how to defeat the dark mystical forces that empowered the webs. In an instant the answer came, not in words, but in the purest form of understanding.

Pulsating mystical energy blasted from Red's eyes. Every muscle in her body expanded with so much power that it caused the webs to weaken. She finally thrust her arms and legs outward and burst free of the cocoon prison.

"I AM THE ALPHA HUNTRESS!"

The nerves in Red's body felt electrified with astonishing power as she jumped to her feet. She found herself standing atop a stone altar that resided in the center of a dark cavern. Glowing moonstones tainted by vile spellcrafts lined the walls from floor to ceiling.

"Welcome back, Alpha Huntress," Eyona said from behind Red. "I was beginning to wonder if you were ever going to free yourself from my webs."

Before Red could react, something sharp pierced right into the center of her back. A dizzying nausea hit her so fast that she went limp and dropped to her knees.

Eyona laughed wickedly. "I hope that didn't hurt too much, my dear."

"What did you do to me?"

Red's vision became twisted and blurred. She could hear Eyona's feet clicking around on the stone ground, but it was hard to tell where exactly the witch was.

"Not to worry," Eyona said. "I just gave you a tiny shot of my venom to calm you down. Your little heart was beating away so fast, I was worried that it might give out before we finish our game."

"I'll show you how I *calm down*." Red's legs wobbled as she stepped down from the altar. A sniff of the stale air revealed that Eyona was just a few feet away. As much as Red wanted to squash her like a bug, there wasn't a chance of her doing that in such a weakened state.

"Careful now, I wouldn't want you to fall down and break your pretty little crown," Eyona said.

"Why did you keep me alive when you could have easily killed me?"

"Who says I'm not killing you right now?"

"I can feel your venom inside me. It's not enough to end my life. So what's the real story?"

"You're becoming more connected with the Alpha Power with each passing moment."

"Yeah, and I'm getting real attached to the power, so don't go getting any ideas about ripping it out of me like you tried to do when I was a child." Red continued to stumble and fumble around the chamber. Her hope of finding something that could be used as a weapon was coming up empty.

Eyona snickered. "Keep searching. You might even find your little sword if you try hard enough."

"I have no idea what you're talking about. Can't you see I'm a helpless little girl? I can't see a thing. Just how you want me to be."

"Holding on to a glimmer of hope that you might be able to escape is just how I want you to be."

"Lady, what is your story anyway? How can a freak show like you be Wolfgang's mother?"

Red's vision was beginning to clear up. As much as she wanted to rush Eyona, she knew it was best to keep pretending to be helpless. If the witch wanted to see her bumbling around, Red was going to put on the best show possible.

"That is a story far too long to tell, considering how little time you have left to live," Eyona said.

"Oh, please. Just think of it as my last request."

"I don't *do* last requests."

"Well then, unless you're going to get to some kind of point here, I sure wish you'd shut that squawking hole you call a mouth."

"Spoken like a true Riding. I know you take pride in hearing me say so."

"You got that right, lady." Red faked a trip to keep up the image that it was a struggle to stay on her feet. "So are you going to let me in on the reason for all of this? Or does it just amuse you to see me stumbling around like a helpless fool?"

"I do find a certain pleasure in seeing you in such a pathetic state. I'm merely waiting for you to run out of fight. It shouldn't be long now."

"Then what will you do to me?" Red asked.

"My son will take back what is rightfully ours. And I'm going to make sure that whatever little feelings he thinks he has for you won't stand in the way."

"That won't be so easy. He's in love with me," Red said.

"You silly girls are all alike. A boy smiles just right, and you think he's in love with you."

Red glanced up and saw her sword bound to the ceiling by a mesh of Eyona's webs. It was well out of her reach. "If he doesn't love me, why did he try to help me escape from you in the forest?"

"Don't be foolish. Wolfgang would never betray his beloved mother for a pathetic Riding."

"I swear on the grave of my own mother it's true. He loves me more than he will ever love you," Red said.

"*Liar.* Say that again, I'll kill you where you stand."

"Ask him yourself."

"You can ask him when he arrives to take the Alpha Power from you."

Red heard the clicking of Eyona's feet approaching her from behind. "I hear you there." She aimlessly flailed her arms around. "Stay away from me, you stinking witch."

"Strange that your eyesight has completely left you, considering how little venom I used. I like my prey to see what I am about to do to them."

"You must have used more than you thought. Maybe you're getting clumsy in your old age," Red said.

"There's only one way to know for sure."

Eyona held her long, pointy fingernail near Red's face. Red fought the urge to flinch as it got closer and closer to piercing her eye. A half-inch before it made contact, she lost control and grabbed Eyona's wrist.

"Pity." Eyona said. "You almost had me convinced." She stabbed her nail into the side of Red's neck.

"It was just a game." Red's vision blurred out of focus as she felt the sting of venom pumping into her veins. "You knew I was faking it all along."

"Of course I did, little huntress. I gave you just enough slack to believe you could get away. I do hope you enjoyed my little theater of death. I call it *killing with hope.*"

"I'm not dead just yet, witch," Red mumbled.

The dose of venom was far more potent this time, making Red feel as helpless as she had been inside the cocoon. She was now certain that Eyona had complete control of the situation. There was no chance Red could physically fight her way out of this trap. To survive the ordeal she would have to come up with a different tactic, though she had no idea what that could be.

"Don't give up now, Alpha. If you think real hard, just maybe you can think up a clever plot to escape." Eyona slammed Red down on the altar and dangled a strange black stone over her eyes. "I know your vision is a bit blurred, but I'm sure you can see this well enough."

Red gazed into the stone as it began to swirl with dark mystical energy. Its hypnotic power filled her mind with terrible images of dread and horror. She felt like snakes were slithering all around, and heard the groans of hideous creatures lurking in the shadows.

"Now, Alpha Huntress, go back in time to the night of your own birth. See the faces of those around you."

Red's thoughts drifted back through time. Her life rapidly flashed before her eyes in reverse order. She soon heard the cries of her newborn self. When the world came into focus, she saw her mother and father smiling down on her. Her perspective shifted back and forth between her newborn self and watching as an outside observer.

"We will call her Red," Jenna Riding said. "Just like the one that came before her."

They were in the forest clearing where Red had spoken to the first Red Riding. Her newborn self was lying atop the stone pedestal that had held the Omega Gem in her previous vision. A group of witches and warlocks surrounded her. They wore long red cloaks and chanted a strange incantation in a language Red couldn't understand.

Grenda looked down on Red through glowing white eyes. "Tonight the power of the Alpha will be yours. You will rise to be our high protector."

Red looked to the sky and saw the moon was engulfed in a blazing inferno. A burst of red energy exploded from the surface and soared across the night sky like a shooting star. It was the Alpha Power in its purest form. The lunar deities had chosen the one who was to receive it. Red heard them proclaim the name, and it was not her own.

"The time is upon us." Grenda said.

The witches and wizards chanted louder and faster. They raised moonstone-studded wands and staffs to the sky. The Alpha Power hovered above the forest in the distance. A spark of white light shot off into the night sky. The Seether clan had just tried to steal the power for Ice, but the lunar deities rejected her.

"We're not the only ones trying to do this tonight," Grenda said. "Our time is running short."

Grenda chanted a tongue-twisting incantation in a strange language. The Alpha Power turned from its distant course and headed their way.

Through the eyes of her newborn self, Red saw a blazing light descend down onto her. The lunar deities peered into the deepest depths of her heart to decide if she was worthy to receive the power. It was a moment of terror far greater than any Red could have imagined. When the power finally entered her body, it felt like the fire of a thousand suns burning in her soul.

"We've done it, loyal servants of the Riding Clan," Grenda said. "The daughter of Ethan and Jenna, bloodline descendant of Red Riding, will rise to become the new Alpha Huntress. She will save us from the coming evil of Ragnarok."

Ethan and Jenna looked down at Red, smiling with great pride.

"We will always be with you," Jenna said.

Red blinked and was back in the cave, looking up at Eyona. Her vision was still blurred, and she couldn't move a muscle.

Eyona squeezed Red's face. "I see from the look in your eyes that you did not know of the dark deeds of your clan. It's a pity that they used you in such a treacherous way."

"It can't be true," Red said.

Eyona raised her arms in victory. "The power intended for my son will restore the glory of the Helheim Clan. For fifteen years we've waited for the chance to reclaim what you Ridings stole from us. Finally, on this glorious night, my son will rise as the true Alpha Hunter. He will use his power to bring our lord Ragnarok back into this world."

"I don't believe you. It's a trick to get me to give up the power. It won't work," Red mumbled.

"It's no trick, Red of the Riding Clan." In his werewolf form, Wolfgang entered the dark chamber. He wore a black hooded cloak, and his eyes were glowing red with pure evil. "We have the power to take it from you, just as your grandmother took it from me."

CHAPTER 24

Red Riding, your clan is guilty of tyranny against my family. Justice will now be served."

It was plain to see that something about Wolfgang wasn't quite right. He stood by his mother's side with a lifeless gaze in his eyes. Red figured that the spellcraft making his eyes glow had also bewitched his senses.

"What have you done to him, witch?" Red's voice sounded weak and distant.

"Do you honestly care, considering he's about to rip the Alpha Power right out of you?" Eyona asked.

"From the looks of it, he won't be doing it by his own choice," Red said.

Wolfgang looked Red in the eyes. "Red Riding, your clan is guilty of tyranny against my family. Justice will now be served."

"That sure doesn't sound like the Wolfgang I know. You still in there, Wolf Boy?"

A hint of confusion came over Wolfgang's eyes. "Your clan is guilty of tyranny against my family."

"Yeah, yeah. Justice will now be served. Stop repeating yourself. Do you hear me talking to you, Wolf Boy?"

Wolfgang's face twitched. "Your clan is guilty of tyranny …"

Neo Edmund

"I got that part, Wolf Boy, tyranny against your family. Your freak show of a mother has got you under a major spellcraft, Wolf Boy."

Eyona put a hand on Wolfgang's shoulder. "Don't fret, my darling boy. The bad girl is trying to trick you. We both know how devious these Ridings can be."

"Don't listen to her, Wolf Boy. Listen to me. Do you remember how you tried to save me from your demented mommy back in the woods?"

Eyona snickered. "Still trying to play your way out of this, I see. Your relentless will to survive so amuses me. Let's see how you handle this twist in the game."

Eyona put a dagger into Wolfgang's hand. It had a glimmering silver blade and a hilt studded with illuminated moonstones of every color in the spectrum. Red was running out of time. She had to end this game sooner, rather than later, or Wolfgang was going to do something they would both regret.

"Wolfgang, listen to me," Red said. "Remember your secret friend from when you were a little boy? Remember what you called her?"

Eyona whispered into Wolfgang's ear. "We know what must be done here. Make mother proud. Become the Alpha Hunter."

Wolfgang looked at the shimmering blade in his hand. "Red Riding, your clan is guilty of tyranny against my family. Justice will now be served."

"Wolf Boy, I know you remember the little girl that you played with as a child. You had a special name for her. Say it to me right now."

"My special friend?"

The glow in Wolfgang's eyes flickered. Red was getting through, but it wasn't enough to overcome the power of the spellcraft that had enchanted him.

Eyona let a screech. "What is this nonsense you're going on about, Riding?"

"You'll find out soon enough, you creepy old hag."

Eyona gripped Red's face. "You're going to lose this game, and none of your pathetic little deceptions will change that."

If there was a chance to survive the ordeal, Red had to keep this going for as long as possible. "You're messing up your own twisted game, witch. I know you get off on the hope of your victims. If you keep telling me I'm going to lose no matter what, I might start buying it. Then you'll just be left with a hopeless little victim. Sounds like an awfully boring game to me."

Eyona let a dismissive laugh. "So you have figured me out. It makes no difference. We are well beyond that part of the game."

"I say the game is just getting rolling, and now it's my move." Red looked Wolfgang in the eyes. "Wolf Boy, tell your mother about the little girl from your childhood. I know you remember her."

Wolfgang's head twitched in confusion. "The little girl. She was my friend."

Eyona ground her teeth. "Enough. I will purge whatever lies you have bewitched his mind with after we're done."

Wolfgang raised the knife above his head. "Red Riding, your clan is guilty of tyranny against my family. Justice will now be served."

"Wolf Boy, you don't want to do this."

Eyona slid the tip of her fingernail across Red's throat. "Before you die, I must thank you for making this game so much fun."

"It's not over until I say so," Red said.

"That is where you are wrong, Alpha. Finish this, Wolfgang. Mother demands it."

Wolfgang looked Red in the eyes, ready to thrust the knife downward into her chest. "I will now take back what your family stole from mine."

"Wolf Boy, that little girl was your greatest friend. You loved her with all of your heart."

"She was my greatest friend." Wolfgang's head twitched as the glowing in his eyes flickered.

This time it was significant enough for Eyona to take notice. She held the tip of her nail over Red's heart. "One more lie, I'll finish you off myself."

"Then do it. If you can." Red closed her eyes and did all she could to remain calm. After a long moment Eyona removed her nail from Red's throat.

Red opened her eyes and saw the witch was trembling in absolute rage. "What's the matter, witch? Does Wolfgang have to do it himself?"

"Silence, Alpha. You will not win," Eyona said.

"I already have. There's no way Wolfgang is going to kill me because he loves me more than you. And I love him." Red dug down and found the strength to pull up to a sitting position. She grabbed Wolfgang and kissed him with all the love she had in her heart. Seconds later she heard the clink of the knife dropping onto the altar next to her.

Wolfgang took Red into his arms and embraced her. "I called you *Little Red Riding*." The glow in his eyes faded away. "You were my greatest friend."

"Curse you, Alpha," Eyona screeched. "You Ridings have crossed me for the last time. If my son is too weak to take the power, then you will both die."

Wolfgang picked up the knife and placed it into Red's hand. "I can't do it. She's still my mother."

"Wolfgang, I'm so sorry." Red concealed the knife behind her back.

"Mother is disappointed, Wolfgang. Your punishment will be to watch me strangle the life from your precious little girlfriend."

Wolfgang turned to face his mother. She was holding out all ten of her fingernails and moving in for the kill.

"Please, mother. There has to be another way to restore the Helheim family name."

"Foolish boy. Do you think I care about the tainted name of your vagrant father's clan?"

"You told me we were doing this to restore our family's honor to the people of Wayward."

Red's hand trembled as she tightened her grip on the knife. She could tell Wolfgang was drawing Eyona closer. There would only be one chance.

"The Alpha Power is all this was ever about," Eyona said. "Our honor will be restored when Ragnarok comes back to enslave the people of Wayward. They will have no choice but to bow to us. It is not too late to do the right thing, my precious boy. Kill the Alpha, and all you ever wanted will be ours."

"Not a chance, mother. What you want and what I want are two different things."

"Then you will watch the girl die, and I will find another way." Her words like daggers, Eyona shoved Wolfgang aside and raised her fingernails to stab Red. "Say hello to your mother for me, Alpha Huntress."

"After you, witch." Red buried her fears deep down inside and thrust the blade into Eyona's chest.

Eyona let out a piercing scream. "Wolfgang, how could you betray your own mother?!" She frantically grabbed for the knife, but was in far too much shock to pull it out.

"You're not my mother. You're just another power-obsessed monster like my father." Wolfgang took Red's hand, and they turned away.

Eyona thrashed around as her life began to fade away. "You may have forsaken me for that wretched Riding girl, but you won't get away with it. This will be our tomb."

A sound of thunder blasted out. The ground began to quake. Red and Wolfgang looked back to Eyona. She had her arms raised high. Mystical energy blasted from her fingertips. The moonstones lining the cavern walls ignited with pulsating energy.

"That can't be good," Red said.

"She's going to bury us alive. We have to get out of here," Wolfgang said.

"Wait, I need my sword." Red looked up to where she had seen her sword earlier. It was still bound to the ceiling by Eyona's webs.

"I'll get you another one. We gotta go before this whole place comes down." Wolfgang tried to pull Red along.

"No, we might need it. Now come on, I don't have all my strength back yet. You'll have to get it down for me."

Wolfgang flailed his arms in frustration. "Fine, but if we die in here, I'm going to be so mad at you."

"You'll be kindly rewarded later."

"I'm going to remind you that you said that."

The ceiling was beginning to crumble. Wolfgang took a deep breath and ran flat-out toward the cavern wall. He planted a foot on a rock and jumped upward with all of his might.

Red cheered as he just managed to get a grip on her sword. As he dropped back down, the webs binding the sword to the ceiling rebounded, springing him back upward. It took a moment of struggling before the webs finally broke and he dropped to the rocky floor.

Wolfgang wiped the sweat from his brow. "That went well."

"It was impressive." Red took the sword from Wolfgang and slipped it into the sheath over her back. "Now let's get out of here."

"Thought you'd never ask."

As they dashed toward the cavern exit, Wolfgang looked back at Eyona, lying face down on the ground and seemingly dead.

"Wolfgang, I'm so sorry," Red said.

Wolfgang wiped a tear from his eye. "It had to be done. I couldn't let her kill you."

Hand-in-hand, Red and Wolfgang ran out of Eyona's chamber and entered a dark tunnel with a low hanging ceiling. Rocks were cracking and crashing down all around them. The ground quaked so hard that it was difficult for them to keep their balance.

"So which way, Wolf Boy?"

"Just follow me, Little Red."

Wolfgang took Red's hand, and together they raced off down a long tunnel. Time and time again, they had to dive and leap clear to evade falling debris. A huge boulder crashed down in their path, missing them by mere inches. They turned to head in the opposite direction, but another huge rock crashed down, trapping them in the middle.

"So what now, fearless leader?" Red asked.

"You tell me, Alpha Huntress." Wolfgang said.

Red took a closer look at the massive bolder blocking their escape. There was only one choice. "We bust through it."

Wolfgang shook his head in outright disagreement. "There's no way we could even put a crack in that rock. Let's try to push it."

"We have no time. You can punch or kick. We go on my call." Red stepped back, her eyes locked on the boulder.

Wolfgang was going to protest. Red gave him a stern look, telling him that they were not going to debate it.

"Fine, I guess I'm kicking," Wolfgang said.

"Then that means I'm punching."

Red had to focus to keep herself stable on the trembling ground. She could only hope the power of the Alpha would allow her to break through such a massive object.

"Ready—*1 … 2 … 3!*"

A burst of energy radiated around Red's fist. It was so intense that Wolfgang took a nervous step back. When Red's fist made contact, the boulder exploded into a shower of shattering debris. For the half-minute it took for the air to clear, she stood trembling in shock and awe.

Wolfgang looked at Red with an astonished gaze. "That was insanely cool."

A sudden shudder of fear shot through Red's body. Something evil was coming their way, though she had no idea what it was. "Wolfgang, we have to get out of here."

Through the cloud of dust, Eyona emerged. Her eyes were as black as death, and she was trembling with rage. She darted at Wolfgang, jamming all ten of her fingernails into his chest. He didn't make even a whimper as his mother pumped her deadly venom into his veins.

With one last twitch, Wolfgang collapsed to the floor.

Eyona shrilled out a vindictive laugh. "I told you this place would be our tomb, Alpha."

"It will be yours before ours." Red drew her sword and let loose a malevolent roar. She unleashed a fury of lightning quick attacks, hacking off all six of Eyona's arachnid limbs. "That was for my mother, Jenna Riding."

Eyona fell to the ground. She looked up at Red with hate-filled eyes. "You may have defeated me, Riding, but you will never have my Wolfgang."

A single swipe of Red's sword is all it took to take Eyona's head clean off.

"You mean *my* Wolfgang."

The cave stopped quaking as the black energy faded from Eyona's eyes. Red shoved her sword into the sheath over her back as she dashed to Wolfgang. He was barely conscious and twitching in shock.

"Wolfgang, look at me. I'm getting you out of here."

"I always loved you." Wolfgang's eyes flickered shut.

"Listen to me, Wolf Boy, you wake up right this instant." Red slapped his face hard enough to make him stir a little. "Fine, if you can't walk, then I'll carry you."

Red strained to pull Wolfgang up off the ground. He felt a lot heavier than she had expected. For the next several minutes, she dashed through the dark caverns, stumbling over fallen debris and maneuvering under low hanging rocks. When she finally saw moonlight illuminating the cavern walls, she knew the exit couldn't be far away.

Fatigue and exhaustion were already setting in as she lurched out of the cave into the dark of the night. The rocky terrain outside was nothing like any place she had ever seen. With little hope of finding her motorcycle, her only chance to save Wolfgang would be to run all the way back to Granny's house.

Without a clue which direction to go, Red cleared her mind and let the spirits of the forest tell her the way. She ran over rocky paths—stumbled down steep embankments—waded across a waist deep river—and leaped over a treacherous ravine. It didn't matter how exhausted she became, or how treacherous the obstacles were that blocked her way, she outright refused to stop running.

Red thought about the dark truth Eyona had revealed to her in the cave. A deep sense of resentment began to swell inside. She believed the tragic events that destroyed her family took place because of their choice to steal the Alpha Power. It made her wonder how things would have turned out if Wolfgang had received the power. There was no way to know if he would've become a terrible tyrant because of his parents' influence, or if he would have risen to become a heroic leader.

What Red did know for certain is that there must be good in his heart if the lunar deities had chosen him over all others to become the Alpha.

After what felt like hours of running, Red found the path that led to Granny's house. Her heart pounded like it was going to explode. Emerging from the forest, she couldn't see a bit of light coming from the windows of the house. The front door was a mere twenty feet away when her body gave out and she collapsed to her knees. No matter how hard she tried, her gasping was too rapid and labored to call out for help.

"It's okay, Red. I know you tried," Wolfgang said weakly, not opening his eyes.

Red refused to fail after having come so far. She forced aside her pain and found the last bit of energy left inside. The incoherent scream that came from her was so loud all the creatures in the land could have heard it. The front door of the house soon swung open. Grenda emerged with a look of terrible dread in her eyes.

"Granny, you have to save him."

Red began to fade in and out of consciousness. The next thing she knew, Ethan was picking her up in his arms and carrying her into the house. He was speaking to her, but she couldn't hear a word he was saying over the sound of her heart pounding in her chest. The last thing she saw was Grenda kneeling down next to Wolfgang, right before the door slammed shut and the world faded to black.

CHAPTER 25

In the moment before she woke, Red thought she was still in the city, living in an orphanage. The events of the last few days seemed far too surreal to have happened. It made more sense to believe she had conjured it all up in her overactive imagination.

As her eyes opened and came into focus, she was astonished to be looking up at the ceiling of her bedroom in Granny's house. She was still in Wayward, far, far away from the life of loneliness she had left behind. Her name was Red Riding, a super-powered Alpha Huntress with an epic battle against evil awaiting her in the Moon Temple.

Her body ached as she pushed herself up to a sitting position. The pain brought back the memories of what had happened in Eyona's cave. The fear she felt during her battle would haunt her for a long time to come. She would not soon forget the many lessons learned along the way. There would be little chance of surviving in this treacherous world if she continued to blindly leap into action.

She let out a long sigh of discontent upon glimpsing her reflection in the mirror. The ratty and ripped clothes that hung on her body were bad enough. Seeing her face caked in so much dirt that she couldn't recognize herself was far worse. The frazzled state of her hair was a matter beyond words she would ever mutter out loud.

Her true concern was for Wolfgang. From what she recalled he had died in her arms the night before. She could only hope that Grenda had managed to pull off a miracle. The idea of having to face his death was more than she could endure. There was far too much unfinished business between them.

"Granny, are you here?"

Red stepped out of her bedroom and into the hallway. The savory aroma of Grenda's blueberry muffins scented the air. The house stood so still and quiet that one could have heard the tapping of an ant's feet crawling across the floor.

"Father? Dote? Ash? Is anybody here at all?"

She stood at the top of the staircase, desperate to hear a response, but there was not a bit of sound in the house. A hollow feeling struck in the pit of her stomach as she walked down the stairs. Wolfgang was lying on the couch as still as a corpse, and with a ghost-white complexion.

"Wolfgang?"

Red's eyes filled with tears as she slowly walked across the room. She begged to see the faintest bit of movement, or hear a sound that would let her know he wasn't gone.

"You better not be dead, or I am *so* going to kick your butt."

She approached Wolfgang and stood breathless for a lingering moment. Her hand trembled as she reached out to touch him. Beads of sweat formed on her forehead. A ringing erupted in her ears. Her heart pounded so hard she could feel it in her fingertips. The tension was so intense it was enough to make her scream.

"Would you move already? Take a breath or something. Don't just lay there looking …"

Red poked a finger into Wolfgang's side. He instantly lunged up to a sitting position. It was so startling that Red screamed out, flipped backward into the air, and landed in a crouch on the other end of the room.

"Red, what is your problem? I'm trying to get some shuteye here."

"You're alive." Red shrilled with joy and dashed over to Wolfgang. She threw her arms around his chest and smothered him with a hug.

"Go easy, Red. You trying to strangle me?"

Red slugged him in the arm. "How could you go and make me think you were dead?"

Wolfgang recoiled and rubbed his aching arm. "Of course I'm alive. Why wouldn't I be?"

"You don't remember? I ran across Wayward with you in my arms for hours. You're a lot heavier than you look."

"What are you going on about, Little Red?" Wolfgang's face was overcome with a troubled look. "Why did I just call you that?"

Red had a nervous twinge. "So then you don't remember?"

"Remember what?"

Wolfgang felt around on his chest and cringed from a stinging pain. He frantically pulled up his shirt, revealing ten round bandages. Each covered the spots where Eyona had stabbed him with her fingernails. "What did you do to me?" Wolfgang began to rip away the bandages.

"You shouldn't do that," Red said.

Wolfgang pulled the last bandage away, revealing ten round black scars on his upper chest. "Who did this to me?"

Red took a nervous gulp. "Don't you remember? In the cave? With your ..."

Wolfgang shook his head. "No. She wouldn't do this to me. Not my own mother. Tell me my mother didn't do this."

Red wiped a tear from her eye. "Wolfgang, I'm so sorry."

"Now I remember." Wolfgang sat back and pressed his hands over his face. "My mother tried to force me to kill you. She told me we could take the Alpha Power back, but that's before I knew you. You have to believe me, Red."

"I do believe you." Red put an affectionate hand on Wolfgang's shoulder. "You were being controlled by your mother's spellcraft."

Wolfgang leaped up in a frantic fit. "Red, you don't understand. I was in on the plan from the beginning. I saved you at the ball so Ice wouldn't get the power. My mother only put the spellcraft on me because I was wimping out."

"That's not true. You realized it was a mistake and decided to do the right thing."

"Plotting to kill you to restore my family's so-called honor is not doing the right thing. All I did was prove that we Helheims are the bottom-feeding scum that everybody in Wayward thinks we are."

Red grabbed Wolfgang and pulled him close. "Stop saying that. You are not like them. I can see the good in you. Someday you'll be able to see it, too."

Wolfgang tried to pull away, but Red tightened her grip and wouldn't let go.

"You're making a huge mistake, Red Riding."

"It's mine to make, Wolf Boy."

As they gazed into each other's eyes, Red moved in for a kiss. The instant before their lips met, the front door swung open. Ash and Dote entered and stopped cold. They gave Red a look of deep disappointment.

"You've gotta be kidding me," Ash said.

"This is hardly the time for getting all kissy-face," Dote said. "We need to have a serious talk, young lady."

Ash pointed a finger at Red. "You can't just go running off into the woods at night without telling people where you're going."

Red had been worried that her friends would be upset over the way she took off the night before. From the look in their eyes, it was a lot worse than she'd expected. "Listen, I know I made a huge mistake."

Ash gave Red a stern glare. "You're darn right you did. I can't even tell you how freaked out we were."

"How could you make us worry like that?" Dote asked. "We're your best friends and the first members of your clan."

"We sat up all night worrying about what could have happened to you," Ash said.

"For all we knew, you could be lying dead in a ditch somewhere," Dote said.

"You need to understand that Wayward is not a safe place to just go gallivanting around alone at night. Or the day, for that matter," Ash said.

"If this ever happens again, you're going to be in serious trouble," Dote said.

"More trouble than you can even imagine," Ash said.

Ash and Dote spoke in unison, "We're deeply disappointed in you, Red Riding."

Red looked away in shame. "You're both right. I didn't stop to consider how my actions could affect other people. I've been alone so long. This friendship thing is still new to me. I promise that it will never happen again. It was selfish and immature. I put myself in terrible danger because of it."

"I'm glad we had this talk and set you straight on some things," Ash said.

"Wait. Did you say you were in terrible danger? Dote asked. "As in you very nearly died sort of danger?"

"Tell us what happened," Ash said. "Don't leave out a single detail."

Wolfgang looked to Red with a shameful glare. "Go ahead, Red. Tell them all about what I did."

Ash raised his fists, ready to fight. "Yeah, tell us. I'll bust him up if he laid a hand on you."

"Easy there, boy." Red smiled at Wolfgang. "He saved my life from a dangerous monster."

"That makes you a hero, Wolfgang," said Dote.

"Yeah, we're all totally impressed," Ash said with a tone of sarcasm.

Red turned away and slumped a little. "I hope you two can forgive me, because you're my best friends. I would be lost without you."

Dote hugged Red in her loving, yet strangling way. "Red, don't be sad. We only got mad because we care so much."

Ash put his arms around Dote and Red. "You know we could never stay angry with you."

"I knew you three would make up," Grenda's spoke out.

Red looked up to see Grenda and Ethan walking down the stairs.

"Papa, you're all healed." Red dashed over and hugged Ethan.

"Red, I was deathly worried about you. Running off like that was dangerous," Ethan said.

"Not to worry," Ash said. "We already set her straight on that. She won't be doing it again."

Wolfgang cleared his throat. "As precious as this all is, we don't have time for it. Ragnarok is going to make a big play for getting back into Wayward. Unless you're all cool with that, we need to make some major plans."

Red casually shrugged. "The way I see it, if he needs me to pull him through the gate, all I need to do is stay clear of the Moon Temple."

Wolfgang clenched his teeth. "Grenda, I'm getting the idea that you didn't fill Red in on how this all works."

Red glared at Grenda. "No, she's kept a lot of things from me. Like not mentioning that she stole the Alpha Power from you and gave it to me."

"Well played, Granny," Ash said. "I always knew you were a crafty little lady."

Dote gasped. "A spellcraft like that must have come with a terrible cost."

"So now you know the truth," Grenda said. "Saves me the trouble of having to tell you about it later."

Red paced in a fit of anger. "That's all you have to say about it? You're lucky I don't walk out of here and never come back."

"Go easy on her," Wolfgang said. "She did it for the greater good, and we all know it. I've let it go. I think you should, too."

Red closed her eyes and calmed herself. "I've had all the half-truths and deceptions I can take. As the Alpha Huntress, I order all of you to tell me everything you know about what's going on here."

Granny cleared her throat. "Okay, Alpha Huntress. Here it is, so listen up real good. The clock in the Moon Temple is counting down. It's about a day and a half shy of five years."

Wolfgang added, "There are also five celestial stones, one marked Alpha. At 9:59 tomorrow night, at the moment of our births, that stone is going to power up. At the same time, the gate will open a bridge to a prison inside the moon where Ragnarok is trapped."

Ethan said, "The celestial stone will remain open for seven minutes. The first danger you face is that if somebody were to destroy the stone during that time, the Alpha Power would be free for the taking."

Dote said, "The next danger you will face is far more dangerous, because during that time you could help Ragnarok come back into this world."

Ash added, "Or you can keep him trapped in the moon until the next stone opens a year from now."

"Oh" is all Red could say.

"The good news is that you'd never help Ragnarok," Dote said.

"Wasn't that my point to begin with?" Red asked.

"It's not so simple," Wolfgang said. "Ragnarok knows you wouldn't do it willingly, so he's going to find a way to force you to do it."

Ash gave Wolfgang a suspicious glare. "And how would you know that?"

Wolfgang flailed his arms. "Because that's what power-obsessed gods bent on world conquest do. Am I wrong here?"

"He's right," Ethan said. "If given the chance, Ragnarok will use all of us against you."

"You mean he would try to kill you?" Red said.

Grenda put a comforting arm around Red. "As much as I hate to say it, that old tyrant will stop at nothing to get back into this world. You cannot allow that to happen, no matter what the cost. Even if we have to sacrifice our lives."

"Granny, you can't mean that," Red said.

"I can, and I do." Red saw from Granny's eyes that she meant it.

The idea that Ragnarok would kill Red's loved ones consumed her heart with a surge of fury. It reminded her of the feeling of hatred that swelled inside her during the vision where she had become the tyrant queen.

Red wondered if losing those she loved all at once could be the very path that would lead to such darkness. With this terrible truth staring her right in the eyes, the time had come to face her destiny.

"If Prince is still here, please ask him to join us," Red said.

"He's outside sharpening his rapier." Ash opened the front door and shouted, *"Hey, Prince, get your pretty boy butt in here. The Alpha Huntress needs you."*

Red cracked a much-needed smile. She looked at the photos of her mother on the mantel. There was no question what Jenna Riding would do if she had been given the Alpha Power. This truth gave Red a feeling of pride. She resolved that she had come to Wayward in search of her family and a better life. There was no way an evil lunar god was going to take it from her without a fight.

"Fear not, Alpha Huntress." Prince charged in through the front door with his rapier at the ready. He dive-rolled across the floor and took a battle stance. "I will slay all who have invaded the sanctity of your home."

It was so absurd that everybody just stood grinning at him.

Red stepped up to Prince and nudged his sword aside. "Easy there, *Sir-Just-A-Little-Too-Eager*. We're not under attack."

Prince sheathed his weapon. "My most sincere apologies. The way the boy cried out so frantically, I feared the worst."

"Hey, I'm not exactly a boy here," Ash said. "If there's hero work to be done, I'm not staying on the sidelines. The choice is mine to make. This time nobody is going to tell me otherwise."

Ash's words brought Red an unexpected revelation. It wasn't up to her to decide if he should risk life and limb in battle. She didn't have to ask her friends to make such a sacrifice to stand by her side. The choice was theirs to make and theirs alone. Her job was to honor their decision and stand tall as the best leader she could possibly be for them.

With this thought in mind, Red turned to face her clan. "A great evil is coming our way. As the Alpha Huntress, I must rise up and face it. I would be honored if each of you would stand by my side as the warriors of my clan. Those who will join me in this dangerous quest, take my hand now and pledge your allegiance."

Red extended her hand.

Grenda was the first to step up and declare her allegiance.

Dote and Ash didn't hesitate to step up as well.

Ethan smiled with great pride as he took his daughter's hand.

Prince knelt down and offered his hand in service.

They all looked to Wolfgang, who stood alone in the corner.

"Why are you all looking at me like that?" he asked.

"You with me or not, Helheim?" Red asked.

Wolfgang's face was overcome with disbelief. "You actually want *me* to be in your clan?"

Red looked Wolfgang in the eyes. "I don't care where you came from. I only care where you're going. You can either be like your parents, or you can stand with me as Wolfgang of the Riding clan."

Wolfgang took a step toward the group. "Do you all feel this way?"

Ash sighed. "Red trusts you, so I'll *try* to keep an open mind."

Dote smiled. "I never had any issues with you. I think it would be fun to have you on our team."

Prince shrugged. "I'm the new guy, so I don't have an opinion either way."

Ethan gave Wolfgang a hard glare. "I'll go along with Red's choice, but I'll be keeping a close eye on you. Take even one step off the path, it will be your last."

Grenda smiled. "It's your decision to make, young man. All I expect is that you honor the choice you make."

"Then it's settled." Wolfgang stood tall and took Red's hand. "Alpha Huntress, High Protector of Wayward, I pledge my life to the service of your clan."

Red smiled with great pride. "We seven stand as the first members of the Riding clan. I am honored to lead you, and to fight with you."

"Awesome." Ash said. "So what happens now?"

"I need to prepare for battle," Red said. "I suggest you all use this time to do the same."

Ethan and Grenda led Red upstairs into her parents' bedroom. From a hidden closet, Ethan took out a silver suit of armor. It was identical to the armor Red had worn during her vision in the Moon Temple. The single plate extended down past her waist and curved up like a skirt just above the knees. Underneath was light chainmail to protect her legs and arms.

"This armor was your mother's," Ethan said. "It's not the most comfortable thing to wear in battle, but it will protect you from most any blade."

Grenda put an amulet hanging on a silver chain around Red's neck. It was studded with a glossy green moonstone. "This will make your armor emerge whenever you take on your werewolf form and vanish when you change back to your human form. Just remember that this moonstone was obtained at a great cost. Consider it irreplaceable."

Ethan put a red-hooded cloak over Red's shoulders. It was made of thick velvet. "This belonged to the first Red Riding. It was once passed down to your mother. She wore it in many battles. It is time for you to do the same."

Red looked at herself in a full-length mirror. The armor and cloak made her feel like a true hero. The life of adventure she had always craved was at last upon her. It was now time to face the reality of her calling head-on.

"I'm ready for you, Ragnarok," she said with confidence.

Armed with her sword, Red left her parents' room and marched down the stairs. Ethan and Grenda followed close behind, both gleaming with great pride. As Red entered the living room, Ash, Dote, Wolfgang, and Prince stopped cold and looked up at her in awe.

"Whoa, you look so …" Ash was unable to finish his sentence.

"It's like you're all …" Dote was also unsure how to put it into words.

"You're totally …" Wolfgang stuttered.

Prince stood up like a soldier saluting his commander. "She has the look of the Alpha Huntress, the high protector of Wayward Woods."

Red looked to her clan. "To defeat Ragnarok, I need to find something called the Omega Gem. I have no idea where it is and will need your help to find it."

Grenda shook her head in grave concern. "As far as I know, the last one to have it was the first Red Riding."

"Nobody even knows for sure if it actually exists," Wolfgang said.

"I know it exists," Red said. "One way or another, I will find it."

Ash spoke up. "Is it a glossy red gem, a little bigger than a gumball, glowing all mystical-like, and if you look into it, you can see the moon?"

Red eyed Ash, a little surprised. "I don't know about seeing the moon in it, but yeah, that would be it."

"It's at Ice's palace. She's got it on the nightstand next to her bed," Ash said.

"Whoa there, creepy boy," Wolfgang said. "Ice told me you were stalking her house, but I had no idea it went that far."

Ash shrugged. "It's a cool place to explore. I get bored easily."

Dote gave Ash a disapproving glare. "I don't know what's weirder, the fact that Ice keeps a stone of such great power on her bedroom nightstand, or the fact that you know it's there."

Red sighed. "Let's just forget about the weirdness right now and figure out how we're going to get it away from Ice."

Ash paced around. "I'm pretty sure that after our little escape the other night, they've got my entrance locked up tight."

"That's okay with me," Dote said. "I don't want to go back into the sewers."

"I'll second that," Red said.

"The Seether's palace is a full day's journey," Ethan said. "If we're going there, we'd better get to walking."

"Forget that foolishness," Grenda said. "I ain't hiking clear across Wayward. No, there's only one way this clan is traveling tonight."

CHAPTER 26

I t was early afternoon as Grenda led Red and the others down a rocky forest trail. The tension was so high that they walked for well over a half-hour without a word spoken among them. Soon the air reeked with an odor so foul it made their eyes burn and twitch.

"What is that stench?" Ash asked, scowling. "It smells like something died out here."

Red looked at Ash a little oddly. "The puke stink in the sewers of Ice's palace doesn't bother you, but *this* is a problem?"

"I've built up an immunity to that smell," Ash said. "This stink is something else entirely."

"Poor little Dorkus of the Ashley Clan," Wolfgang said. "Is the big, bad smell of garbage upsetting your fragile aristocrat nostrils?"

"Helheim, don't even get started on my family," Ash said.

"Aristocrat, as in rich people?" Red asked.

"I guess you haven't remembered that part yet," Dote said. "Ash is super-rich."

"I am not super-rich," Ash said.

"More like gold-plated underwear rich," Wolfgang said.

"You guys are totally exaggerating," Ash said.

Wolfgang belted out a laugh. "Your family owns half the land in Wayward, including the part of town I live in."

"My family doesn't own the land," Ash said. "Just the buildings that are standing on it."

"Where I come from, that's what we call rich," Red said.

Ash sighed. "Okay, so my family is a little bit rich."

"Super-rich," Dote said.

"Gold-plated underwear rich," Wolfgang said. "Maybe one of these days you can tell us all the story about how your family tried to boot my family out of town."

Ash gave Wolfgang a glare. "Oh, don't you even go there."

"Ash, you tried to kick Wolfgang out of Wayward?" Dote asked.

"Why would you do that?" Red asked.

Ash batted a fist in frustration. "That was my grandfather. It happened before I was even born. Don't go holding what my family did against me."

Wolfgang gave Ash a shove. "Try to remember that the next time you go rubbing my family's past in my face."

Ash chuckled. "You can't be comparing my family's business ventures with the evil crap your family has done. And is still doing to this day."

"I wouldn't expect a silver spoon boy to know the difference," Wolfgang said.

"Listen up, Helheim. Just because my family is rich doesn't mean I'm a spoiled brat. It's true that I could have anything I want just by pointing at it. But have I ever once done that?" Ash pointed to Dote.

"Not once that I've ever seen."

"And there it is," Ash said. "Rock-solid proof that I'm nothing like my family. I plan to make my own way in this world. Mark my words, I will never take a cent of the money my family has set aside for me."

Wolfgang eyed Ash curiously, "How much money we talking about?"

"More than you could ever count," Ash said.

"How about I start slugging you in the face and we see who loses count first," Wolfgang said.

Red pushed Wolfgang and Ash apart, glaring. "You two are going to put an end to this squawking, or I'll be the one counting out the hurt. Hear me, you pair of girly boys?"

"Girly boys." Wolfgang grunted.

"You don't have to resort to name-calling," Ash whined.

Grenda cleared her throat. "You'd best all keep down that squawking before you scare off our rides." She pulled back a tree branch, revealing a towering hill of garbage in a forest clearing. A flock of grungy rodents were feasting away on the rotting waste. They were well over six-feet in length and had grungy wings.

"What are they?" Red had to fight the urge to gag from the stench.

"Ratgulls." Wolfgang said. "You've got to be kidding, old woman."

Grenda backhanded Wolfgang across the face. "Watch your sass, Helheim."

Wolfgang bitterly ground his teeth. "That's it. I'm out."

Red grabbed Wolfgang by the jacket and yanked him back. "You're not going anywhere, Wolf Boy."

"You don't get it," Wolfgang said. "She thinks we're going to fly across Wayward on those stinkin' things."

Red cringed in disgust at the thought. "Granny, that's not true, is it?"

"Unless you know of a better way, it sure as heck is true," Grenda said.

Dote whimpered, shuddering. "But they're so yucky."

"They're also dumb as a rock and easy to command," Ethan said. "It won't be a pleasant ride, but it will get us there much quicker than walking."

"What of it, Alpha?" Ash asked. "As much as I hate the idea, I'll go along with whatever you decide."

"Well ..." Red let a long sigh. "They are gross, but I don't see a better choice."

"Then it's settled," Grenda said. "Follow my lead."

Dashing out of the bushes, Grenda ran for the nearest ratgull. In one spry leap she got onto the creature's back and clutched a handful of its fur with both hands. The beast bucked around in protest, so she gave it a swift kick in the side, forcing it to submit.

"Looks easy enough." Red ran toward a ratgull and tried to jump on its back. The creature spun around to try and scare her away. It only took one light whack to get the beast to stop fighting and let her climb on its back. "I guess it could be worse."

Wolfgang, Prince, and Ethan were already mounting their own ratgulls. Ash was having a hard time getting his to submit, but he was soon able to persuade the creature to let him climb on. Dote was pacing around, afraid to even try to approach one of the grungy creatures.

"Dote, why don't you ride with me?" Red said.

"Oh, yay." Dote dashed over and climbed on behind Red. "You are the best friend ever, Red Riding."

"So now what do we do?" Wolfgang asked.

Grenda grinned. "You hang on for dear life and try not to fall off. I'll handle the rest." She smacked the ratgull in the head. "Fly, you dumb critter."

Red took a deep breath. "Why do I feel like we're going to regret this?"

Grenda's ratgull took off running and spread its wings wide. The other ratgulls instinctively dashed behind it. Red cried out a shrill of fear and excitement as they took flight. She had to grip on tightly as they flew almost straight up, climbing higher and higher until they reached the treetops.

The sight of Wayward from high above the trees was the most magnificent thing Red had ever seen. From what she could tell, the majestic wooded landscape spanned off to infinity in every direction. Dusk hadn't set in, and yet the blazing red full moon was right above them. Red knew of the evil forces that dwelled under its cold surface, but she was too awe-inspired by its lunar magnificence to care.

"Wayward will not fall into darkness tonight." Red proclaimed.

The ratgulls began ascending higher as the landscape sloped upward. The air grew so cold that Red could see her own breath. She looked back to make sure the others were still with her. Grenda was grinning with delight. Wolfgang, Ethan, and Prince looked like warriors prepared for battle. But Ash looked ready to throw up as he clung to the fur of his ratgull.

"Don't worry," Dote said, noting Red's worried look. "Ash may be a little wimpy at times, but he always comes through in the end."

"I hope you're right. Without his help, we have no chance of getting the Omega Gem," Red said softly.

As they soared over a rise of trees, Red saw a sight more astonishing then any she could have ever dreamed. A great metropolis built of brick and stone was down below. Many of the buildings towered as high as the treetops. Pipes vented hot steam from the roofs of houses and shops. The cobblestone streets were abuzz with pedestrians and horse drawn-carriages. There were even a few vehicles similar to the automobiles from the world Red had left behind.

"What is this place?" Red asked.

"That's Wayward Village. It's pretty much the center of all civilization," Dote said.

"Sure hope I get to visit there one day soon," Red said.

Ice's palace soon came into their view. From high above, it looked even bigger than it had from the ground. It towered on a hilltop with a steep cliff at the back end. Red spotted the opening to the sewer drain they had jumped from during their escape. It was so high up one would assume a fall would be impossible to survive.

"Ash, how do we get in?" Red yelled.

"We land in the center courtyard. From there I can get us in through a secret entrance," Ash said.

"We do that, they'll see us coming," Ethan said.

"I've been thinking it over all the way here," Ash said. "As far as I can figure, it's the only chance we've got."

Red pulled out her sword and raised it high. "If that's the way it has to be, then we go in fast and hit the ground running. Prepare for battle."

Wolfgang transformed into a werewolf and raised a clawed hand. "I'm so ready for action."

Ethan pulled out his battle-axe and held it high in one hand. "As am I."

Dote conjured a sphere of mystical energy in her hand. "My mother will be so proud, when I tell her about this."

Ash closed his eyes and took a calming breath. "I've got your back to the end, Red Riding."

Prince drew his rapier and kissed the blade. "I will bring great honor to the Knights of the Alpha Huntress."

Grenda led the group into a steep dive, heading toward the front wall of the palace. The guards on the towers scrambled into action, arming themselves with bows and arrows as their leaders shouted warnings to those below.

Red tightened her grip on her sword. "This is it. We're going in."

The guards on the towers fired a volley of arrows.

"We've got incoming." Ethan warned. "Take evasive maneuvers."

"No. Stay on course." Grenda said. "I'll handle this."

The arrows were mere seconds away. Grenda raised her hands. They began glowing with mystical energy. She fired out a burst of lightning bolts, blasting the arrows to dust.

"Now it's my turn." Dote flung an energy vortex at the nearest guard tower. The force of the impact sent the guards soaring into the air like rag dolls.

"Dote, that was amazing," Red cheered.

"That was my most powerful spellcraft *ever*," Dote said.

An alarm blared out as they descended toward the courtyard in the center of the palace. A dozen armed guards scrambled into defensive positions.

Red didn't wait for her ratgull to land before she leaped to the ground. A guard charged at her and swung his sword. She countered with a flying elbow to his face, knocking him unconscious.

Ethan belted out a thundering battle cry. "It's been far too long since I've stormed a castle." He grabbed the nearest guard by the shirt and flung him into another guard, knocking them both out cold.

Prince dueled with a pair of armored guards. "I smite thee in the name of the Alpha Huntress."

Grenda was using a pair of mystical energy whips to beat down several attackers. "Red, we'll keep these jokers busy. Go do your thing."

"Ash, it's time to make me proud!" Red called out.

"Then follow me." Ash ran toward a patch of bushes in the far corner.

"This is almost too easy," Wolfgang said.

"You won't hear me complaining about it," Red said.

Red, Dote, and Wolfgang caught up to Ash. He was crouching behind a tall hedge, straining with all his might to pull off the cover of a ventilation shaft. It was a mere three feet in height and width.

"*This* is your big secret entrance?" Wolfgang asked.

Red skeptically peered into the dark shaft. "Ash, where does this go?"

"Inside. Unless you know a better way." Ash climbed into the vent and waved for the others to follow.

Red concealed her doubt and gestured for Wolfgang and Dote to get inside. She then joined them and replaced the vent cover. The inside of the shaft was not only dark and dusty; it was such a tight squeeze that they had to crawl along on their knees.

"Red, I've got a weird feeling about this," Dote said.

"Me, too, Dote. I just don't know what else we can do."

Ash led the others through an ongoing maze of air ducts. They went up and down and every which way until Red found herself completely lost.

Dote tapped a nervous finger on the tip of her nose. "Why do I feel like we've gone down this tunnel a hundred times already?"

Red rubbed her eyes as she was overcome by a strange feeling of dizziness. "Ash, are you sure we're going the right way?"

"I'm taking us the long way around to avoid the guard stations. Just trust me on this one. The Omega Gem will be ours before you know it."

The thought of this filled Red's heart with fear. Getting her hands on the gem would allow her to defeat Ragnarok, but to do so would expose her to a force that could turn her into a terrible tyrant. She felt a chill from the inside out as she realized the thing that could save Wayward also had the power to bring about its demise.

CHAPTER 27

J ust follow me and don't fall behind," Ash said as he stomped on a large spider. He continued to lead Red, Dote, and Wolfgang down the endless maze of ventilation shafts that ran through Ice Seether's palace.

Red was certain that something was out of sorts as the minutes passed like hours. "Ash, if you don't get us out of here soon, I'm going to rip a hole in one of these walls."

"Don't go freaking out now," Ash said. "It's just around this next bend."

After another minute or two of walking, Ash finally signaled for the others to stop near a vent cover. On the other side, they could see the legs of two guards standing in a corridor.

Ash gestured to Red that he was going to push the vent open. She was to grab one of the guard's legs and pull him inside. He then motioned to Wolfgang, indicating to grab the other guard and knock him out.

Red and Wolfgang looked to one another and shrugged in agreement.

As soon as the vent opened, Red grabbed a guard by his pants and pulled him inside. Before the man could react, Ash clubbed him in the face. The other guard peered down into the vent with a perplexed expression. Wolfgang grabbed him by the shirt and pulled him inside.

As Red jumped out of the vent into the dark hallway, she heard a hard thud and knew the other guard was out of the game.

"I guess that worked out well enough," Red said. "Where to next?"

With Ash leading the way, they dashed down a long hallway covered with royal blue carpet. The strangest paintings Red had ever seen lined the walls from floor to ceiling, each depicting extreme close-ups of people's faces.

Dote glared downward to avoid looking at the portraits. "This hallway is giving me the creeper-jeepers."

"The Seethers call this the Hall of Faces," Ash said. "There's an old urban myth that the faces were stolen away from their owners by an old witch. She immortalized them in these paintings."

They rounded a corner and came upon two guards standing at the far end.

"Halt in the name of her royal highness, Ice Seether!" one commanded, raising a hand to signal them to stop.

An energy vortex shot past Red from behind. The guards were hit head-on and sent flying backwards into a wall. Quite startled, Red snapped a look back to see Dote had both hands extended, and they were glowing green.

"That's my favorite spellcraft." Dote stumbled a little. "The problem is that it makes me feel sleepy when I do it."

"It was totally impressive," Red said.

As they passed the fallen guards, Red was relieved to see they were still breathing. The idea of causing them serious harm felt wrong. She figured they were just employees doing their job and certainly not responsible for the things that the Seethers did.

They arrived in a hallway with floors and walls lined in dark purple velvet. At the far end, stood a twenty-foot wooden door with a white ivory archway. Two royal knights stood before it, in werewolf form, with glowing red eyes.

Red looked to Ash. "Let me guess. Ice's bedroom?"

"You got it."

"We gotta make sure her guards don't have a chance to call for backup." Wolfgang sprinted off down the hallway toward the guards.

"Hey, wait for me." Red dashed after him.

Roaring furiously, the knights pulled out their swords. Wolfgang did a high-flying jump-kick and pummeled the knight on the right. Red slid feet forward for the last few yards. The knight on the left swung his sword, but she passed right underneath it. She finished the fight with a powerful kick to the knight's gut.

Red and Wolfgang looked at one another and grinned.

"We make a pretty rocking double act," Red said.

"I still say this is going just a bit too easy," Wolfgang said.

Ash and Dote ran up to join them.

"I so wish you could have seen how cool that looked," Dote said.

Red approached a huge spiraling mechanism attached to the door. It was made of solid iron and had a spinning dial with hieroglyphics carved into it.

"This looks sort of like a combination lock used to secure a bank vault," Red said.

"More like a bunker," Wolfgang said.

"Ice can get a little obsessive when it comes to home security," Ash said.

Red spun the dial. "Any idea how we get inside?"

"Allow me." Ash nudged Red aside and began turning the dial. He spun it three times to the left, three times to the right, and four times back to the left.

The lock disengaged with a clunk.

Red and Wolfgang looked at one another and shrugged.

"I don't even want to know how he knew that," Wolfgang said.

"I'm going to just smile and be glad he did," Red said.

"If you think that was weird, wait until you get a look at what's inside," Ash said.

It took Red's and Wolfgang's combined might to push open the massive door. They stood in awe as they took in the bizarre sights of the large stone chamber.

Dote looked up in disbelief at a wall lined with enough bladed weapons to arm a squadron of soldiers. "Obsessed much with the killing stuff?"

"This is new." Ash took a wide step around a rug made from a beast that resembled a grizzly bear, but was several times larger and had vastly more teeth.

Red approached a wall, covered from top to bottom with the mounted heads of hundreds of slain creatures. "Is there anything in Wayward Ice hasn't killed?"

"Several," Wolfgang said. "Have no doubt they're all on her hit list."

Dote stood trembling. "Can we just get the gem and go? All this dead stuff is giving me nightmares, and I'm not even asleep."

"Agreed," Ash said. "Let's not end up as the next trophies on Ice's wall of death."

In the center of the chamber stood an extravagant canopy bed. The legs and poles were made of three-inch-thick animal bones. A white curtain made entirely of animal skins hung over it.

"Major creep show," Red said.

Next to the bed sat a large nightstand, also crafted from the bones of slain beasts. The glowing Omega Gem sat perched in the severed claw of a raven. Red gazed into its glossy reflective surface and saw an image of the full moon.

"Just like I told you." Ash said.

Red took a careful look around the chamber. "Is it me, or does this all seem just a bit too easy?"

"I'm pretty sure I've been saying that since we hit the ground," Wolfgang said.

"Well, now *I'm* saying it." Red took a quick sniff of the air. There weren't any obvious signs of danger. Not that it offered her much comfort, considering their surroundings.

Dote whimpered. "Just grab the darn gem and let's get out of this place."

As Red reached out for the Omega Gem, she could feel its power calling to her. It wasn't until her hand made contact that she realized she had made a terrible mistake. An intense shockwave of mystical energy blasted out, knocking her to the floor with a painful thud.

"What a dirty rotten spell," Dote said.

Wolfgang and Dote dashed over and helped Red to her feet. The gem flickered and vanished in the blink of an eye.

"Whoa. What happened to it?" Ash searched around the nightstand.

"Great job, Dorkus," Wolfgang said.

"How was I supposed to know it was going to do that?"

"We have to find it," Red said. "How can I defeat Ragnarok without it?"

"The answer is *you don't*, foolish peasant girl," Ice said. They turned as she strutted in through the chamber door, grinning maliciously and holding Prince's rapier.

Red pulled her sword and pointed it at Ice. "What did you do with the Omega Gem?"

"You still don't get it." Ice snickered. "It's a fake, you little dummy."

"You're lying." Red said.

"Sadly, I am not. But don't feel bad. Even I was fooled when I first held it. My sages assure me that it has no real power."

Red slumped in defeat. "Then we came all the way here for nothing."

"Dearest Red, don't be that way. You left our little party the other night so abruptly that I never got a chance to show you my room. I do hope you're impressed."

"Impressed is not the word I would pick. Major freak show is more like it."

Ice smiled quite proudly. "So then you do like my trophies. I killed every one of them all on my own, you know."

Dote gasped when she noticed Prince's rapier in Ice's hand. "Is that the sword that belongs to my pretty prince?"

Ice playfully swung the rapier around. "Oh, poor dodo bird. I do hope he wasn't somebody special to you."

"Not yet, but I was making plans," Dote said. "What did you do to him, you albino freak show?"

Ice gave a dismissive laugh. "Is that the best insult you can come up with, dodo bird? Red already used the term freak show when she complimented my decor. Do try to be original next time."

Wolfgang approached Ice. "Are you just going to stand there cackling like a jaded witch, or are you and me going to have us a rematch?"

"Come now, little wolfy. Did you miss the part where I was talking about being original? We've already done that dance."

Wolfgang cracked his neck to the side. "Don't disappoint me and go running away with your tail between your legs."

"Bored now." Ice said. "How about we stir the pot a bit. Red, do you have any clue why this vagrant is following you around?"

"Try stirring another direction," Red said. "Wolfgang and I have already been down that road."

Ice snickered. "Oh, no. Don't tell me we have a case of puppy love going on here? That is so quaint."

Red grumbled. "Now I'm getting bored. We gonna fight now, or what?"

"No need to jump right to the primal thing," Ice said. "How about I pick a fun subject to lighten things up. Let me think. How about the coming of Ragnarok in only a few short hours?"

"Check your calendar," Red said. "Our big birthday bash isn't until tomorrow night."

Ice giggled. "Oh, now this is the part of the game where I say something shocking, then you totally freak out and call me a liar."

Dote's face was overcome with a look of dread. "Oh no. I knew something was going on inside the vents."

Ice pointed the rapier toward Dote. "Zip it, dodo bird. My spellcraft. My punch line."

Red took a nervous gulp. "What did you do to us?"

"It was so simple," Ice said. "When I saw you coming on your little flying rodents, I knew that your little Dorkus here would try to use the vents to sneak around the house like he always does. So, in my brilliance, I put a little *déjà vu* spellcraft down there. I had you all running in circles, over and over and over and over."

"So then how long were we in there?" Red asked.

"A whole day," Dote said.

Wolfgang clenched his fist. "I knew it was too easy."

"Surprise, birthday sister," Ice said. "Sorry your granny and friends couldn't stay around to join in the festivities. My guards had to escort them off the property."

"You mean, they're not dead?" Dote asked.

"Of course not. If you want them back, I'm sure you'll know where to find them." Ice extended her arms. A flash-bang explosion ignited. The chamber rapidly filled with thick smoke. "See you around, Little Red Riding."

"Ice, I am so going to get you for this," Red said.

Red couldn't see a thing in the smoky haze. A sniff of the heavy air revealed that Ice had already fled the chamber. She then caught four distinctive scents. Ice's elite guards, Mia, Naoki, Suki, and Yuki, had entered the room.

"Ash! Dote! Get out of here!" Red yelled out.

Red could smell her friends nearby. She dashed off in their direction, but an unseen attacker smacked her in the face with a wooden staff. A flurry of invisible attacks followed from every direction. She blocked as many of the strikes as she could, but smoke filled her lungs and slowed her down. The final blow sent her crashing face-first to the floor.

Then, just as quick as the attackers came, they were gone.

"Ash, Dote, Wolfgang? Where are you?" Red cried out.

A sniff of the air didn't help a bit this time. There was too much smoke to smell anything. After a couple of minutes of aimless searching, the haze cleared enough so Red could see. Just as she feared, Ice had captured Ash and Dote. Only Wolfgang remained. He was lying half-conscious on the floor, with a nasty gash on the side of his head.

"Get up, Helheim." Red nudged Wolfgang with her boot. "It's time to go."

"Oh, sure, I'm fine." Wolfgang sat up and clutched his aching head. "Thanks for your concern, by the way."

Red walked toward the door. "They took Ash and Dote. I'm pretty sure they have Granny and my father, and Prince, if he's still alive."

Wolfgang stumbled after Red. "You know she's going to use them against you."

"Of course I know that!" Red shouted so loud it made Wolfgang flinch.

Wolfgang took a calming breath. "I'm sorry that things got all screwed up, but don't go taking it out on me. I'll do whatever I can to help you, if you'll let me."

Red also took a calming breath. "I'm sorry, I didn't mean to bark at you."

"Don't let that angst go so easy, Alpha Huntress. You're going to need it tonight. Ice is going to have an army waiting out there for you."

Red ground her teeth. "I hope you're right. I'm so ready for a major fight."

"What about the Omega Gem? How will you defeat Ragnarok without it?" Wolfgang asked.

"I don't think I'm supposed to defeat him just yet."

Red recalled how the first Red Riding told her that the search for the Omega Gem would be a long journey. She felt foolish as it became clear that she had again jumped into action without thinking things through. "Tonight I only have to stop Ragnarok from getting into this world. It's time to go to the Moon Temple."

Wolfgang nodded in agreement. "Then we go together. And I know exactly how we're going to get there."

CHAPTER 28

Red was certain the moon was on fire when she caught a glimpse of it in the night sky. It was sweltering crimson and loomed just above the trees that lined the rocky path she had been speeding down for over an hour. The voices of the lunar deities were calling her toward the inevitable battle awaiting her in the Moon Temple. The Alpha Power surging through her body gave her strength unlike any she had ever imagined possible.

"Faster!" Wolfgang called out to the horses that pulled their carriage along, the same one that had carried Red and Dote to Ice's grand ball. He was sitting by Red's side in the driver's seat with the stone cold expression of a warrior ready to face his destiny.

The fearless confidence in Wolfgang's eyes made Red believe they had a chance to survive the night. A smile came to her face as she recalled their brief time together. He was not the same guy she had met a mere five days ago. The disgrace of the Helheim name no longer defined his existence. Wolfgang was now on a new path where he could carve out his own destiny.

"They're almost here," Wolfgang warned.

A surge of fear overcame Red when she got her first look at the swarm of phantom faeries now pursuing them. They were winged creatures with the size and form of a full-grown human. Their skin glowed with a reflective luminescence that made them look like they were on fire. Her skin tingled as she stiffened involuntarily, as her grip tightened on her sword and she mentally tried to prepare herself. *I am the Alpha Huntress. I am the Alpha Huntress.*

"Red, I don't get it. If Ice wants you to go to the Moon Temple, why is she trying to stop you?" Wolfgang asked.

"I don't think she's trying to stop me. She's trying to slow me down, so I get there after she has a chance to destroy the Alpha Stone and claim the powers for herself. Then she can make me watch her help Ragnarok through the gate."

"If we weren't talking about Ice Seether, I'd say that sounds totally insane," Wolfgang said.

"When you're dealing with crazy people, you gotta think crazy." Red stood up on the roof of the speeding carriage. She locked her eyes on a phantom faerie that now flew alongside them. "Are you sure these things aren't humans with wings?"

"Not even close. Phantom faeries are mindless beasts that only care about eating and killing," Wolfgang said.

Red clutched her sword. "Then I won't feel bad about hacking every last one of them to pieces."

"Don't go thinking this is going to be easy, Alpha. There's a good chance they'll rip our carriage to bits and try to eat us alive."

Red buried her fears deep down inside and focused her thoughts on saving her family. "Then I guess you'd better keep this thing moving no matter what happens."

A phantom faerie glared at Red through its blazing red eyes and wailed out a vicious screech. It swooped in and swung its razor-sharp claws. Red's armor provided excellent protection from the attack, just as Ethan had promised. She countered with a swipe of her sword that chopped the beast's arm off and then followed up with another slash that hacked its wings in half, sending it spinning into the trunk of a tree.

Another phantom faerie grabbed Red from behind. She responded with a backward thrust of her elbow that knocked it away. She spun around and swung her sword with so much force that the creature's head flew off into the woods and its body fluttered off in another direction.

The swarm of phantom faeries began to viciously slam into Red from every side. She lost her balance and crashed down onto the roof. While trying to catch her breath, she spotted a phantom faerie flying near the underside of the carriage. It swung a claw and slashed the wooden wheel into splinters.

"Wolfgang, I think we're in major trouble," she said.

Red looked over the other side of the carriage just as a phantom faerie clawed the other back wheel to bits. The rear of the carriage collapsed to the ground. It caused such a jolt that Red had to jam her claws into the roof to save herself from being thrown.

A phantom faerie tugged at the reins in Wolfgang's hands. Wolfgang slashed his claw into its wing. "If they take out another wheel, the carriage is done for. And we might be, too."

Red saw a phantom faerie swooping down along the front of the carriage. She fearlessly jumped over the edge and caught a handle on the side. Right as the beast raised a claw to slash the front wheel, Red swung her sword and lobbed its wing off.

"Wolfgang, keep an eye on the other wheel," she warned.

A phantom faerie grabbed Red from behind and pulled with all its might. She let go of the carriage and locked an arm around the winged beast. It screeched out and swooped upward, carrying Red high enough to leap away toward the top of the carriage. In midflight, she swung her sword and hacked its wing off, sending it screaming away.

Red landed on the carriage's roof in a battle-ready pose. She was relieved to find that the remaining phantom faeries were gone.

Wolfgang grinned at Red. "You didn't think I was going to let you have all the fun?"

Red kicked away an unconscious phantom faerie that was dangling off the side. "Looks like we're clear for now. But this carriage is done for."

Wolfgang pulled the reins and slowed the carriage to a stop. "We gotta get out of here before more of Ice's minions find us."

Red and Wolfgang hopped down to the ground. They worked quickly to unhook the two ghost-white stallions that had been pulling the carriage. Their hands touched as they both reached for the final piece of the harness.

The way Wolfgang looked into Red's eyes made her heart flutter. "Red, I want you to know how much tonight means to me. Nobody has ever given me their trust like you have."

"I didn't give you anything. You've earned my trust. Tonight you'll bring great honor to your name."

"No matter what happens, I will stand with you. My life is yours, Alpha Huntress."

"Let's just hope it doesn't come to that, Wolfgang Helheim."

They stood in silence, gazing into one another's eyes. Red slowly moved in for a kiss, but Wolfgang turned away.

"We've only got an hour to get to the temple." Wolfgang jumped up onto a horse and rode off in a flash.

"Wait for me, Wolf Boy," she called after him.

With her heart fluttering, Red leaped onto the other horse. She raced off and was soon riding by Wolfgang's side. Together, they rode across the majestic landscape on their way to face their destiny.

Red had come to love Wayward with all of her heart and would fight tooth and nail to protect it from evil. She knew the moment would soon be upon her where she might have to choose between the survival of her loved ones and stopping Ragnarok from thrusting her new home into eternal night.

"The Moon Temple is just ahead," Wolfgang said. "We'd better ditch the horses and go in on foot so they don't hear us coming."

"The Alpha Huntress *is not* sneaking into battle tonight. They already know we're coming, so I want them to hear our thunder when we arrive."

Red and Wolfgang roared out as their horses leaped over a tall hedge. The Moon Temple was now directly ahead. Blazing red light blasted out of the stained glass windows. It illuminated an army of heavily-armed werewolves guarding the main door.

"I thought you said this was going to be tough," Red shouted.

"These guys are vicious beasts. They'll take us out without a second thought," Wolfgang said.

Red's adrenaline spiked as they charged into the horde. The hands of countless werewolves grabbed and pulled at her arms and legs. As her horse lost its balance, she stood up and vaulted high into the air. In mid-flight, she hacked down a werewolf that was twice her size. The instant her feet hit the ground, she again swung her sword, taking off the arm of a werewolf as it tried to grab her.

Moving at lightning speed, Red hacked and slashed her way through the onslaught of attacking werewolves. Wolfgang was nearby, battling the horde without the use of a weapon. He preferred to fight with his claws and a flurry of martial-arts style punches and kicks.

The final werewolf charged up behind Red and batted at her head with a hatchet. She dropped down to her knees just in time to evade the strike. With a backward thrust of her sword, she stabbed her attacker through the chest. Finally, spinning around and swinging her blade wide, she lobbed its head off.

Wolfgang stepped up next to Red. "Not bad, Red Riding. You might save Wayward after all."

"Before I can do that, we need to get inside the temple."

"Easier said than done."

Red and Wolfgang turned to face the temple door. Mia, Naoki, Suki, and Yuki strutted down the front steps in werewolf form, armed with staves, and outfitted in sleek battle armor.

Everybody stopped cold and locked eyes for a tense moment. Mia was missing the hand Prince had hacked off. The look of rage in her eyes made it clear she was on the hunt for vengeance.

Red took a battle stance. "I'm going through those temple doors. You can either step aside, or we're going to move you out of the way."

Mia raised her weapon. "Bring it on."

She and her counterparts dashed off in different directions and vanished.

"They've gone stealthy on us," Wolfgang said.

"I've gotta learn that trick," Red replied. Going on pure instinct, she raised her sword just in time to block a series of invisible attacks.

Wolfgang stumbled and fumbled as the girls pounded him with attacks from every direction. "Red, how are you blocking this stuff?"

"Stand back-to-back with me and listen for the sound of their staves cutting through the air."

"Easy enough for you to say, Alpha girl."

Wolfgang dashed over and took position behind Red. Sensing another attack, Red raised her sword and blocked it. She tried to counterstrike, but her attacker dashed away. Wolfgang blocked an attack with his forearm. He swung a fist wide, hitting nothing but air.

"They're trying to keep us busy, and we're running out of time," Red said.

"Then pick your moment and go for the door," Wolfgang whispered. "I'll do my best to hold them off."

"I've got a better idea," Red whispered. "I say we both run for the door and let them chase us. Then at the last second, we turn and pounce."

"Sounds just crazy enough to work."

"Then we go on my call. Don't hesitate for a second."

"I'll be racing you all the way."

Red blocked another attack and swung her sword. She then heard the sound of Wolfgang blocking an attack. *"Now!"*

Red and Wolfgang sprinted toward the temple door. Red could sense Mia and her counterparts racing after them. When her feet hit the steps, she turned and thrust her sword out. One of the invisible girls ran right onto her blade. Wolfgang turned and slashed a claw, inflicting a strike on one of their attackers.

The two wounded girls materialized. Suki was on her knees, gripping her stomach from Wolfgang's strike. She was injured, but it wasn't a fatal strike. Yuki was not so fortunate. She stood impaled on Red's sword. The blade had pierced her heart. She stumbled backward and clutched both hands over the deadly wound.

Red gasped in horror and dropped her sword. "No. I didn't mean to do *that.*"

Mia and Naoki materialized and dashed over to Yuki. They held her in their arms as she took her final breath.

Wolfgang placed a hand on Red's shoulder. "This wasn't your fault."

Suki and Naoki picked up Yuki from the ground. They walked away toward the forest and vanished.

With hate-filled eyes, Mia stood staring at Red. "You will suffer for what you've done to my sisters."

"Mia, don't!" Red shouted.

Mia dashed up the wall and landed behind Wolfgang. She stabbed her claws deep into his back. He wailed out in pain and dropped to his knees. Red picked up her sword and swung it in his defense. Mia blocked the attack, slamming Red into the wall. She then slashed her claws several times into Wolfgang's chest and throat.

"*Noooo!*" Red roared.

Mia bitterly locked her eyes on Red's. "Now we are even, Alpha Huntress."

Red lunged at Mia and swung her sword. Mia somersaulted backwards, just avoiding the attack. She raced away toward the trees and vanished from sight. Red dropped her sword and dashed over to Wolfgang. He was bleeding badly and laboring for every breath.

"Wolfgang, I'm so sorry. It was a stupid plan."

Wolfgang smiled lovingly at Red. "What are you talking about? It totally worked." His voice was weak and strained.

"I'm taking you to get help." Red tried to pick up Wolfgang, but he pulled away.

"You cut that out. The Alpha Huntress doesn't cry in the face of battle."

"I can't leave you here to die."

Wolfgang wiped a tear away from Red's eye. "When I agreed to come along, I was choosing to risk my life. I gave you my word of honor. I won't take it back now. I can't. The best way you can help me now is to stand up tall, march through those doors, and let Ragnarok hear your thunder."

Red kissed Wolfgang on the forehead. "I won't fail you."

"I love you, Little Red Riding."

As he said it, Red realized she loved him, too. "I love you, Wolf Boy," she answered. She hoped they'd both survive long enough to do something about it.

Red turned away from Wolfgang and picked up her sword. She closed her eyes and cleared her mind and heart of fear and doubt. When her eyes again opened, she had the stone cold expression of a warrior of legend.

CHAPTER 29

The Alpha Huntress stormed into the Moon Temple with her sword held high, ready for the fight of her life. She had planned to let out a furious roar to announce her arrival. Instead, she stood frozen with a perplexed glare of confusion. The chamber was deathly silent and there was no sign of anybody around.

High on the wall, a clock counted down from—

5 YEARS / 0 MONTHS/ 1 DAYS
0 HOURS / 14 MINUTES / 59 SECONDS

"That can't be right," she muttered. If the time was correct, it meant Ragnarok wasn't coming for another twenty-four hours. It also would mean Ice had fooled her into believing she had been trapped in the palace vents for a full day.

Red couldn't deny that it made more sense to believe it was all a trick, rather than buying into the idea of a *déjà vu* spell. This didn't mean she was taking any of what she was seeing at face value. Ice was a master of elaborate deception.

With her sword clutched tight, Red took a few steps further into the temple. She found it peculiar that the air was void of even a hint of odor, and the clicking of her footsteps on the stone floor didn't echo like they should in a chamber so large.

Topping the strangeness of the situation, the five celestial moonstones sitting upon the marble pedestals had been reduced to piles of dust. The last time she had been in the temple, they had vibrant colors and a wide range of textures.

A strange tingling sensation overcame Red as she stepped closer to the Alpha Stone. It began in the tips of her fingers, then ran up her arms and down her legs. By the time she stood in the center of the five pedestals, the feeling was buzzing throughout her entire body. It was so unpleasant that she wanted to get as far from the stones as possible.

"I bet that's exactly what you want me to do, right, Ice Seether?"

The last time Red had stood before the Alpha Stone, it was scorched red with jagged edges. It was now dusty white and smooth on all sides. As she reached out to touch the stone, an intense bolt of energy shot through her body, forcing her to take a big step backward.

Refusing to be intimidated, Red again reached out for the stone. The tingling made her feel a bit nauseous. When her hand made contact, an ear-piercing buzz sounded. It was so dizzying that she nearly fell to the floor. In the brief instant before she stepped away, she caught a glimpse of somebody standing on the altar.

Taking a deep breath, Red gave the Alpha Stone a quick tap. An ear-piercing buzz again blasted out. It lasted for less than a second, but this time she clearly saw Ethan and Prince standing near the pillars of the moon gate.

"Ice Seether, I've had just about enough of your games," Red said and slammed a hand down on the Alpha Stone, forcing herself to endure the continuous buzzing. Ethan and Prince were still standing near the moon gate, then she saw Dote and Ash at one end of the altar and Grenda on the other.

As for the clock, it was counting down from—

5 YEARS / 0 MONTHS / 0 DAYS
0 HOURS / 13 MINUTES / 19 SECONDS

Unable to endure the mind-scrambling buzzing any longer, she finally took her hand off the stone. Silence returned in an instant, and all of her clan members vanished. She feared that they were under some sort of enchantment, which would explain why they weren't fighting to escape. She suspected Ice was using a spell similar to the one Grenda had placed on her home.

With only thirteen minutes remaining on the clock, Red paced around in a frantic whirlwind, trying to think up a way to break the spell. Her eyes lit up with excitement as she recalled what had happened when Wolfgang had rapidly opened and closed the front door at Granny's house. The protection spell had caused a strange humming that made the floors and walls tremble. Dote had warned him to quit, or the place would be blown to bits.

With fearless resolve, she dashed over to the Alpha Stone and began tapping a hand on its smooth surface. On the altar, her clan rapidly vanished and reappeared. The buzzing tone quickly became too painful to endure, but she forced herself to keep going.

"Red, that's enough," Ethan cried out.

Red stopped tapping on the stone and looked up to see her father standing next to the moon gate. "Papa, what's going on here?"

"It's over. Granny cast a spell that will prevent the moon gate from opening," Ethan said.

"Is that so?" Red gave him a suspicious look. His hollow eyes were void of all emotion. "So where is she now?"

"Your granny is already heading back home. If you hurry, you can catch up with her."

"Then come down here, so we can leave together."

"You go on ahead of me. I'll be along soon enough."

"Tell Ice Seether I know she's here. I'm not buying her freaky little head game."

Red began tapping her hand on the moonstone. The buzzing forced Ethan to press his hands over his ears and drop to his knees in pain.

Prince appeared next to the moon gate with his hands pressed over his ears. "Alpha, you must stop doing that."

Ash and Dote also materialized at the far end of the altar with their hands pressed over their ears.

"Red, please stop that!" Dote cried out.

"You're going to ruin everything," Ash said.

Ignoring their pleas, Red began to tap her hand as rapidly as she could. A low-pitched humming rang out. The walls and floor began to quake violently. The stained glass windows cracked under the stress. The others were all on their knees in terrible pain. Red wanted to stop more than anything, but feared doing so would give the spell a chance to recover.

Grenda emerged near the altar. "Red, please stop. You're going to kill us all."

Red had no doubt that her granny was under a spell. If Grenda were in her right mind, she would have told Red to do anything necessary to ensure Ragnarok didn't get through the gate. Red had to be willing to sacrifice all of their lives to prevent evil from winning the night. In her heart, she knew that her clan would agree with this choice. Giving up now would only dishonor the vow they had all made.

"Ice Seether, show yourself, or I'll blow this place to the moon."

Red slammed a hand down on the stone and didn't let up. A violent spiraling vortex erupted. It made her head swell with dizziness. Guilt filled her heart when she saw her loved ones lying on the floor in terrible pain, but she just didn't have any other choice. She looked up and saw that the clock was no longer shifting between the two conflicting times.

It was now counting down from—

5 YEARS / 0 MONTHS / 0 DAYS
0 HOURS / 11 MINUTES / 5 SECONDS

Red locked her arms around the stone as the vortex pulled her feet up into the air. Her clan was then sucked up off the floor and began spinning around the chamber. A deep rumbling erupted. Blinding light ignited, making it impossible to see. The quaking was so violent that she feared the temple would crash down at any second.

It all finally ended with a sonic boom.

Everything faded to black.

There was nothing other than the sound of dead silence.

Red was quite certain she had reached the end of her path.

Then, she flopped to the temple floor. The vortex faded away. When her eyes came into focus, she saw her clan lying scattered throughout the chamber. They were alive and stirring, as if just waking from a deep sleep.

She looked up at the clock: only six minutes remained.

"Well played, Red Riding." Ice strutted down the steps of the altar, clutching her jeweled scepter. Her eyes glowed purple with mystical energy. "I must confess that I am quite impressed. I didn't think you had it in you to take it all the way."

Red stumbled to her feet. "It's about time you showed your freak show of a face. I was starting to think you were going to stay in hiding, like a coward."

Ice giggled. "Red, it's time for you to stop thinking like a foolish peasant. I wasn't hiding out of pathetic fear. This was a test, and you passed with flying colors."

"Right. And I suppose the flock of phantom fairies and werewolves outside were all part of the test, too."

"Don't forget about the creepy old goblin, the bridge troll, the fire orcs, and especially the little scuffle with Wolfgang's mommy."

Red gasped in disbelief. "No way. That can't be true."

"Oh yes it can," Ice said with a tease. "Ragnarok has been masterminding this since the beginning. And you've proven yourself each step of the way. I must admit I had hoped you would fail and I'd get the Alpha Power, but you have proven your right to ascend to the status of royalty. Our master will be quite impressed when he arrives."

Red snarled, "I sure hope you don't think I'll be helping that monster through the gate, because that's just not going to happen." She spotted her sword jammed into a wall, much too high for her to reach.

"Awwww. Did my birthday sister lose her little toy?"

"I'll get it back soon. When I do, it's going right through your heart, if you have one."

"Red, don't be like that now. Do yourself a favor and accept the inevitable. Ragnarok will be your master one way or another. The sooner you stop fighting that, the less you will have to suffer."

"After putting my clan in such terrible danger, he'll be the one suffering."

Ice walked over to Prince, still lying on the floor. "It's hilarious to hear you say that, considering how willing you were to sacrifice your so-called clan to defeat my spells."

"The sacrifice was their own choice."

"Well then, let's find out how far they're willing to go." Ice shot a beam of mystical energy from her scepter. A green moonstone embedded in a choker around Prince's neck ignited with a pulsating purple luminescence. "Just remember that you chose this path. I do hope you can live with it."

"Ice, don't do it." Red watched in fear as the choker began to tighten up around Prince's throat.

"Release me, wretched witch," Prince wheezed as he gagged and pulled desperately at the silver chain strangling his throat. It took only seconds before he began to lose his strength and black out.

"Ice Seether, you're so gonna get it for this!" Red yelled out.

"As if that's ever going to happen," Ice sneered, as smug as ever.

Ice blasted Red with a beam of mystical energy from her scepter. Red flew backward several feet and slammed full-force into a wall with a painful *thud*.

Ice laughed hysterically. "In just over four minutes the moon gate is going to open. You're going to help Ragnarok come back into this world, or I'm going to kill your friends."

Prince looked Red in the eyes. "You can't let her win, my huntress." With a final gag, he fell lifeless to the floor.

"Ice Seether, you're a monster!" Dote screamed out as she stumbled toward Prince.

She was halfway to him before Red grabbed her. "Dote, let me handle this."

Dote put her arms around Red and broke into dreadful sobbing. "Red, this is all wrong. You can't let such evil win. Promise me you'll make this right."

"You have my word on it, Dote."

Ice again laughed. "Don't blame me because things got all out of joint tonight. As you said, the sacrifice was his to make. *You* chose not to save his life. Now the big question we must ask is who will be next."

Red gasped in fear as she noticed the others had amulets chained around their necks. "Ice Seether, I'm warning you. Leave this temple, or this will be the last thing you ever do."

Ice pointed her scepter at Red and Dote. "No, this is *your* last chance, Red Riding. Do as *I* say, or watching your precious little loved ones die will be the last thing *you* do." She blasted a beam of mystical energy from her scepter.

The amulet around Dote's neck lit up and squeezed her throat. "You're going to have to do a lot better than that to take me out." Dote held out her hands and blasted Ice with an energy vortex.

Ice stumbled off balance and almost dropped her scepter, and in doing so broke the beam that was choking Dote.

"Oh, dear, I nearly forgot the little dodo bird has a bit of spunk to her." Ice shot an energy blast from her scepter at Dote, this time trapping her inside a mystical bubble.

"Ice, where are you getting all this borrowed power from?" Dote fired an energy vortex from her hand. It rebounded off the inside of the bubble and hit her in the face, knocking her out cold.

Red looked up at the clock to see it was passing the three-minute mark. To survive this ordeal, she had to get the scepter away from Ice.

"Red, listen to me," Ice said. "I'll give you one last chance to play nice. I don't want to be your enemy. To be candid, I've become quite fond of you. Together, we could rule this land. You can even keep the Alpha Power. Ragnarok will reward me with enough power to make us equals. Well, as equal as a pureblood like *me* and a peasant girl like *you* could be. I'm even willing to let your little friends live. You could keep them as play things for your amusement."

Red found it humorous that Ice was offering to share power with her. If she were to become a tyrant queen, the demise of Ice Seether would be her first act of power. "That's a really great offer," Red said. "I hate to admit that there's a part of me that would love to take it. All that power is a tempting thing."

"Then let us stop this foolish fighting, my birthday sister. We can bring Ragnarok back into this world together," Ice said.

Red looked Ice right in the eyes. "My choice has already been made for me. My clan decided they would rather die than let evil win this night. I'll honor their choice, even if I have to die with them. So let's finish this."

"Have it your way, Alpha Huntress." Ice fired a beam of energy at Ash's amulet. It surrounded him in a mystical sphere that began to get smaller and smaller.

"You're going down, Ice Seether." Red charged at Ice with furious intent.

Ice fired a burst of energy from her scepter. Red leaped high and soared over the attack. She inflicted a powerful kick into Ice's chest. Ice stumbled backward, losing her mystical hold over Ash.

"Red, I have had just about enough of your nonsense." Ice turned her scepter and blasted another burst of energy at Red, sending her soaring head-first into a pillar.

Red clutched her throbbing head. "I can't let it end this way."

Ice strutted across the chamber with her scepter aimed at Red. "Now I will show you the true meaning of suffering."

Just as Ice was about to blast Red, an energy bolt struck her from behind. She screamed and turned to see Grenda standing behind her, hands raised.

"And I haven't even gotten started," Grenda said.

"Is that so? Let's see how you handle this, you prune-faced hag!" Ice called out.

She fired an energy burst from her scepter. The amulet around Grenda's neck began to glow. She flew straight up and was tightly bound to the ceiling by mystical energy.

"Release her, Seether." Ethan dashed at Ice with his axe held high.

Ice fired a shot from her scepter. The amulet around Ethan's neck lit up, causing him to lose his strength and collapse to his knees. The energy binding Grenda to the roof dissolved, dropping her to the floor.

"Now it's my turn." Grenda blasted a mystical cyclone from her hands. The blow was so hard it knocked Ice to her knees.

Ice screeched, "I will not be defeated by a bunch of impure peasants!"

"Get over yourself, psycho girl." Ash charged up and tackled Ice to the floor. "This is for trying to take me out with your stupid magic bubble."

"How dare you put your hands on me, Ashley," Ice whined.

Ice fired a burst of energy into Ash's face. He groaned and fell backwards with his hands pressed over his face.

The clock was dropping past the one-minute mark. The Alpha Stone began to illuminate with a red glow.

Red looked up toward her sword. There was only one chance for her to end this nightmare, and it had to be now. Letting out a furious roar, she charged across the chamber. Ice fired a blast at Red, missing by inches.

When Red reached the wall, she planted a foot at its base and began to run straight up. Ice blasted another shot, again missing Red, but this time the shockwave sent the Alpha Huntress soaring upward. She reached out, just managing to get a grip on her sword.

Plummeting toward the floor, Red did a quick tuck and roll to get her feet underneath her. With only ten seconds on the clock, she flung her sword like a javelin. It soared across the chamber so fast Ice didn't see it coming. The blade pierced right into her heart.

"Impossible." Ice twitched in shock and lost her grip on the scepter.

"Ice Seether, I warned you it would end this way." Red dashed over and kicked the scepter across the floor.

Ice raised her arms and broke into a fit of maniacal laughter. "You think you've won, Red Riding? Just wait till you see what Ragnarok's going to do to you." In a bright flash of white light and smoke, she vanished from sight. The sword fell to the floor with a clunk.

Red looked up to the clock just as the seconds counted down to zero. "Ragnarok, the Alpha Huntress is here. Show me what you've got."

CHAPTER 30

"Wake up, Red."

Red found herself alone in a pitch-black void. There was nothing around her to see, or touch, or even smell. The emptiness was so absolute that she couldn't feel the ground beneath her feet. The boundless realm of isolation consumed her heart with a grim feeling of loneliness that she hadn't known since her arrival in Wayward.

"Where am I?" she asked.

"That's the big question, isn't it, Red." The soothing voice of a man spoke from nowhere and everywhere. "Where do you think you are?"

"I have no idea. This must be another one of Ice Seether's games."

"Who is this Ice character you keep speaking of?" the man asked.

Red took a nervous gulp. "Why don't you tell me who you are? And where you are, because I can't see you."

"We've been through this many times before. You're still having a great deal of difficulty accepting it."

Red walked aimlessly, reaching her hands out into the black void, but she couldn't find the man, or anything at all. "I don't understand this. Tell me what's going on here."

"You have to focus, Red. If you fall asleep again, I fear you may never wake."

"What are you talking about? I'm not asleep. Ragnarok, I won't fall for your tricks."

"You don't actually believe this Ragnarok is real, do you?"

"He has to be. I was in the Moon Temple. I'm the Alpha Huntress. I have to stop him from coming through the gate."

"Think about what you just said. A Moon Temple? You're an Alpha Huntress? Does any of that make a bit of sense to you?"

Red's heart fluttered in a panic. "No. It's real. I was there. I have to go back. Wayward needs me."

"Red, you must calm down, or you're going to slip away again."

"Don't you tell me to calm down!" Red shouted. His words reminded her how angry she had gotten when Wolfgang had told her to calm down. Nothing about what was happening felt right, and she wasn't going to just accept it because some strange voice was telling her she should. "I won't calm down, and you can't make me."

"I'm sorry this is so upsetting to you, but we're running out of time. If you don't wake up soon, it will be too late."

"Running out of time for what?" This made Red even more suspicious. She recalled the clock counting down in the Moon Temple.

"Before you slip off into sleep again and we can't get you back. If that happens, you will surely die."

"If I've been dreaming for so long, then what happened to me?"

"You had a terrible accident. A woodsman found you unconscious in the forest. You ran your motorcycle into the trunk of a tree. You've been drifting in and out of sleep for nearly a week."

"No. That can't be true."

Red thought about her passage through the great tree. It was far more realistic to believe she had merely crashed. The notion of a mystical portal transporting her to another world was rather absurd. She had suspected from the beginning that it was all just a wild dream.

"Are you still with me, Red?"

"What if I don't want to admit it's a dream? What if I decide to just stay in Wayward forever?"

"I'm afraid that's not possible. If you stay asleep any longer, your mind will fade away until there is nothing left."

"Well, if I'm not in Wayward, then where am I?"

"You're safe at home. I'm the one taking care of you."

Red considered his answer. It just felt wrong. "I'm sorry. I can't remember where my home is."

"Why don't you wake up and see for yourself?"

"And how exactly do I wake up?"

"You merely need to prove that you truly believe it was all just a dream. You must admit that there is no Wayward, or an Alpha Huntress, or a Moon Temple, or any of that other foolish nonsense."

"But it all feels so real. I couldn't have just dreamed it up."

"Red, think carefully. The last time we spoke, you told me you'd met a wolf. You talked about walking down a path in the woods to your granny's house. You spoke of a large man with an axe who saved you from terrible danger."

"It sounds like one of the stories I've read," Red said grimly, with a tear in her eye.

"That's right. You've read many stories. Think about all that's happened and you will know where these dreams have come from."

"So now I have to stop dreaming." The idea of accepting that she was nothing more than a hopeless orphan almost felt worse than dying.

"Sounds like you're finally ready. I'm holding a hand out to you. All you have to do is reach out and take it. In the blink of an eye you'll wake up at home, safe in your bed."

"Take your hand?"

"It's as easy as that."

Red closed her eyes and slowly extended a hand. A feeling of warmth filled her heart as she recalled her adventures and the love she experienced during her time in Wayward. *She saw the faces of her granny, her father, and her beloved friends Ash and Dote ...*

She recalled dancing with Prince at the ball and her battle with Ice Seether ...

She remembered kissing the goblin and all the dangerous creatures she had battled …

She thought about Wolfgang, and her mouth curved into a fond smile …

"It was a truly wonderful adventure," she said.

Above all the things Red recalled in that moment, one memory stuck out more than any other. It was from her vision when she had stood before the gate in the Moon Temple and Ragnarok was reaching a hand out to her.

"Set me free." His wicked voice echoed out in her mind.

Red's face tightened with anger. She was now certain that this was all a cruel deception.

"I'm ready to meet you, Ragnarok."

Red opened her eyes and was back in the Moon Temple. She was standing before the gate. It was now emanating a swirling barrier of lunar energy. On the other side, she had expected to see a monster towering ten feet tall with burning red eyes and jagged metal armor. Instead stood a boy the same age she was. His face was so pure, it was hard to believe he was the most evil force ever to walk the Earth.

"Alpha Huntress, you must set me free. Together we will rule over all of Wayward," Ragnarok said.

Red's every last doubt about her life was gone in an instant. The fate of her new world depended upon the choice that she was about to make. She looked down to see her arm reaching through the mystical barrier. Ragnarok was gripping her hand. His skin was soft and warm and felt oddly familiar. She looked into his eyes and saw a reflection of herself as the tyrant queen.

"I will make you a god," Ragnarok said. "You will be the Empress of Wayward. All the riches of this world will be yours for the taking. You will never endure another night without a place to sleep or food to eat. Nobody will ever be able to harm you again."

The temptation that swelled in Red's heart and mind was nearly more than she could endure. A surge of energy began to flow through her body and soul. The power was so immense it made her twitch and tremble. It felt like her skin was on fire. Her blood boiled in her veins. In that moment, she understood what it felt like to be a god.

"There is little time, Alpha. Pull me through, or all will be lost," Ragnarok said.

Red recalled how Grenda told her the gate would remain open for seven minutes. She looked at the clock to discover only a single minute had passed.

0 YEARS /0 MONTHS/ 0 DAYS
0 HOURS / 6 MINUTES / 1 SECONDS

"Think of all the suffering that you can save yourself from enduring," Ragnarok said.

Red noticed an intense crimson light illuminating the chamber. She looked back to the Alpha Stone. It was pulsating with swirling mystical energy. Grenda, Ethan, Ash, and Dote were standing at the bottom of the altar, gazing up at her. She could see the terrible fear in their eyes. Without a word spoken among them, she knew they were urging her to turn away from evil.

Ragnarok squeezed Red's hand. "You must now know that we are destined to stand together as one. You will not merely be helping me. You will be helping yourself."

"What does that mean?"

"It means that our destinies are intertwined in a way that you cannot yet begin to understand."

Red looked into Ragnarok's dark blue eyes. Her reflection was so crystal clear that it was as if she was looking back at herself.

"Alpha, I can give you the power to defy death itself. As Empress, you will decide who lives and who dies. You will never have to fear the demise of those you care for. They can be with you for all time."

Red's eyes grew wide with desire. If the promise of infinite power and riches wasn't enough to push her over the edge, the ability to assure her loved ones would never perish very well could have. Her mind swirled with dark thoughts as she recalled the vision where she had sat upon a throne as the high ruler of Wayward.

The purpose of the terrible dreams Red had been having since her arrival in Wayward became clear to her. She now understood why it was necessary to see the forest burning to the ground—and to see those she loved face their demise. It was all to teach her why she had to turn her back on evil in the darkest moment of temptation.

"It is time to face your destiny," Ragnarok said.

Red took a calming breath. "It is an awfully tempting offer. I want to say yes more than anything, but I am the Alpha Huntress, high protector of Wayward. Before I came here, my clan made a choice, and now I must honor it. I will let them all die, if that's what it takes to send you back to your lunar hell."

Red finally released Ragnarok's hand and turned her back on him.

"NOOOOOOOO!" Ragnarok tried to reach through the gate, but the mystical barrier blocked his hand. "Red Riding, you have made a deathly mistake. Your loved ones will now die, and you will be the one to kill them."

An explosion of lunar energy shot out of the moon gate into the chamber. The amulets around the necks of Red's clan began to glow. Their eyes turned as black as death.

"Ragnarok, what have you done to them?" Red shouted.

"It's not what I have done that you should fear. It is what you are about to do to them."

Ethan raised his axe and charged flat-out at Red. She jumped high, just in time to avoid being hacked in half. As soon as her feet hit the floor, Grenda shot an energy bolt that forced her to dive-roll clear. Dote unleashed a powerful vortex, missing Red by inches. The assault was so fast and intense, Red had to fight the urge to strike back.

"Listen to me," Red cried out. "You all have to fight this. Don't let Ragnarok destroy us."

Ash ran up and tried to punch Red, again and again, but she was able to block his attacks. His assault became so vicious that she finally lost control. She lashed out with a powerful punch to Ash's gut that knocked him to the floor.

"Ash, I'm so sorry."

Dote walked up to Red, with her hands glowing bright green, and blasted her point-blank. Red soared across the chamber and slammed into a pillar. The pain consumed her with a surge of aggression that was so primal it made her want to lash out in rage.

Ragnarok wailed out a wicked laugh. "It's not too late, Alpha. You can still save your friends."

Red looked up at the clock. Three minutes remained before the gate would close. She then noticed that the breastplate of her armor was cracked down the center. With a furious roar, she ripped it off.

A stinging pain stabbed into her upper back. She spun around to see Prince, slouching like a lifeless zombie and stabbing at her with his rapier. Even with her chainmail preventing injury, his strikes only heightened the rage growing inside her. She dodged his next attack and countered with a vicious punch to his face, knocking him to the ground.

Grenda blasted Red with a burst of black lightning. The pain that surged through Red's body was so intense it made her roar out in rage. Before she could recover, Dote fired a vortex that knocked Red flat onto her back. Ethan charged up and swung his axe at Red, again and again. Terror consumed her heart as she rolled clear, just avoiding his strikes.

"I can't take much more of this." Red's mind was swelling with primal rage.

Ragnarok laughed again. "It won't be much longer before you can't contain the wolf. Oh, the terrible things you will do once the beast takes control."

The words pierced Red's heart like a searing hot knife of fear. He was right, and she knew it. With two minutes left before the gate would close, she was seriously considering letting Ragnarok have his way.

Just then, a bolt of Grenda's black lightning hit her from behind. She wailed out a mindless *roar*. Her ability to restrain her rage was gone.

Ethan swung his axe at Red. She reached up, caught his arm, and threw a powerful kick to his leg. There was an awful sound of crunching bone. He grunted in immense pain and collapsed to the ground.

"Look what you've done." Ragnarok said. "Now we shall see how you deal with the others."

Red's mind was void of rational thought as she looked at Grenda and Dote. They were on the far end of the chamber, hands glowing brightly, and ready to strike. The world went into slow motion as Red dashed their way, dodging and leaping clear of their mystical attacks. She would destroy them both in only seconds, and there wasn't a thing that could stop her.

All was lost until the voice of the first Red Riding spoke in Red's mind, *"You must let go of your rage. Once you fall down the path of darkness, there will be no turning back. Call on the power of the Alpha and you will see another path."*

True to her word, the Alpha that came before Red showed her an answer that she had not considered. As she soared over the wave of mystical energy, her eyes fixed on the glowing amulet around Grenda's neck.

"I understand."

Red hit the ground and dove, rolling back to her feet. Ethan was staggering toward her on his broken leg. He swung his axe with brutal force. She dodged the attack and tackled him to the floor. With both hands, she gripped the thick silver chain binding the amulet to his neck.

She tried with all of her might to snap it in two, but the spellcraft used to create it was too powerful. Her arms then began to glow with mystical power, giving her so much strength that it felt like she could have ripped a hole in the earth itself.

With a furious roar, she finally broke the chain.

In a single blink, Ethan's eyes returned to normal. He abruptly fell to the floor, clutching his injured leg. "Red, what's happening here?"

Red flung the broken amulet into the moon gate, hitting Ragnarok in the face. "I'm just about to stop evil from winning the night."

"This is not over, Alpha!" Ragnarok roared.

Red looked at the clock. A full minute remained. "You're right. I gotta work fast."

Moving at inhuman speed, Red dashed over to Ash. He was still lying on the floor, clinging to his injured abdomen. He reached up and tried to stop Red as she grabbed the amulet around his neck. With a mighty pull, she ripped the chain off his throat.

"Red, I feel like I'm going to hurl," Ash said.

"Hang tough, Ash. It's almost over."

Grenda fired a blast of black lightning as Red dashed toward Prince. He made a feeble attempt to stab her with his rapier. She bashed the weapon from his hands and twisted his arm around his back. With a quick yank, she ripped the amulet off his neck. Prince went limp and dropped to the floor.

"Just a little bit longer, Ragnarok," said Red.

Armed with Prince's rapier, Red dashed toward Dote and Grenda. They blasted searing blue flames her way. Red clawed up a wall and executed a spiraling somersault. She could feel the blazing heat of the flames as she soared across the chamber.

Red landed in front of Dote and thrust the rapier into her amulet, shattering it to dust. In a single continuous motion, she spun the blade around and destroyed the amulet around Grenda's neck. Grenda and Dote collapsed to their knees, disoriented and gasping in exhaustion.

Red dropped the rapier and looked to the gate. "It's over, Ragnarok. You've failed."

The clock was counting down from 33 seconds.

"Well played, Alpha Huntress," Wolfgang said from behind.

Red turned just as he was approaching the Alpha Stone. "Wolfgang, you're alive."

"You didn't think a few scratches were going to take me out?" Wolfgang picked up Red's sword from the floor.

Red took a nervous gulp. "What are you doing?"

Wolfgang tapped the tip of the sword on the Alpha stone. "The power was supposed to be mine. I could bust this stone open and fight you for it right here and now."

"Do it, Wolfgang. Do it now." Ragnarok yelled. "It's not too late to free me. Together, we can bring glory to the Helheim name."

Wolfgang placed a hand on the Alpha Stone. Its immense power flowed through his hand. "That's just what my mother and father would want me to do."

"Wolf Boy, please don't do this," Red begged.

"I'm only doing what has to be done." Wolfgang raised the sword high above his head and slammed the blade into the Alpha Stone, smashing it into a thousand tiny glowing shards.

"Impossible." Red felt the Alpha Power leaving her body. She watched in dread as a glowing vortex began to swirl above her head.

"Destroy her and free me." Ragnarok screeched out. "I only have seconds left."

Red looked at Wolfgang with tear soaked eyes. "If this is what you want, I won't stop you."

Wolfgang pointed the sword at Red. "There's only one thing I want from you." He dropped the weapon and grabbed Red around the waist. He kissed her with all the love and passion he had in his heart.

Ragnarok roared. "You will suffer for this treachery, Wolfgang Helheim."

The remaining seconds that the gate would stay open ticked away.

"Alpha Huntress, you will see me again." An inferno of flames consumed Ragnarok and sucked him back into his lunar prison.

The vortex around the gate faded away.

Wolfgang stepped back as the Alpha Power swirled around Red. When it entered her body, her eyes ignited with a blaze of glowing energy that lit the chamber. She let out a furious *howl* so loud it rattled the walls.

Then, in a flash, it was all over.

Wolfgang gazed into Red's eyes. "You did it, Red Riding. With the Alpha Stone destroyed, nobody can ever try to take the power from you again."

Red placed a loving hand on Wolfgang's face. "I couldn't have done it without you, Wolfgang of the Riding Clan. You've brought great honor to your name."

Gazing into his eyes, Red recalled that she had yet to understand the strange connection that trailed all the way back to their childhood. She turned to see Grenda, Ethan, Ash, and Dote were smiling at her. They were bruised and beaten, but very much alive. One after another, they kneeled down and bowed their heads in respect.

Red stood tall and proud. "I thank you all for your valiant courage. We have won the night, but the real war has yet to even begin."

They all looked up to the clock, which was now at—

4 YEARS /11 MONTHS/ 364 DAYS
23 HOURS / 57 MINUTES / 9 SECONDS

"We can worry about that another day," Grenda said. "I think it's time for a big ol' group hug."

Red embraced her friends and family in love and victory. It was by far the finest moment of her life. One that she believed, without a doubt, was all real. There was such a thing as a perfect day, and she was living it in all its glory.

Prince stumbled over and joined the group, alive and looking quite bewildered. "Did I miss anything important?"

"My pretty man!" Dote shrieked with joy and kissed Prince quite affectionately.

Red turned and placed a hand on the moonstone marked *II Skoll and Hati*. She could feel a strange vibration that told her two lunar deities would soon arrive in Wayward. They would unleash chaos the likes of which Red couldn't begin to imagine. With Ragnarok still alive and the final fate of Ice Seether unclear, she would need to embark upon a quest to locate the true Omega Gem.

"I'm ready to face it all," She said, straightening with confidence.

While the path ahead was paved with uncertainty, Red knew that no matter how perilous the journey would become, she would always have the love and strength of her clan of family and friends to help her through the darkest of hours. With them by her side, she would stand tall and proud as the High Protector of Wayward Woods, the Alpha Huntress forever known as Red Riding.

About the Author

Neo Edmund has worked in the entertainment industry for over a decade as a Film Writer, Animation Writer, Comic Book Writer, Film Development Executive, Novelist, Blogger, and Public Speaker. He has written for companies including: Disney Interactive, Hub Network, Spike TV, History Channel, Discovery Channel, Animal Planet, JumpStart Interactive, Platinum Studios, Genetic Entertainment, Zenescope, and Silver Dragon Books. Several of his graphic novels are listed among titles that meet the United States Common Core Standards for English Education. He attended UCLA where he majored in Screenwriting, English Creative Writing, and Film Production. He lives and works in Los Angeles, California.

88888570R00169

Made in the USA
Columbia, SC
13 February 2018